TIME TO RUN

"Melton...doesn't miss a beat in this involving story."
—*Publishers Weekly*

"Melton's compelling protagonists propel the gritty and realistic storytelling...Excellent!"
—*Romantic Times BOOKreviews Magazine*

"This book will twist all of your heartstrings...you won't be able to put *Time To Run* down...a must-read."
—**FreshFiction.com**

"Exceedingly riveting...enthralling...you'll find yourself racing through it from one exciting scene to the next...my favorite."
—**RomRevToday.com**

"An exciting tale starring a fine lead couple...fans will enjoy this wonderful thriller."
—*Midwest Book Review*

Also by Marliss Melton

Forget Me Not

In the Dark

Time to Run

Next to Die

MARLISS MELTON

DON'T LET GO

FOREVER

NEW YORK BOSTON

Copyright © 2008 by Marliss Arruda
All rights reserved. Except as permitted under the U.S. Copyright Act of 1976, no part of this publication may be reproduced, distributed, or transmitted in any form or by any means, or stored in a database or retrieval system, without the prior written permission of the publisher.

Cover design by Dale Fiorillo

Forever
Hachette Book Group USA
237 Park Avenue
New York, NY 10017
Visit our Web site at www.HachetteBookGroupUSA.com

Printed in the United States of America

Forever is an imprint of Grand Central Publishing. The Forever name and logo is a trademark of Hachette Book Group USA, Inc.

First Printing: April 2008

10 9 8 7 6 5 4 3 2 1

*Honey, you've found your way into several
of my characters before, but never as blatantly as this.
Some women may be jealous that I'm married to
my inspiration. Others will be glad you're mine
and not theirs. We've seen good times and bad.
But you're still the love of my life, and I'm ever
so grateful that you didn't let go when you could have.*

Acknowledgments

As usual, the creation of this story is due to a wonderful group effort. Thank you again, Navy SEAL Commander Mark Divine, for editing and inspiring my action scenes. Your generosity and professionalism make you a credit to the Teams. Thank you, Sharon, for selflessly educating me on the Myers-Briggs Personality types and Socionics relationships, both of which continue to help me with characterization and conflict. Last but never least, a million times, "Thank You!" to Janie, for being with me every step of the way on this adventure that we dreamed up together.

DON'T
LET GO

Prologue

◆

Five Years Ago

Despite the heat blowing out of the vents near the old Volkswagen's floorboards, Chief Petty Officer Solomon McGuire shivered in his woolen peacoat. He'd grown up in Camden, Maine, where the winters were ruthless. The milder weather in Virginia Beach seldom troubled him, but the memories of the mission he'd just come from sat in his chest like a block of ice, freezing him from the inside out.

Petty Officer Blaine Koontz from Kentucky had been one of those younger guys that made older SEALs feel tired and used-up. He was five and a half feet of boundless energy. His freckled face and grinning countenance made every deadly objective seem like kid's play.

Hooyah! We get to parachute with a low open into enemy territory; run four miles with sixty-pound rucksacks over the dunes; set a perimeter around the oil well guarded by Iraqi National Guards and take it. No problem! We can do it!

And they had. Only, as they'd scurried across the open sand toward the oil well, a bullet had caught Koontz in the side of the head. It hadn't killed him right away. He was still alive and rambling when Solomon held him still so the corpsman could tape his fractured skull.

After sixteen years of being a SEAL, Solomon thought he'd heard and seen everything. He was wrong. The exclamations tumbling out of Koontz's mouth had raised the hairs on the back of his neck. It seemed that Koontz hadn't been so happy-go-lucky after all. The twenty-two-year-old had flirted boldly with the Grim Reaper for a reason: Death couldn't be a fate any worse than Koontz's sadistic father.

Koontz hadn't died until a NightStalker dropped into hostile airspace, dodging rocket-propelled grenades to pick him up and whisk him away. Though his death had shaken Solomon, time for grief was a luxury he and his men could ill afford, so they had pressed on to finish the mission—a mission that had lasted seventy-two sleepless hours. Not only had the SEALs commandeered the oil well, but they'd had to defend it from counterattack, until the Army's Seventh Infantry Battalion arrived to relieve them.

Solomon, known for his relentless pursuit of an objective, was beyond exhausted. The memory of Koontz's childhood horrors abraded his frayed nerves as he increased his speed through the suburban sprawl under a cold, January moon.

The entrance to his neighborhood came into view, and he downshifted, turning the corner without touching the brakes. He ached for relief. Relief that would come the instant he scooped his infant son into his arms and gazed down at the innocent contours of his cherubic face. Relief that would be complete once he found release in his wife's soft arms.

His son was Silas. And he was Solomon's joy.

His wife was Candace. At one time, he'd fancied her the center of his universe, and his every thought had revolved around her. But that was before he came to realize that her beauty was as shallow as her conscience. She was the mother of his son, however. It had been his choice to marry her, and he stood stubbornly by his decision.

His brick two-story home stood at the end of a cul-de-sac. Every month, the mortgage sucked away half of his paycheck, but Candace had wanted it, so he'd bought it for her. The windows were dark at this late hour, his little family sleeping. Solomon cut the engine and glided into the driveway.

Dragging his rucksack behind him, he got out and followed the granite walkway that cut across the frost-covered lawn. With stiff fingers, he unlocked his front door, his heart beating faster to know that one-year-old Silas was upstairs, tucked into his crib. He could almost feel the warmth of his sturdy little frame against his chest, smell his sweet, baby scent.

As he pushed his way inside, the warmth he anticipated failed to greet him. The air inside was cold and undisturbed; the silence tomblike; the smells faded.

With a stab of fear, Solomon flicked the light switch. Glaring light confirmed what his other senses were telling him. "Candace!" His anxious voice echoed off the empty walls and high ceilings. "No!" he breathed, dropping his rucksack.

He took the stairs three at a time, raced down the wide hall, and threw open the door to the nursery. The relentless moon displayed a room as empty as the rest of the house. There wasn't any need to turn on the lights. The bear-on-the-rocking-chair border was all that remained.

"Oh, God," he groaned, lurching back into the hallway and stalking to the master bedroom. He barreled through the double doors and stared. Gone. Everything was gone.

With a shiver, he pivoted, going back to the nursery. "Silas," he moaned, feeling as if his very bowels had been ripped from him. He fell onto his knees where the baby's crib had stood, bowed his face into his hands, and wept.

Chapter One

✦

Las Amazonas, Venezuela

The double doors of the chapel at La Misión de la Paz slammed open, startling the occupants within. The interloper raced out of the hazy sunlight, his brown limbs coated in sweat, breath coming in gasps that punctuated his announcement. *"Guerillas se acercan. ¡Hay por lo menos cincuenta y llevan armas!"*

Guerillas are coming. There are at least fifty of them and they're carrying weapons. Translating the message, Jordan Bliss straightened from the pupil she was instructing and looked at Father Benedict to gauge his response.

The priest's benign countenance hardened with concern. "You should have left two weeks ago," he said to her, catching her eye. "Now you'll have to hide with us."

"My choice, Father," she gently reminded him, her gaze sliding toward the reason for her stay, four-year-old Miguel, who sat clutching his slate. She could not have left him, regardless of the political turmoil in Venezuela and the growing threat toward Americans.

"Come," urged Father Benedict, who was British and only slightly less at risk. "Bring the children. We'll all hide in the wine cellar. Pedro, run and fetch Sister Madeline," he added in Spanish. "Hurry."

Jordan gathered the children, instructing them to leave their slates beneath the pews. She scooped Miguel into her arms. Thin as a rail, he scarcely weighed her down, especially when he coiled his limbs around her.

"This way," indicated the priest, hurrying toward the sacristy, which was separated from the sanctuary by a curtain. Once within, he kicked aside the worn rug that covered the stone floor. A wooden hatch was nestled in the flagging, providing access to the cellar below. He lifted it, exposing steps that disappeared into darkness, releasing a musty smell.

Jordan's fear of closed spaces made her balk. The children bunched up behind her, instinctively silent.

"Take these candles," the priest instructed, thrusting several waxen pillars at her. "Matches," he added, his voice remarkably steady. She stuck them into the deep pockets of her cargo shorts. Lifting a cloth off a basket, he withdrew a loaf of bread meant for services that night. "We'll need this."

God knew how long they would be down there. Or whether the guerillas headed in their direction would avidly hunt them down or simply move on.

"Go ahead," said the priest, with a nod at the steps.

With panic threatening to close off her airways, Jordan instructed her little troop to hold the rickety banister and follow her. She took her first step into the bowels of the earth and then another.

A spider's web brushed her cheek as a dank coolness swallowed her. Shivering, she clutched Miguel closer while shaking off her fear for his sake, and for the others.

Down, down into the black hole they went until coming to a floor of hard-packed dirt.

As she gazed up at the light, tremors rippled through her. What if she never saw the sun again? A scurry of footfalls heralded the approach of Sister Madeline.

"I caught sight of them," the nun divulged, in her no-nonsense voice. "They're a horde," she added, with typical British understatement.

An angry horde, Jordan thought, a cold sweat matting her shirt to her back.

Sister Madeline bustled down the steps. "Whom do we have with us?" she inquired.

"The orphans," Jordan murmured.

"We should let them go," Sister Madeline suggested, glancing up at the priest.

"No," whispered Jordan, clutching Miguel more fiercely.

"Their cries might betray us," the nun argued.

"It's too late to send them up," Father Benedict pointed out as he, too, descended. "Besides, who would care for them? They would end up on the streets again. Pedro," he called to the hovering teen, a youth hoping to join the priesthood, "close the door and lock it. Put the rug over the hatch and hide the key. Tell no one where we are. When the guerillas leave, let us out again."

"*Sí, padre,*" answered the boy. With reluctance and apology wreathed upon his indigenous features, he gently lowered the door. It wasn't so dark, not with rays of sunlight slipping through the cracks. But then the rug was tossed over the hatch, dousing them in blackness so deep and thick that it paralyzed every muscle in Jordan's body.

"Let us light a candle and pray," recommended Father Benedict, his voice swimming out of the darkness. It unlocked Jordan's frozen joints.

She stiffly put Miguel down, eager to drive back the void. But the task, given her shaking hands, proved virtually impossible. The flare of her trembling match revealed the pale faces of her adult companions and the gleam of four sets of children's eyes. They feasted their gazes on the wick, then looked around once the candle was lit.

Their hiding space was perhaps ten by seven paces, laced in cobwebs and peppered with holes that housed bottles of sacramental wine. *We have plenty to drink,* Jordan thought, swallowing a hysterical giggle.

The priest sat, folding his long limbs to make more space. Jordan hunted for a place to put the candle, out of reach of the children. Finding a crack in the wall, she wedged it in like a torch. "Sit down," she instructed the children, doing the same.

Miguel scrambled into his customary seat—her lap, his hair tickling her nose. Jordan's eyes stung with regret that she couldn't shield him from harm any better than this.

"Beloved Father," began the priest, his voice quiet and grim yet amazingly calm, "look down upon us and cast your mantle of protection over us, we pray you..."

As his sonorous voice droned on, Jordan's thoughts wandered. She hushed Fatima, who whimpered in fear as she burrowed into Jordan's side. Prayers couldn't hurt, Jordan acknowledged, but neither would they necessarily help. God knew she'd expended many a prayer to keep from losing her pregnancy and then her marriage.

Unlike the priest and the nun, Jordan wasn't in Venezuela to save souls. She was here to continue a healing process that had begun last summer, only to be cut short when her teaching job necessitated a return trip home.

This summer, she'd come back—not for healing but to complete the adoption process she'd begun nine months before. In doing so, she'd turned a deaf ear to government warnings that the political environment was unstable. Her refusal to acknowledge the dangers could well end up getting her killed.

The *rat-tat-tat-tat* of gunfire suspended Father Benedict's prayer. They all listened, holding a collective breath. Had the guerillas killed one of the villagers visiting La Misión? Or were they merely announcing their fearsome arrival?

The threat of a disturbance had seemed so unlikely in this remote jungle mission, though for weeks newspapers had warned of Populist uprisings, urging Americans to leave the country.

Jordan didn't concern herself with politics. The children of Las Amazonas needed her even more than her students at home did.

She touched each child, rubbing their narrow shoulders to comfort them. She would protect them with her life, if necessary, especially Miguel, who was exactly the age her baby would have been. Small and defenseless, he had found a special place in Jordan's heart. She was so close to being able to take him home with her. Come hell or high water, she wouldn't leave him now.

Suffolk, Virginia

Special Agent Rafael Valentino read the freshly painted sign at the head of a tree-lined driveway.

SECOND CHANCE, HIPPOTHERAPY RANCH

With a stab of his finger, he curtailed the haunting aria from the opera *Carmen* and turned down the graveled driveway, braced for disappointment.

The Jillian Sanders he knew was a nurse in Fairfax, not a horse rancher in Suffolk, Virginia. Still, having seen the name on a roster of incoming calls, he'd decided to pay this house call in order to see for himself.

Mature oak trees gave way to a butter-yellow farmhouse in need of a fresh coat of paint. The front porch listed. Bushes and shrubs overran the walkway. A newly constructed barn stood fifty yards away, displaying a ruddy stain and a fence so recently erected that the tempered wood still looked green.

Rafe cut the engine and reached for the file. Jillian Sanders had made thirty-one phone calls requesting FBI assistance.

As he approached the front door, he listened, hearing only the sloughing of wind and the twitter of a bird. The heels of his Ferragamo shoes sounded out of place on the planks of the sagging porch.

Before he could knock, the door popped open. "Yeah?" said a boy of perhaps fourteen, his gray eyes hostile.

"Special Agent Valentino, FBI," said Rafe, softening the rasp produced by his injured vocal cords. "I'm looking for Jillian Sanders."

"She's in the barn," said the boy, eyeing the scar on Rafe's neck.

"Who are you?" asked a young girl, poking her head out from under the boy's arm.

"He's the bogeyman," said her brother.

"Nuhn-uhn."

"Well, he could be. Go back to your room and play. We don't talk to strangers."

"You can't tell me what to do."

With a grimace, Rafe backed away. How long had it been since he'd overheard siblings squabble? Eight years, now, long enough that the memories had faded.

Crossing to the barn's open doors, Rafe peered into the mellow shadows. The faint odor of horse manure mingled with the scent of fresh straw. "Hello?" he called, following a scuffling sound along an isle of empty stalls.

The ears and eyes of a huge bay crested the dividers. The horse gave a whinny, and the stall door slid open. A woman peered out.

"Rafael!" she gasped. Her long, golden hair was caught up in a ponytail. She wore shorts and a T-shirt stretched taut across her pregnant midsection, but he would have recognized her anywhere.

"Jillian." A feeling of intense satisfaction rushed through him.

"Oh, my," she breathed, putting a gloved hand to her heart. "I never thought I'd see you again."

"Nor I," he admitted, loving the sweet timbre of her voice, the periwinkle blue of her eyes.

"What brings you to Suffolk?" she asked in delight.

"I transferred from D.C. eight months ago," he explained.

"You're here because of my phone calls," she guessed.

He indicated the file. "I wondered if it might be you." Not only had she soothed him in the ER as he'd choked on his own blood, but she'd visited him daily in the weeks following his recovery.

"I'm so happy to see you again," she said, pulling off her glove, extending her hand.

Savoring the warmth and softness of her fingers, Rafe realized this was the first time they'd ever touched.

"Do you live here in Suffolk?" he asked, releasing her regretfully. "I thought your husband was with the Fairfax police."

She looked away, putting her gloves down. "I moved here to start a therapy ranch. It's for veterans who've lost limbs in the war. Riding helps them regain muscle and get their balance back."

"I had no idea," he admitted, intrigued. He eyed her belly inquiringly.

"You caught me mucking out the stall," she apologized, ignoring the look. "Come into the office," she suggested. "I have so much to tell you."

Ten minutes later, with the promise that the FBI would do everything in their powers to help locate her sister, Jillian watched Rafael leave.

With graceful ease, he slipped into the Cutlass and donned his seat belt. She had never seen him dressed in anything but pajamas, yet it came as no surprise that he wore a designer silk suit of unrelenting gray, a snowy white shirt, and no tie. Even in pajamas there had been something elegant about him.

As he smiled at her, a lightness buoyed her heavy heart, easing the crush that kept her so despondent. How nice to have seen him again, a friend she'd cherished for a short time and then lost, especially since she'd lost so much lately.

With a deft hand on the steering wheel, he backed up and pulled away, and her sorrow returned.

She hadn't even told him she was widowed. Every morning she awakened to the panicky realization that her family's welfare rested on her narrow shoulders. Her baby, Gary's surprise legacy, would be born in two short months, and she had so much left to do before she could give their baby the attention it deserved.

With a weary sigh, Jillian turned to gaze at the barn. She must've been crazy to think she could honor her and Gary's dream alone. But now that she'd started, she had no choice but see it through.

Las Amazonas, Venezuela

"What's the plan, Senior Chief?" whispered Petty Officer Vinny DeInnocentis as he slapped at a mosquito boring through the camo paint slathered on his neck. With night falling, the insects were swarming worse than ever.

Solomon McGuire, aka Mako, took his eyes off the rebel-occupied Misión de la Paz long enough to send Vinny a glacial stare. Given the pale, almost colorless gray of his eyes, glacial stares required little effort on his part.

"What?" the kid demanded with inner-city bravado. "We've been lyin' here for like six hours, watching these jackasses scare the locals. When're we gonna pursue the objective?"

"We haven't been lying here," Solomon corrected him. "We've been observing."

"True," Vinny acknowledged, giving Solomon brief

hope that he might one day make chief, but then he added, "and I have observed that a big-ass beetle is climbing up my right leg heading straight to my balls. There's a venomous snake dangling five meters over our heads, and the vines that we're hiding in look a lot like poison oak."

"It's trumpet flower," Solomon retorted, nonetheless attuned to Vinny's restlessness. "We're going to penetrate at zero one hundred hours. You, Teddy, and Gus will sweep the enclosure while I locate the recovery targets. We find them, flexicuff them, and get them out. Harley and Haiku will meet up with us at the rendezvous point."

Vinny's white teeth flashed in the gloom. "Hooyah, Senior Chief. I gotta get this bug outta my pants," he added, shaking his leg in what looked like a rendition of the hokey pokey as he backed out of the vines.

Solomon thumbed his interteam radio to contact the sniper team. "Four hours to Operation Extraction," he warned the spotter and shooter.

"Roger," Harley murmured back. Now that darkness was falling, he and Haiku were making their way along the top of the mission wall, over a ceramic-tiled roof of the outdoor kitchen, up and into the bell tower of the seventeenth-century chapel, an ideal vantage point from which to guard the recovery team's blazing entrance and subsequent search.

Solomon set his watch to perform a countdown.

Chapter Two

✦

Three hours and fifty minutes later, Solomon watched the seconds tick down on the face of his MTM Extreme Ops Black SEAL watch. He and his recovery team were poised beneath the fragrant vines of a bougainvillea bush, swimming in adrenaline. *Nine. Eight. Seven...* They were loaded with gear, wearing gas masks. *Three. Two. One.*

At his nod, Teddy detonated the breaching charge. The ancient wrought-iron gate popped open. Vinny, Teddy, and Gus hurled smoke grenades out of the tree line into the courtyard. Summoned by the disturbance and hissing smoke bombs, rebels raced into view and reeled back, disoriented and confused.

From the bell tower, Harley belted out the first stream of bullets while the masked specters of the recovery team stalked into the mission with their MP5s blazing.

Behind the protective wall of their fire, Solomon began his search.

A quick sweep of the medieval-style kitchen revealed that it was empty. His men blazed their way toward the chapel, laying out half a dozen rebels who'd put up a resistance that lasted less than five seconds.

Vinny and Teddy flattened themselves against the stucco wall of the church as Gus, a lieutenant, kicked the double doors open and tossed in a flash bang. Simulating a stun grenade, its purpose was to disorient occupants and encourage their evacuation. Solomon peeked inside, just in time to glimpse through his NVGs the orange-red silhouette of a man darting behind a partition.

Time to question a rebel, he thought, as Gus signaled for him to enter. They left Vinny and Teddy to guard the door as they slipped along a peripheral wall toward the cowering man. "Come out with your hands up, and you won't be harmed," Solomon called out in Spanish, as they drew closer.

Flipping up his mask, he determined that the emerging figure was just an adolescent and probably not a rebel, given that he wore the robe of a cleric. He held his arms high above his head, quaking from head to toe.

"We're looking for gringos," he said, watching the youth's reaction.

His panicked gaze darted to the right.

Solomon took note. "Where are they?" he asked again, and Gus hefted his gun threateningly.

"*Abajo,*" squeaked the youth.

"Below?" Solomon countered.

"In a cellar," Gus guessed.

"*Aquí,*" the boy confirmed, shuffling back into the alcove and pointing at the floor.

"Show us," commanded Solomon. "Quickly."

With fluid movements that indicated this was an accustomed task for him, the boy drew a key from his robe, pulled aside a rug that covered the floor, and unlocked a trapdoor, pulling it open. "*Soy yo,*" he called down, identifying himself and adding that he was in the company of American soldiers.

Given the odor rising out of the cellar, those in hiding had been down there for days. Solomon knelt, pulling out his penlight. Gus peered over his shoulder as they strobed the area below.

At the base of a run of rickety steps, they counted three Caucasian adults and four indigenous children all blinking into his light.

"Jordan Bliss?" Solomon asked, centering his light on the adult male.

"No, sorry," answered the man, who was obviously a Brit. "I'm Father Benedict. Miss Bliss, our teacher, is there." He nodded.

Miss? He should have guessed.

The beam of Solomon's penlight revealed a woman in her early thirties—reddish brown hair, pretty features, eyes that braved the beam to regard him with suspicion. "Who are you?" she demanded in a voice rusty from disuse as she hefted a boy child in her arms.

"Navy SEALs," he answered curtly. "I'm Senior Chief McGuire. This is Lieutenant Atwater. We're here to extract you and the British citizens."

"Praise God," exclaimed an older female.

"Did you hear that, *niños*?" Jordan Bliss whispered to the little ones. "These men are going to help us."

"Just adults, ma'am," Solomon corrected her, gruffly, in a tone that brooked no argument. "No children. Let's go."

She looked at him like he'd shot her in the heart. "No," she protested, on a note as obstinate as his. "We *can't* leave the children here."

Solomon glanced up at Gus as he fingered the flexi-cuffs in his vest pocket. It was standard operating procedure to cuff and even gag, if necessary, the recovery targets to keep them from jeopardizing the operation.

"We are under orders to extract *you,* ma'am, and these two British citizens. No one else," Gus explained, saving Solomon the trouble.

"Take them, then," she retorted, her knuckles white as she backed away, drawing the children with her. "I need to go to Ayacucho anyway."

"They're orphans," the priest explained, sending Solomon a look that held great power to influence. "They've no one to look after them. And the rebels are a vicious lot, according to Pedro."

Solomon sneaked a peek at his watch. He thumbed his mike. "Status check." He did not have time for this.

"No movement in the courtyard," answered Haiku, "but we can hear what sounds like reinforcements coming, one klick out. Copy."

"We have the targets sighted," Solomon reported, weighing his options. Gus, though an officer, lacked experience in search and rescue. This was Solomon's call.

"I won't leave without the children," Jordan Bliss repeated.

He wanted to snap back that he was going to grab her, will she or nill she, but with the priest gazing at him so expectantly, he heard himself say, "We'll take the children as far as the Landing Zone. No farther. Everyone out."

As he helped them up the stairs, Gus flexicuffed the older children to each other to decrease the chance that one or two might get lost in the rain forest. He let the little one remain in Jordan's arms.

"Listen to me," he growled, inspecting them quickly, "and make sure the children understand this. We are going to hike six miles to the Landing Zone, moving fast, with no time to stop, for any reason. There will be no talking. No crying or whining. Do I make myself clear?"

"Very," said Jordan with equal heat.

He glared at her. "Let's go," he said.

"*Vayan con Dios,*" murmured the youth, as they left the nave, heading for the chapel doors.

Jordan's arms ached. She had a permanent kink in her spine, but she would not put Miguel down to be swallowed up in Las Amazonas's dense foliage. The older children, latched together, struggled to keep pace, as it was.

Senior Chief McGuire, Lieutenant Atwater, and two heavily armored SEALs escorted them out of La Misión into the pathless rain forest at a pace just short of a jog. They were joined by two more SEALs, who startled a gasp out of Jordan as they materialized without warning.

Miguel echoed her gasp with a disoriented wail.

"Hush, baby, hush," she soothed, terrified that the senior chief would demand that they ditch the children. Even in the murky forest, she detected the frown he cast over his shoulder.

Heartless man. Did he even care that she was carrying thirty extra pounds? The mud sucking at her boots felt like glue. The air was so wet she could scarcely draw enough oxygen out of it to feed her aching lungs.

"How're you doing, ma'am?" inquired one of the SEALs drifting alongside her. Bristling with weaponry and carrying a pack, he hardly sounded winded. Unlike the other four SEALs, he didn't wear special binoculars, either. He peered, instead, through the infrared scope mounted to the top of his rifle.

"You want me to carry him for you?" he offered, kindly.

"No, thank you," she replied, laboring on. "Miguel's afraid of strangers."

As well he should be. His shadowy history had taken shape at the end of last summer, six months after Father Benedict had discovered him in the care of the older street children. Small for his age, with enormous brown eyes that reflected innocent confusion, Miguel would not speak, other than in whispered words to his companions. It took Jordan's tireless devotion to coax even a heartfelt giggle out of him. The last thing she wanted was for some stranger to manhandle him and send him scuttling back into his shell.

Leaving him at the mission last summer had nearly broken her heart. Miguel had become her second chance to give love and be loved in return. She'd immediately taken measures to adopt him, which Venezuela's new government had made possible. But with the Moderates now struggling to keep a foothold, she feared the laws would revert back, putting an untimely end to the painful process of home studies and document gathering, all requirements to securing his dossier.

She had to convince these SEALs that she'd adopted Miguel already, though she still awaited the approval of the court in Ayacucho. Praying the priest and the nun would understand the purpose behind her lies, Jordan hurried to the front of the pack. A frond slapped her wetly in the face. She stumbled over a root. "Excuse me," she called, to slow down the senior chief.

He swung his masked face around, reminding her of Darth Vader—evil aura and all. "What now?" he demanded, curtly.

"I have to tell you something," she panted. "I've adopted this child, Miguel," she lied. "He's my son, and I won't leave him at the Landing Zone. He's coming home with me."

"Show me his adoption papers," he demanded.

"They're in Ayacucho, being held by the adoption agency. I have to pick them up," she explained without exactly lying.

The SEAL ignored her. Glancing at the compass on his watch, he adjusted their direction and pushed on.

Panic made Jordan's extremities tingle. "I won't leave him," she said, chasing after him. "This isn't even the way to Ayacucho. I need to go east."

"We'll talk about your options when we get to the LZ."

He was implacable. "What's wrong with you?" she demanded with maternal fervor. "Were you raised by wolves? Did you never have a mother?"

He rounded on her, so swiftly, so abruptly that the others bumped into them.

"Do I need to cuff and gag you?" he threatened, startling Miguel awake. The boy loosed a wail of fright.

"Hush, baby." Jordan immediately sought to quiet him. "It's all right."

But the stress of being locked up for four days only to be rudely awakened in the jungle, terrorized by a stranger toting a submachine gun, was too much for Miguel. His cries grew in strength, rising up through the dense vegetation to echo beneath the jungle canopy.

Senior Chief McGuire went rigid. "Make him stop," he ordered hoarsely.

"You're the one who frightened him with your threats,"

Jordan retorted. "Don't you know how to speak in a civil voice?"

"Jordan." Father Benedict stepped between them. "Please don't argue with the senior chief," he pleaded. "I've decided to take all the children to Puerto Ayacucho. I'll collect your dossier from the agency there and keep Miguel safe until you can return for him."

She refused to hear the offer, let alone consider it. No. This was the summer she was going to bring her baby home with her.

Turning away, she drew all the children in her wake, soothing Miguel as she went. "Hush, baby. Hush. You're safe now. You're safe. No one's going to hurt you." She prayed she was right. If she left without him, she risked losing him forever in a country ripping apart at the seams. It was unthinkable. She couldn't survive another separation.

They came abruptly on the LZ, a clearing hacked out of the jungle and burned weekly to keep Mother Nature from taking back what was hers. Solomon spied the silhouette of a Chinook helicopter, backdropped by a sky now the color of pewter. Its rotors spooled lazily at their approach, stirring up a breeze that smelled of mud and rotting fruit.

With a glance at his watch, he thumbed his mike. "Put the women on the helo," he said to his men. "The children stay with the priest." He spoke loudly enough for Jordan Bliss to overhear him.

She drew up short, causing all the children to bunch up behind her.

"It's nothing personal," he called, turning his head to intercept her horrified look. "My orders don't allow for extra passengers." Through his thermal-sensitive NVGs, he saw that she glowed more green than red, as if the blood in her veins had drained right out of her, leaving her cold.

"I won't leave Miguel!" she insisted, a tremor in her voice, as she gripped the boy fiercely. "I'll go to Ayacucho with Father Benedict."

The priest stepped over to intervene. "Give him to me, Jordan," he persuaded, holding out his hands. "It's time for you to leave. You shouldn't have stayed this long in the first place."

She clutched the boy harder, shaking her head in silent, vehement refusal.

Solomon sent Teddy and Vinny a surreptitious signal. In the next instant, they descended on Jordan and wrested the boy from her arms.

"No!" she shrieked, kicking and flailing as Teddy hoisted her off the ground, carrying her into the chopper's wind. Vinny handed off the wailing child to the priest and followed.

With a bad taste in his mouth, Solomon nodded at Father Benedict and turned away. He watched in amazement as Jordan wriggled like a cat out of Teddy's arms and sprang free. In the next instant, she was racing for Miguel, her arms outstretched, screaming out his name.

The indigenous boy cried back, his face wet with tears, mouth agape with confusion and terror, as he struggled in the priest's hold.

With a whispered curse, Solomon intercepted Jordan's path. With a lunge and a hook, he caught her up from behind, coiling her in a hold that no amount of twisting or kicking could compromise. "No!" Her cries of raw pain ricocheted inside his head, reawakening memories that had barely faded after five years.

Like a lioness, she fought him, knocking askew his helmet, raking his face with her nails. The heels of her boots pummeled his shins as she writhed in his grasp and, still, he managed to wrestle her to the thundering Chinook, where Vinny and Gus contributed hands to haul her, screaming continuously, into the cabin.

No sooner were they inside than the helicopter rose, racing the sunrise as it bore them up, up, up into the brightening sky. The lush terrain rolled beneath them like a dark ocean, and still Jordan Bliss fought with every ounce of strength to claw her way to the open door.

"Hold her down!" Solomon yelled, closing the hatch.

With the noise of the rotors muffled, the woman's anguished cries seemed to come from inside his own head.

"You son of a bitch!" she screamed, directing her fury at Solomon, even as both Vinny and Gus struggled to keep her from attacking him. "Make them go back!" she ordered, with hoarse desperation. "Make them go back!"

Solomon set aside his gear and helmet. "Let her go," he said, tired of watching her useless struggles.

The instant the two men released her, Jordan dropped to her hands and knees, obviously spent. She pinned Solomon with eyes that brimmed with tears. "Please, take me back," she pleaded, groveling now.

"I can't," he said, hating the words coming out of his mouth. "It's not up to me."

With a moan of despair, she lowered her head onto the grooved, metal floor, drew her knees up in a ball, and sobbed—deep, rasping sobs that drove Solomon to the cockpit to share a word with the crew.

By the time he rejoined his men, Jordan was strapped into the bench, her head lolling, limbs splayed and limp. Sunlight streamed into the cabin's windows, sparking red highlights in the hair that hung over her pale, fatigued face.

"I gave her a shot of Lorazepam," Vinny confessed, seeing Solomon's startled look. "I couldn't take it anymore, Senior Chief."

Solomon nodded. He didn't blame Vinny one bit.

He eased down onto the bench between Jordan and the praying nun. Gus flipped through a manual in the corner seat. Haiku and Teddy took inventory of their arsenal. Harley, who manned the mounted M15 machine gun, looked up from his position on the floor.

"What?" Solomon demanded, reading disapproval in the bald chief's stern expression. "You would have done that differently?"

"Yes, I would have," said the sniper, disdain in his eyes and voice.

"Then you would have had to turn right around and dump the kid off again," Solomon predicted.

"Maybe not," said Harley, with a challenging glare. "What do you think, sir?" he asked Gus, who glanced up from the manual he was reading.

"It's the senior chief's call," said Gus, taking a neutral position. "Life's not all black-and-white."

Solomon glowered out the window. He didn't need Harley's disapproval or Gus's philosophizing. He'd made a decision based on regulation, expectation, and discipline. At the same time, he knew how it felt to have a child ripped out of his life, out of his future. He hated what he'd done.

Chapter Three

✦

Jordan burrowed deeper into the cozy cocoon she floated in, resisting the pull of consciousness. There were reasons why she didn't want to waken; oblivion was so much sweeter than reality.

Her head rested on a densely muscled shoulder, her face buried against a manly-smelling neck. Was it Doug who was holding her so tenderly? Her ex-husband was a big, strong, high-school football coach. Sweeping a hand up the rock-hard chest, she remembered his infidelities, and with a cry of protest, lifted her lolling head to demand he let her go.

The painted face glancing down at her brought it all back. Navy SEAL Senior Chief McGuire was carrying her across a hot and windy tarmac toward an airport terminal. The helicopter's rotors descended a musical scale behind them. Two SEALs preceded him; three more followed behind, escorting Sister Madeline.

"Put me down," Jordan croaked. The last thing she remembered was one of the SEALs sticking a needle in her thigh. It was this man—this bastard—that had prevented her from bringing Miguel. She started to struggle.

"You won't be able to stand," he warned.

"Let go of me!" she raged, her fury swelling to think that she may have lost Miguel forever, just as she'd lost her baby.

He stopped in his tracks. "You want me to put you down?" he asked, with an arctic glare.

"Yes!"

"Fine then." He dropped an arm, releasing her legs. Her boots touched the sun-warmed cement. She twisted her upper body free and—to her astonishment—kept right on going. Quick as lightning, he looped an arm around her, catching her in middescent. He set her on her feet again.

"Don't touch me," she hissed, prying free of his hold, determined to stand on her own.

He put his hands up to signify surrender and watched her keel right over. This time he didn't move to catch her.

"Oooph!" Jordan landed on her hip, pain radiating from her pelvis.

With a shake of his head, the senior chief just turned and walked away.

Two more SEALs hurried over to scoop her up. "You okay, ma'am?" asked the dark-haired, brown-eyed one who'd stuck her with a syringe full of God-knew-what. He was all concern now.

Jordan couldn't answer. Okay? She'd never be okay again.

The bald SEAL's blue eyes flashed with disapproval at the now-retreating senior chief. But his gentle touch conveyed concern.

"Up you go," said the first SEAL, and together they hoisted her between them. She moved her legs automatically, amazed not to feel the pavement under her feet. How odd.

The African-American SEAL held the door for them, ushering the trio and Sister Madeline inside, out of the windy heat.

Air-conditioning, marveled the part of Jordan's brain that functioned autonomously. It'd been months since she'd experienced that luxury. The smell of coffee and maple syrup wafted from a food court at the rear.

The SEALs lowered her onto one of a half dozen sofas in what was obviously a gate at the airport. The bald SEAL stalked away; the younger one crouched in front of her, checking Jordan's vital signs and her pupils. "You'll feel better in a couple a' hours," he reassured her. "How 'bout a cup of orange juice?" he asked, like he was offering her the elixir of youth.

She just looked at him. How could she eat anything, knowing Miguel was probably hungry and thirsty and terrified without her?

With a commiserating grimace, he stood up and followed the others.

Jordan keeled over on the cloth-covered couch and closed her eyes. A patch of sunlight fell warmly across her face.

Miguel. She'd played with him and held him and watched him flower for two summers in a row. He'd become as much a part of her as the baby who'd been attached by an umbilical cord. Now that he was gone she felt just as incomplete as when she'd miscarried.

Hot tears welled up under her closed eyelids and seeped

between her lashes, wetting the cushion beneath her head. A shadow robbed her face of warmth.

She cracked an eye and discovered Senior Chief McGuire standing over her with a cup in one hand and a half-wrapped breakfast biscuit in the other. She closed her eyes again. "Go away."

"Sit up," he said, ignoring her.

"Leave me alone."

Instead of leaving, he cupped her shoulders and pulled her up into a sitting position. "You need to eat," he said, lowering himself into the sunny patch she'd lain in. He plucked the food items off the floor.

"Says who?"

"Says me." He shoved the cup at her.

She realized suddenly that her mouth was parched. Her fingers shook as she accepted the cup. She had to close her eyes at the sensation of citrus juice gliding over her tongue, sliding coolly down her throat.

She took a tentative bite of the biscuit that was thrust into her hand. Hunger, revived by the smell of food, made her suddenly ravenous. "Where are we?" she demanded around a mouthful. The stunted cactus visible through the window told her nothing.

"The Dutch Antilles," he said, curtly.

An ocean lay between her and the child of her heart. The realization robbed her of her appetite. She started to wrap up the rest of the biscuit.

"Finish it," said the SEAL.

She glared at him, her eyes stinging. "I am not one of your soldiers," she retorted. As their gazes clashed and held, she was hit by how unrelentingly male he was. The breadth of his shoulders, the thickness of his upper arms, summoned an annoying awareness of herself as a woman, filthy and in bad need of a shower, while he, sometime in the last few minutes, had managed to wipe the paint off his face.

"A representative of the FBI is coming to collect you," he said, in a gruff, resonant voice. "And escort you home."

"Whatever." Her home was wherever Miguel was.

"You need to get cleaned up," he added.

His own scrubbed face was strangely arresting. Patrician features, a dark moustache, and neat black eyebrows combined to make him ruthlessly handsome. His silvery eyes were nothing short of hypnotic. She wrested her gaze upward, noting the silver hair above his forehead that streaked back into darker hair like a fin.

Mako. The name popped into her head. No wonder the others called him that. He looked just like a shark.

"Where's the bathroom?" She struggled to rise.

"Over there." He stood up also, watchful, but not touching as he nodded toward a door. "I tossed a flight uniform inside so you'd have something to change into." The words *there* and *uniform* betrayed New England roots.

As Jordan shuffled toward the ladies' room, her legs tingled and revived. She could feel Mako's gaze on her as she fumbled with the handle and pushed her way inside.

She winced to see her reflection in the mirror—bedraggled hair, puffy face, and disillusioned eyes. Her life was supposed to be getting better, not worse.

With a fresh onslaught of tears, she twisted the faucet on and set about washing up. She would get through this, she promised herself. No matter who or what tried to get in her way, she wouldn't rest until Miguel was back in her arms, where he belonged.

Rafael Valentino had to take Senior Chief McGuire's word that Jordan Bliss was in the restroom. "Good luck," the SEAL had said, seeming all too happy to foist the woman off on someone else.

Rafe eased into a chair and waited. This wing of Curaçao's Hato International was used exclusively by U.S. and NATO forces. At the moment, it stood deserted. He didn't know what to expect as the restroom door squeaked open. He drew a startled breath as a darker-haired version of Jillian edged through the opening. Her pale, exhausted countenance brought him quickly to his feet.

She looked like she'd been to hell and back.

"Jordan Bliss?" he asked, approaching her.

Indigo-blue eyes reflected confusion. "Who are you?"

"Special Agent Valentino, FBI."

"Where did the SEALs go?" The plastic sack she held sagged to the floor, as if too heavy to hold.

"Back to Venezuela. They have orders awaiting them."

The freckles on her nose stood starkly against her pasty complexion. "They went back?" Abandoning the sack, she stumbled to the exit and feebly thrust it open.

With a cry of disbelief, she beheld the spot where the helicopter had sat. She let the door fall shut, slumping wearily against it.

"I'm a friend of your sister's," said Rafe, with an urge to take her into his arms before she collapsed. Her vulnerability reminded him of Jillian's.

"Jillian?" She turned her head to look at him.

"Yes, Jillian. She's been worried sick about you."

"Is she okay? The baby!" she cried.

"She's fine," he reassured her. "And very pregnant. She's looking forward to having you home."

"Of course," Jordan agreed, without enthusiasm.

"I have a plane waiting," he added, indicating the private jet outside. "Is there anything you need before we go?"

"Just my clothes." Pushing off the door, she went to retrieve the sack.

As the tiny twin engine sliced through the thin atmosphere over the Gulf of Mexico, Jordan felt the effects of the tranquilizer waning. It might have been the sugar in the powdered donuts Valentino set before her at the start of their flight, but as they entered U.S. airspace, with the Mississippi River snaking far below them, she felt revived enough to ask, "So, how did my big sister get six Navy SEALs and the FBI to yank me out of Venezuela?"

The darkly handsome agent cast her a ghost of a smile. "The SEALs were my idea," he admitted, in his peculiar, gravelly voice. "But your sister gets points for persistence. She called the Bureau thirty-one times."

"I'm not surprised," said Jordan, dryly. "How do you know Jillian? Through Gary?" Her sister had never mentioned a friend at the Bureau, certainly not a distinguished gentleman who didn't wear a wedding ring.

"She was a nurse in the ER in Fairfax when I was treated for shrapnel in my neck." He touched the scar just above his collar.

Jordan realized the injury was the reason for his rusty

voice. "Oh. So…" She pushed back thoughts of Miguel that made conversation so difficult. "How's Jillie doing? Is the barn up yet?"

"The barn is up." He turned down the corner of the page and closed the magazine, giving her his full attention.

A gentleman, thought Jordan—unlike a certain Navy SEAL she'd encountered lately.

"Has she bought those therapy horses yet?"

"She has just one horse that I know of."

"That's our old horse Molly," said Jordon, locking her cold hands together. "You must think I'm an awful sister, leaving her at a time like this," she added, betraying her private guilt.

"It's not for me to think anything," he answered tactfully.

"I had to go back to Venezuela," she explained. "I was supposed to bring Miguel home with me. Did Jillie tell you about Miguel?"

"No."

"He's four years old. An orphan. I met him last summer doing my mission work there, and I…" How could she possibly convey her immediate and overwhelming attachment for the boy? "I knew back then that I wanted to be his mother." Her voice wobbled. "So I got all the documents signed and sent off, but it takes so much time for the Venezuelan courts to respond. And with the new government struggling to stay in power…" She swallowed the lump filling her throat. "I don't know if I'll ever get to adopt him. Or if I'll even be able to find him again."

She had to look out the window to subdue her overwhelming despair. "Still," she added, huskily, "maybe I should've stayed near Jillian this summer. It's got to be hard without Gary there to help."

A long silence followed her lament.

"What happened to Gary?" Valentino finally inquired, his tone remote.

She turned and looked at him, realizing at the same instant that he hadn't known. "Jillie didn't tell you?"

"No." He calmly slipped his magazine into the pocket of his black leather briefcase.

"He was killed in a drug sting. You knew he was a policeman, right?"

"Yes. When was this?"

"It was January, so—seven months ago. She didn't even know she was pregnant. She sold the house in Fairfax and moved into the house we grew up in. That was something she and Gary'd always planned to do, to have a hippotherapy ranch."

A taut silence followed her words. Jordan sensed that she'd caught the agent by surprise, though it was hard to tell by his serene expression.

"Excuse me," he said, unbuckling his seat belt. "I need to have a word with the pilot. Can I get you anything? More milk?"

"No thanks. I still have some." His polite retreat made her wonder if he had feelings for Jillian. Jillie was a beautiful, capable woman, but what bachelor wanted to take on another man's family?

Thoughts of Miguel impaled her again, and she turned her stricken face to the window, grappling with the awful feeling that she'd lost him forever.

* * *

Solomon stared at the patina of moonlight shining on the ceiling. The fact that he couldn't sleep had nothing to do with the whirring of insects outside the barracks or the occasional volley of gunfire as soldiers of the Moderate government drilled in anticipation of a coup. It was Jordan Bliss. He couldn't get the damn woman out of his head.

The memory of her haunted him. Even with her hair matted, her eyes swollen, her nose running, he'd been struck by something ferociously beautiful in her. Physically, she was pleasing, with autumnal coloring, deep violet eyes, and full lips. But beyond the physical, he sensed a wealth of devotion and commitment for a child she hadn't even given birth to.

Had Candace ever loved Silas like that?

He had. With a groan, he realized that the pain of losing a child never really went away. It just got buried under everyday issues and details. But beneath those issues, it remained, a bleeding wound.

And now he lay here, wondering what his son looked like at six years of age; where he was, that not a single private investigator over the course of five years could find so much as a trace of him. From that fateful night Solomon had returned home to an empty house, Candace and Silas hadn't once resurfaced.

Since then, he'd taken life one day at a time, seizing comfort wherever he could find it—in a book, between a woman's thighs, on the wide expanse of the ocean. He never looked beyond the day's end for happiness.

He'd had his orders, and he'd followed them. Yet, orders aside, he had now condemned Jordan Bliss to the same circle of hell he lived in. From now on, the memory of her loss would be the first thing to peg her heart when she stirred each morning. She would dream occasionally that she and her child were reunited, only to have reality snatch that stubborn joy from her breast when she awoke.

Who was he to separate a mother from her son?

Never mind that Miguel was not of her blood. He was a part of her soul. As much as Silas had been a part of Solomon's.

He owed her an apology—no, more than that. His repentance, no matter how honest, could not alleviate her loss or absolve his guilt.

"Forgive me," he whispered at the ceiling, which seemed to ripple when viewed through the wetness in his eyes. "Jordan." Her name felt strangely intimate upon his tongue. The memory of her lithe, wriggling body was so deeply impressed upon his senses that he responded sexually to it. He couldn't think of her as Miss Bliss. That formality had been tossed aside the moment he'd glimpsed into her heart and recognized her selfless spirit.

He experienced a powerful yearning to see her again, to *know* her, in the Biblical sense. "Jordan," he said again, hearing desire in his raspy whisper.

With sleep now hopeless, he swung his feet to the floor, dragged out the chair by his cot, and sat at the crude, metal desk.

"Wha's going on?" muttered Harley, who raised his head off the cot by the wall.

"Nothing. Go back to sleep." Solomon switched on the desk lamp. A search through the drawers turned up two tattered pieces of paper and a military-issue, ballpoint pen.

With the point of a pen centered in the lamp's light, he began to write from his heart, in verse, a talent few people knew he possessed.

"To My Son," he titled the poem.

By the time he'd finished, the light of the lamp was no longer needed. The sky had lightened to a purple-blue that was the exact color of Jordan Bliss's eyes. The lines on the original poem had been scratched through and rewritten. Once the result was neatly transcribed to the second page, he felt a kinship with Jordan that overrode reason. He wanted to comfort her in person.

Hearing Harley stir, Solomon turned the light off, put the pen away, and slipped the paper into the drawer to be mailed later.

He'd absolved himself of his crime. But who could say whether the poem would bring solace or more despair?

Mantachie, Mississippi

"I gotta pee," said a small voice in the back of Ellie's 1983 Chevy Impala.

If Ellie Stuart weren't just furious that her husband had forgotten that he had three sons, plus a nephew, all of whom were too hungry at eleven o'clock at night to sleep, she might have laughed at Silas's predictable statement. The six-year-old had the bladder of a mouse.

"We're here, sweetie," she comforted, even as she signaled a left turn. "You can use the potty inside."

They bounced into an unpaved parking lot, rutted with

potholes and already crammed with cars. Spying Carl's truck up close to the entrance, Ellie's lips thinned. She parked her Impala between Carl's truck and a telephone pole, ordered the boys to clamber out of one side and to hold hands while she pulled the sleeping baby from his car seat.

"Come on," she urged the small troop, tugging them in a straggling line behind her.

The bar was dark and smoky and pounding with sultry music. Heads turned to speculate as Ellie shooed the boys into the bathroom. "Christopher," she told the oldest, "make sure all of you wash your hands with soap. I'll be over there"—she pointed toward the stage, where a scantily clad dancer was circling the center pole—"having words with your father."

"Yes, Mama." Christopher took his responsibilities seriously.

Which was more than could be said of Carl, who was so hypnotized by the dancer's undulations that he failed to notice her approach. "Carl," she said sharply. He swiveled with a gasp. "The boys are too hungry to sleep. I've come for some money to feed them."

His astonishment shifted abruptly into apathy. "I ain't got no money," he protested, hiding the dollar bill in his left hand.

He was going to tip the dancer with it, Ellie realized, her fury mounting.

"Carl Louis Stuart," she hissed, clutching baby Colton fiercely to her bosom, "how can you turn your back on your own children?" she demanded, blood roaring in her ears.

"Who says they're even mine," he sneered, not noticing the frowns gathering on the faces of men sitting near him.

"Three birth certificates and the state of Mississippi, that's who!" Ellie retorted, shuddering with outrage.

"Well, that boy Silas ain't mine," he defended himself. "I don't owe him nothin'. Here, take this." He slapped the dollar onto the counter before him, dug into his pocket, and produced a handful of change. "It's all I got," he insisted.

With fingers that shook, Ellie snatched up the dollar as well as the change.

"Best get yourself a job," Carl added, before she could whirl away. "I sold that heap-o'-junk trailer you live in to Eddie Levi up the road. You got two weeks to move out of it."

"What?" She felt the blood drain from her face. "You can't do that."

"'s been in my name all these years," said Carl, sounding pleased with himself. "I can do as I damn well want."

Hearing his speech slur, she realized he was drunk. In her fury, Ellie snatched up his mug of beer and tossed it in his face. With a roar, he stood up, hands going for her neck.

Men on either side leapt up to subdue him. Grinding her teeth to keep from shrieking, Ellie stalked away. Reasoning with Carl when he was drunk was a waste of time. He had to be taunting her, she reassured herself. He couldn't have sold the trailer out from under them.

Seeing the boys emerge from the restroom, their wide eyes fastened on the dancer as she shrugged her top off, Ellie hurried over to usher them out of the bar. "Let's go," she called.

"How much did he give us?" Christopher wanted to know as they marched in a knot back to the car.

"Just get in," said Ellie, through her teeth. Her throat ached with the need to scream out her frustrations. Only, she wouldn't. Not in front of the boys.

She buckled in the baby, as Christopher, Caleb, and Silas wrestled over seat belts. Settling herself behind the wheel, Ellie counted the money still gripped in her hand. One dollar and seventy-six cents.

Feeling her eyes sting, she blinked back her tears. She could buy a box of macaroni and cheese and feed them all tonight. But what about tomorrow? The boys would starve at this rate.

You could call Social Services, suggested a voice in her head.

Never. She'd experienced firsthand what Social Services in the state of Mississippi did to families. It broke them apart. Her boys belonged together. They belonged with *her*. She'd sell her hair first, take in extra children, do whatever it took to keep from asking for a handout and getting screwed in return.

But if Carl had really sold the trailer, what then? They'd be living on the streets in two weeks. And in that case, she might not really have a choice.

Chapter Four

✦

Rafe Valentino reached for the ringing phone with relief. He couldn't keep his thoughts on his work long enough to be productive. "Valentino," he rasped, praying for a big distraction.

"Hi, it's Jillian." Her voice was soft and subtle and, in some mysterious way, seemed to sink inside of him.

"Well, hello." His heartbeat quickened with pleasure he didn't want to analyze. It was Jillian who was widowed, not married. He hadn't gotten used to thinking of her that way.

"I didn't get a chance to thank you yesterday," she admonished. "You disappeared right off the plane."

"I had an emergency at the office," he prevaricated. "Besides, you were there to greet your sister, not me."

"True, but it would have been nice to thank you in person."

"No need," he reassured her. "Your sister is remarkable. How's she settling in?"

"Oh, not too well. She looks and acts like a waif. She spends all of her time watching the news and nagging the adoption agency to see if Miguel's dossier is back from the courts yet. I don't suppose there's anything the FBI can do to speed things up?"

"That's beyond the scope of our powers I'm afraid," he apologized.

"I thought so," she said, sadly.

An awkward pause filled the phone lines.

"How are you doing?" Rafe asked to fill it. He really didn't want to hear an answer. There wasn't any question that she had to be struggling, that she could use all kinds of help, even his.

"Oh, hanging in there," she said, with just a thread of desperation. "My therapy horses arrive in a week. I'm expecting my first patients shortly after that."

"You'll be busy," he noted, wondering when she was supposed to fit in time for a baby.

"I was wondering if you'd like to come over for dinner this Friday," she offered, unexpectedly, "to welcome Jordan back and to thank you for bringing her home."

"I'll need to check my calendar," he replied, inexplicably panicked. Jillian was available. *Available.* "May I get back to you?"

"Of course." Another awkward pause. "Rafael?"

The way she said his name made him feel like they were sitting next to each other. "Yes, Jillian."

"I'm sorry I didn't tell you about Gary."

His breath caught.

"I just . . . I didn't want to burden you with my situation, that's all. It's so tiring to explain what happened and then have to listen to people stutter through their condolences. I just want things to be normal again, not sad all the time, you know?"

"Yes," he said, though he was a hypocrite to say so. But hearing her practically beg for a reason to be happy, he elected to accept her invitation to dinner. "My calendar looks clear on Friday," he decided. "What time would you like me to arrive?"

"How about six?" she suggested, sounding relieved and grateful.

"I'll be there," he promised, hanging up quietly. He was pleased to have given her something to look forward to.

The record-breaking, late-July heat summoned a trickle of sweat between Jordan's shoulder blades, just as it had in Venezuela. She'd give anything to be there and not at the front door of her condominium in Chesapeake, struggling to insert a key in the lock, weighted down by grocery bags and today's mail.

The lock yielded with a click, and she stumbled inside. The condominium she had bought a year ago still smelled new, unlived in. As she dumped her groceries on the kitchen counter, the mail slipped free to scatter across the floor.

Blinking back tears of frustration, Jordan bent to scoop up the dozens of bills. She hadn't had the courage yet to look into her finances, which were already strained from paying to fly to Venezuela.

An envelope addressed to her in a forceful scrawl caught her eye. She picked it up, her heart accelerating as she took note of the Venezuelan postage.

Laying the bills aside, she sat down at her dinette table and tore open the envelope, praying Father Benedict had written with news of Miguel. In confusion, she frowned at the small wrinkled page inside. A poem appeared to be written on it, entitled "To My Son." Her gaze dropped to the signature at the bottom: Solomon McGuire, and her heart stopped.

McGuire. Mako. The senior chief whom she blamed for her separation from Miguel. Who'd have guessed he had a name like Solomon?

Intrigued, she read the poem, once quickly and then a second time, unable to reconcile the tender, poignant message with the one who sent it. *My boy,* he wrote, *my beautiful, my own.*

In disbelief, she sought a return address, but there wasn't one.

She could scarcely comprehend it. He'd put into words her complete and utter despair at having had Miguel ripped from her arms. But how could he, unless he'd lived through something similar?

With a thoughtful frown, Jordan's assumptions shifted, expanded, made room for the unthinkable. She laid the paper on the table and smoothed out the creases.

Perhaps she was wrong to have blamed him. The senior chief's surliness might have been a reaction to the awful task ahead of him. Who but the most sensitive man could write, *Is he my earthly ideal gone?*

This was his way of apologizing. Only she would rather have someone to blame and rail against, wouldn't she?

But there was something bittersweet in this apology, as well as an underlying communication of intimacy that made her feel exposed, like he'd glimpsed a side of her she'd vowed no man would ever see again.

At a loss as to what to do with the poem, Jordan stuck

it back in the envelope and left it with the rest of her bills to deal with later.

She put her groceries away. As a part of her nightly ritual, she called Jillian and confirmed that she'd be over for dinner Friday night. Then she fixed supper and ate it standing up, her gaze straying thoughtfully to the envelope.

On her way to bed, she snatched it up and carried it upstairs, where she left it on her bedside table while she showered and dressed for bed. Turning out the light, she slipped under the covers and looked at the envelope, glowing like a ghost in the darkness.

The fact that Solomon McGuire, a stranger, recognized her pain made it all the more crushing. Turning her back on his missive, she grieved her loss. The memory of Miguel's smile, his scent, his frail little arms clutching her neck, followed her into her dreams.

One of Solomon's best-kept secrets was that he enjoyed puttering at the desk in his office at Spec Ops. Senior chiefs weren't supposed to enjoy time spent in the office. Paperwork was for lowlier enlisted to generate and officers to sign.

But Solomon took private pleasure in anything associated with reading and writing. He knew for a fact he was better-read than his commanding officer. Lieutenant Commander Montgomery had a master's degree in finance, but he didn't own a library like the one on Solomon's houseboat. Harley, who'd constructed the built-in shelves, had an inkling of the number of books that lined them, but not even Harley knew Solomon had read them all.

Back from a month's TDY in Venezuela, Solomon was pleased to return to a desk overflowing with paper. He shut the door, cozied into his leather desk chair, and started sorting through it. It took an hour to come across a handwritten envelope that had been forwarded to the SPEC OPS building from his previous command post.

The return address of Mantachie, Mississippi, looked entirely unfamiliar, as did the neat script. He slit the envelope with his sterling-plated letter opener, finding two pages inside, a handwritten letter and the copy of a death certificate. Candy's death certificate.

Doused with shock and disbelief, he skimmed the letter, desperate for news of Silas.

You do not know me, sir, but I know of you through Candy, who was once my stepsister. Her father and my mother were married in the early nineties. Candy came through Mantachie two years ago, on her way to Vegas. She left Silas behind, promising to collect him later, only she never did. Last month I got word that she'd died in a car crash a few months before. She'd lived her life like that—going too fast, wanting too much. I'd just as soon keep Silas with me—God knows I love him like my own. Truth is I can't afford to keep him any more than I have a right to. He's your boy, not mine. Please come and fetch him within a week if possible, as I have to move from this address.

Respectfully,
Ellie Jean Stuart

"Son of a bitch," Solomon breathed, examining the second page, a death certificate. Candace was definitely dead. He waited to see how that news would impact him and felt nothing. His love for her had perished long ago.

Silas!

He dove back into the letter, reading it carefully this time, searching for inferences. The message seemed sincere, suggesting that the author was a woman of common sense and moral consciousness, which was more than could be said of Candace.

Excitement started singing through his veins.

Silas was alive! His son, alive! His search was over.

He stood up so swiftly that the room went briefly black. He staggered through his door past Veronica, the secretary, who all but cowered as he thundered on the CO's closed door. "He—he's in a meeting," she hedged, wary of Solomon on a good day.

Solomon could not have cared less. Hearing the call to enter, he shoved the door open and marched inside. "Sir, I need to request emergency leave effective immediately," he stated, even as he came to belated attention before both men present, Commander Montgomery and Admiral Johansen, who appeared less than impressed by his abrupt entrance.

Joe Montgomery sat back in his chair and just looked at him, his thoughts inscrutable behind a face that was badly scarred yet still managed to be appealing to the opposite sex. "What's going on?" he asked.

"I've found my son," said Solomon, marveling at the words coming out of his own mouth. "He's in Mantachie, Mississippi. I need to go get him." He held up Ellie Stuart's letter.

The CO glanced at the admiral, then looked back at Solomon, and said, simply, "Take a week."

Solomon had never disliked Joe Montgomery. They were very different entities who, when paired, made a brutally effective team. But in that brief second that their eyes met and something warm and friendly flickered in the CO's face, Solomon felt a sudden connection.

"Thank you, sir!"

"Dismissed," the CO growled.

"Yes, sir!" with a hundred-and-eighty degree swivel, he marched briskly towards the door and left the room. The grin of unadulterated joy that split his face as he headed for the door had Veronica staring at him like he'd grown two heads.

On the west side of Atlanta, Georgia, Solomon forced himself to stop driving, to find a cheap motel, and to sleep.

He was beset with disturbing dreams in which he found Silas mentally and emotionally crippled; found Silas gone when he got there. At dawn, Solomon got up, showered, and shaved, wanting to look presentable. He grabbed breakfast at a diner and drove eight more hours to Mantachie, Mississippi.

The place wasn't even marked on a map. He'd had to stop twice to ask for directions. At last, with the afternoon sun baking the cab of his Chevy Silverado, he arrived at 909 Hickory Road. One of the nines had fallen off the leaning mailbox.

He turned down a dry, dirt road, one that was sparsely forested, with a low-lying swamp off to the right. It was little wonder no private detective had ever been able to

•

find Silas. The boy had been dumped out here in the middle of nowhere. Anger whipped through him, but with Candace dead, he had nowhere to direct his ire.

The dirt road climbed a brief hill, and there at the top stood a blue mobile home. Half its underpinning was missing, the siding was rusted, one window had been boarded up, and the saddest-looking Impala sedan was parked out front.

Solomon scarcely took in the setting. His attention had been captured by the three boys playing under an immense hickory tree—two with light hair, one with dark. As he slowed his truck, the medium-sized boy shoved the dark-haired boy off his feet and wrested a toy from his hands. Pale gray eyes flashed on the smaller boy's face. *Silas!* thought Solomon, braking abruptly.

He watched with bemusement as his son rolled quick-as-a-cat to his feet and plowed his head into the blond boy's belly, wresting the toy car back again.

That's my boy, Solomon marveled, even as the three dust-covered children looked up at him and stilled, cautiously suspicious.

The door of the mobile home flew open and out stepped a young woman with an infant in her arms. Solomon turned his engine off and eased out into the sultry heat to greet her. His first impression of Ellie Stuart as she made her way toward him was that she was amazingly young to be the mother of this brood.

Worn but clean clothing hugged a body that was lean and strong, outlining full breasts that the little baby grasped possessively. Her hair was a light ginger brown, tied into a single braid down her back.

She stopped by the bumper of his truck to take stock

of him. "Great day, but you look just like Silas!" she exclaimed in an alto voice that came out in slow, syrupy syllables.

Solomon nodded, not sure how to greet this woman. After all, she'd kept Silas from him for years, since Candy had dropped him off.

"Ellie Stuart," she said, stepping up to offer him a work-roughened hand.

"Solomon," he replied, seeing nothing but honesty in the woman's gray-blue eyes.

She nodded. "Silas," she called, "come and meet your papa, now."

Solomon turned toward the approaching trio of dust-covered boys. His mouth felt desert-dry in this wilting heat. Fear and uncertainty made his heart pound. How could the boy standing waist high be the same cherubic baby he'd held in his arms? Yet the silvery eyes, so like his own, were unmistakably the same, as was the line of his mouth, the height of his brow.

Father and son stared at each other from a distance of ten feet.

"Lord have mercy, boys," Ellie muttered, walking briskly up to them and slapping the dust off their clothing. "You'd never know you all had a bath this morning. Now get into the house and scrub that dirt off your faces."

All three boys turned obediently toward the house, but the littlest, Silas, ran ahead of them, slamming the door shut.

Ellie sighed. "I told him you were coming to fetch him sooner or later. I think he hoped I was lying."

"Why'd you keep him from me all these years?" he demanded, letting his frustration show.

Instead of cowering, Ellie lifted her chin at him. "Candace told me things about you—things I hope aren't true," she added with a searching look.

Solomon glowered. "They're not," he retorted. "That boy was my life," he added hoarsely.

The suspicion in her eyes faded. She gave a nod of understanding and resignation. "Silas has been with us since he was four. He's been one of us," she added, her own voice husky, her eyes suspiciously bright.

Solomon sensed her deep sorrow at the impending separation, but she turned toward the house, keeping her emotions under tight rein. "Come on in," she called.

He followed her leggy stride, admiring her outward spirit.

The interior of the mobile home was scarcely cooler than the temperature outside. Not a single light was shining. He guessed right away that the power had been turned off.

As bedraggled inside as it was outside, the trailer was nearly Spartan in terms of furniture but surprisingly tidy considering the number of boys living in it.

"Silas?" Ellie called. "Christopher, Caleb, go find him," she instructed. "Then all of you wash up."

She put the baby in a windup swing and reached in the cupboard for a glass. "All I can offer you is water," she said, matter-of-factly.

Solomon wasn't fooled. He'd already guessed that the silent refrigerator probably stood empty. "Please," he said, nodding at the glass.

She filled it at the sink, then handed it to him.

He drained it in three swallows. "Did she tell you why she left me?" he swallowed his pride to ask.

Ellie gave him a good once-over. "What she told me doesn't really matter, considering it was her problem, not yours. Like I said in my letter, she was never content with what she had. Don't blame yourself for that," she added frankly. "Silas, on the other hand, never complains. He must've gotten that from you," she added.

He found her candidness refreshing. She deserved better than this. "Sounded in your letter like you'd fallen on some hard times," he fished, inviting her to unburden herself.

Her smoky eyes reflected cynicism. "My husband ran off," she admitted, "with a cocktail waitress from Turley's Show Bar. Decided being a daddy wasn't what he wanted, after all."

Despite the careless toss of her head, he detected disillusionment so deep and so wide that he found himself reaching for his wallet.

Her eyes went from questioning to indignant as he cracked it open and pulled out a hundred-dollar bill. "I don't want your money!" she exclaimed, backing up. "Boys! You'd better be washing up."

"Silas won't come out from under the bed, Mama," said the oldest son, who sidled into the doorway, his gaze fastening on the money.

"I'll get him out," she said, pushing past Solomon to head down the hallway. "Watch the baby," she said to Christopher.

Solomon trailed after her. Silas was his responsibility now. He found Ellie in the center of an impossibly small bedroom, down on her hands and knees. "Silas, I told you this was going to happen. It's a good thing, trust me. Your papa's going to take good care of you. Come on out now, or else."

Solomon didn't know what "or else" entailed but it was bad enough to prompt Silas to wriggle out from his hiding place. He crawled into Ellie's embrace and hid his face in her neck. "Hush, baby. It's okay," she said, her voice trembling audibly. Solomon thought of Jordan Bliss. A weight immediately pressured his chest. Jesus, not again.

"Listen," he said, loath to separate another child from his caretaker, "I'm going to write you a check."

As she shot him an outraged look, he added, "It's up to you whether you cash it or not, but it's got my home address written on it. That way you can find me if you want to visit Silas." Stepping over to a dresser, he scribbled out a sum ample enough to see Ellie and her brood through the next few months, at least.

By the time he turned back, Ellie had pulled clothing out of a second dresser and was stuffing it into a paper bag. She took the check without looking at it and stuck it in the pocket of her shorts. "This is all he's got," she said, handing Solomon the bag. "Okay, Silas. Give me a hug and get on out of here." Her terse tone camouflaged the fact that she was close to tears.

As the boy wrapped his thin arms about her shoulders and trembled, Solomon tore his gaze from the heartache etched on Ellie's brow. "Come on, son," he urged in his gentlest voice. He held out a hand to him.

Silas looked at the hand. Eyes filled with trepidation, he nonetheless found the courage to put his little hand into the bigger one.

The instant their palms touched, Solomon's knees went weak. A ferocious tide of love roared through him, so fiercely that he had to fight from crushing his son's fingers. He wanted to speak reassuring words, but with his throat clogged with emotion, all he could do was to blink back tears and nod at Ellie as he herded Silas toward the door.

The formal dining room in the nineteenth-century farmhouse was used strictly on holidays and special occasions. It surprised Jordan to find that Jillian had not only dusted the mahogany sideboard, she'd also dressed the table in a lace tablecloth, topping it with heirloom china and crystal glassware. The essence of cooked apples wafted from the kitchen, betraying the fact that Jillian had also baked their mother's recipe for apple pie. And all of this was to celebrate Jordan's safe return?

Even Graham and Agatha thumped down the stairs wearing their finest. Bemused and a little curious, Jordan was told that Special Agent Valentino was en route and would she please stir the rice so that Jillian could race upstairs to dress?

"Of course," said Jordan, glancing wryly at her own, casual sundress. "I didn't know this was going to be a special occasion."

Valentino's knock came just as Jillian descended the stairs in a pretty pink dress. At the sudden brightening of her countenance, Jordan had a thought: Maybe this was more than just a thank-you.

She watched as Jillian introduced her children— Graham, who grudgingly accepted Rafe's handshake, and six-year-old Agatha, who caught the agent off guard by hugging him effusively. He looked over at Jordan and smiled. "You look much better," he told her kindly.

"Thank you," she murmured, knowing full well that she looked like hell.

"Would you like a tour of the house?" Jillian asked.

"Sure," said Rafael.

They made their way up the stairs, with Agatha right on their heels. As Graham threw himself down on the sofa to sulk, Jordan returned to the kitchen, one ear cocked to her sister's narrative and the agent's kind replies.

They spoke like old friends, Jordan mused, not just acquaintances. Friends who found themselves on unfamiliar ground.

Her speculations continued as she watched their exchange over dinner. Jillian had outdone herself dishing up a savory entrée of duck à l'orange, served with rice pilaf and steamed vegetables. Rafe ate with deep appreciation and impeccable manners.

"Graham would like to know how you got the Navy SEALs to rescue Jordan," Jillian asked, pulling her uncommunicative son into the conversation.

Rafe touched his napkin to his lips. "Well, my colleague, Hannah Lindstrom, is married to a SEAL officer," he explained to the teen, who briefly met his gaze. "Hannah made inquiries and, as luck would have it, six members of Team Twelve were in Caracas, anyway, training the Elite Guard."

Graham grunted and stabbed his fork into his meat.

Jillian tried again. "You mean our military trains their military?"

"Just their elite warriors," he replied. "We want to see this Moderate government succeed. Training their best is one way to keep the Populists from wresting control again."

At the reminder of the unstable political situation, Jordan's appetite fled.

"What are the chances that they might?" Jillian asked, shooting her sister a troubled look.

Rafael shrugged his shoulders. "The Moderates were elected by the barest of margins," he admitted, "and the poor, who support the Populists, probably didn't even vote, which means there may be more support for the rebels than the Moderates can combat."

Jordan didn't want to hear that. She placed her fork beside her plate. How was she supposed to eat and casually discuss the fate of Venezuela when Miguel and the others relied on Father Benedict for every crumb to enter their mouths, for shelter from harm? She'd heard nothing from the priest in the past week, didn't even know if Miguel was alive.

Unaware of Jordan's plummeting emotions, Rafe added, "They also have Cuba and Iran furnishing them with weapons and Colombian cartels financing their resurgence. It's a tenuous situation."

Jordan pushed her chair back. "I'll go warm up the pie for dessert," she volunteered, avoiding Jillian's concerned glance.

When she returned to the table, conversation had turned to the details of Jordan's rescue. "Jordan, Rafael says the SEALs who saved you are stationed in Virginia Beach."

"Are they?" Jordan replied, unsettled to think that Solomon McGuire lived just a stone's throw away. What would he think to know she read his poem every night, perversely comforted by the intuitive knowledge that he'd lost a child himself, once.

"You should write them a thank-you note," Jillian suggested, unaware of Jordan's agitation. "Rafael could give it to his partner to pass along."

Jordan didn't answer. If she wrote to Senior Chief McGuire, she wouldn't know what to say to him. His poem was a comfort, yes, but nothing changed the fact that he'd wrenched Miguel away from her—possibly forever.

"Can I be excused?" Graham demanded unexpectedly.

All three adults looked at him, startled by his angry tone.

"You've hardly eaten anything, honey," Jillian pointed out.

"That's because you guys are boring me to death," he retorted, rudely. "I want to hang out with Cameron."

Cameron was the boy next door—if you could call him that when the nearest house was half a mile away.

"Rinse your plate, then, and put it in the dishwasher," Jillian replied, looking disappointed. "I guess you won't be getting any pie," she added, on a firmer note, something Jordan knew that Gary would've said.

Jordan understood the boy's discomfort. Having a strange man in their home, a man who seemed to know his mother on an intimate level, must seem like a betrayal to his father's memory.

Graham wordlessly shoved back his chair and disappeared.

Jillian flinched and drew a sudden breath.

"Jillie?" Jordan called with concern. "What's wrong?"

"I'm fine." Her sister forced a smile. "It was just a pang. Let's have a toast," she added, reaching for her glass of water.

Jordan and Rafael obliged. Agatha joined in eagerly.

"To the FBI and all its wonderful agents. God bless them all, especially Rafael."

"To Rafael," Jordan echoed, watching the subtle glow return to her sister's face. The agent, on the other hand, appeared self-conscious of praise—or was it more than that? His black-as-night eyes seemed to harbor painful memories.

He tried to dismiss himself. "The meal was delicious," he began, "and I'd love to stay for a second serving, but I have an early flight in the morning."

"Oh," said Jillian, sounding disappointed. "Where are you going?"

"Just to D.C. I'll be back on Tuesday."

"Please say you'll have some dessert," she begged him, looking crestfallen.

"It's Grandma's apple pie!" Agatha piped up. "I helped Mommy bake it and it took all day!"

The agent looked from mother to child, his mouth quirking ruefully. "Well, in that case, I'll stay," he decided.

Jillian's smile lifted Jordan's spirits. "You sit," she said to her sister. "I'll get it." More than anything, she longed to see Jillian happy again. It seemed a miracle that Rafe Valentino did just that.

Chapter Five

✦

Solomon drove toward Anniston, Alabama, in a daze. As the miles rolled beneath his tires, he cast sidelong glances at his son, drinking in every feature of the boy he'd lost and found again.

The pale, silent child huddled on the far side of the truck's cab was as familiar as he was alien. Solomon didn't know what to say to him. They were, for all intents and purposes, strangers. Solomon loved his son; but it didn't follow that the boy felt the same way about him. If anything, he seemed terrified.

When a rivulet appeared on the upholstery, creeping out from under Silas's legs, Silas's fear was undeniable. The boy had just wet his pants.

Solomon groped behind the seat for a roll of paper towels. "Why didn't you say you had to go?" he asked.

Silas didn't answer.

Flexing his jaw, Solomon veered off the highway onto an exit ramp. Thank God, Ellie had sent a bag of clothes with them.

As he stood outside the stall in the men's room at a

roadside McDonald's, Solomon felt uncomfortably out of his element.

He'd known what to do with an infant. Feed him; change him; croon lullabies. Silas was a little person, now, independent in some ways, helpless in others. Solomon didn't know the first thing about caring for him.

His son pushed out of the stall in dry clothing. Solomon inspected him quickly, then scooped up the sodden pants lying on the floor and found a plastic sack in the garbage to stuff them in. Wouldn't this add an interesting dimension to laundry day?

"Wash your hands," he instructed. "You hungry?"

Together they washed their hands in the same sink, Silas's fingers small and sturdy beneath Solomon's touch.

Solomon tried again. "Look here, son," he said, handing Silas a paper towel. "You've got to talk to me," he urged. "I can't read your mind to know what you need."

To his dismay, Silas's little chin trembled. His big eyes filled with tears.

Undone by the sight, Solomon hit his knees right there on the bathroom floor. He pulled the stiff little figure into his arms and held him tight. "I'm scared, too," he rasped in his ear, grateful that his humiliation wasn't being witnessed by anyone else. "The last time I saw you, you were just a baby," he continued roughly, "and I could hold you in my arms and rock you."

To his relief, he felt Silas lean into him.

"Look," he added, picking up the boy as he stood. "Look into the mirror and tell me what you see." He put his face cheek to cheek with Silas's.

Silas didn't say a word, but he took in their reflections—the identical dark hair, the light, silvery eyes fringed with dark lashes. "We're the same," Solomon answered for him. "You came from me, see? We belong together."

The little boy's gaze searched his own. "Did you sing to me when I was a baby?" he asked suddenly.

With a skip of his heart, Solomon realized he'd just heard his son speak, for the very first time—in the thickest Southern drawl imaginable, with a lisp that was a result of his missing front teeth.

Emotion clogged his voice box, making it impossible to answer right away. "Aye, I did," he rasped, at last, displaying his own Maine dialect.

"What did you sing?" asked Silas.

"I'll show you later," Solomon promised, "when we get to Virginia." It would take them another twelve hours to get there. Solomon didn't want to stop this time. He couldn't wait to bring his son home.

By lunchtime the following day, Solomon had started a mental list of things that needed change in his life in order to accommodate a six-year-old. The fact that his home was a houseboat and Silas couldn't swim didn't help matters.

"Auntie said we'd be bait for 'gators if we swam in the creek," Silas had said this morning as Solomon led him for the first time down the pier toward home. The rising sun had turned the marsh that fringed the inlet into stalks of gold.

"There aren't any alligators this far north," Solomon had explained. He'd made his first note to self: *Teach Silas to swim*.

Exhausted and emotionally spent, all Solomon had

wanted to do was to fall into his captain's bed and sleep. But Silas was wide-awake, having slept all night in the truck. Some of his shyness had worn off, making him a fount of unending questions.

"What's this? How's it work?"

The interior of Solomon's houseboat was crammed with curiosities that captivated Silas's imagination. Solomon didn't dare retreat into his bedroom.

Every nook, every cabinet, every drawer and cupboard— and there were dozens, all handmade and hung by Harley, a master craftsman—drew Silas's scrutiny. He discovered the trapdoor that led to the engine room. "No, no. You don't belong down there. It's dangerous." Solomon made another note: *Buy a lock.*

"Come find me!" came Silas's muffled voice as Solomon stood in the galley-style kitchen putting together sandwiches.

Solomon sucked jelly off his fingers and went seeking.

But the living area from which the challenge had been issued stood empty. With rising concern, Solomon cast his gaze about, praying Silas hadn't slipped through the door to traipse along the deck, above the deadly water. "Where are you?" he demanded, as the nightmare played itself out in his head.

"In here!" came the muffled voice.

Solomon's horrified gaze flew to the storage space under the built-in bookcases where he kept his SEAL gear, including a loaded, .5mm handgun.

"Silas!" he thundered, then immediately reined himself in. The boy didn't know any better. He was just doing what any healthy child would do; he was playing.

With a forced smile, Solomon lifted the lid of the smooth, wooden chest. "Found you," he said, a cold sweat filming his forehead. "Come out now and eat."

As he pulled the boy out, he stashed his gun out of sight, under the pile of gear, making yet another note: *Buy hardware for a second lock.*

They sat in the dining nook by a pentagonal window that overlooked Lynnhaven Inlet and consumed their sandwiches. Solomon's thoughts scrambled to address his new circumstances.

His routine necessitated a 4:00 A.M. wake-up, in order to arrive at the Spec Ops facility by zero five hundred hours to oversee physical training. Who would watch Silas when he went to work? The Navy's Family Services Center offered before-and-after-school programs, but what about when he was called away, for weeks and months at a time? Perhaps he could request special permission to remain stateside, but then he'd ruin any prospect of making master chief.

"What grade are you going into, Silas?" he asked his son.

Silas just looked at him.

"You're six now, right? Did you go to kindergarten last year?"

Silas shook his head. "Christopher and Caleb went to school."

A terrible thought skewered Solomon. "You know how to read, though, don't you?" He, himself, had taught himself to read when he was four.

Silas lowered his chin and darted him an anxious look. "No, sir," he whispered.

The thought of Silas not having such a great source

of entertainment at his fingertips dismayed Solomon. Surely the boy ought to be reading by now, at least short little words. He added to his growing list: *Teach Silas to read.*

How in God's name was he supposed to do that, plus all the other sundry tasks, with only four days of leave time left and just a few weeks of summer remaining? Feeling overwhelmed, he scratched his head. He needed help. A nanny. A tutor. Someone who was good with children.

A vision that seemed to hover at the periphery of his thoughts jumped front and center: *Jordan Bliss.* The peanut butter he'd swallowed moved thickly down his throat. She would know what to do with a six-year-old boy. He'd made inquiries—she was a first-grade teacher, *and* she lived near enough to assist him.

His breath came faster. Yes, and having been separated from one little boy, she might have an interest in helping another.

His rational thoughts disintegrated into what was recognizably a primal urge. The desire to mate with her had ambushed him back in Caracas when he'd written her that poem. It hadn't eased, either, in the intervening days as the memory of her feisty spirit and passionate devotion resurfaced again and again. And now he had the perfect excuse to see her.

Jordan reread the e-mail from Father Benedict with tears in her eyes and her heart in her throat. At last, she had word of Miguel, though the news wasn't terribly good:

Dearest Jordan, he wrote, *I'm writing this from within the British consulate in Ayacucho, which is being evacuated at this precise moment as a Populist Army has seized most of the Amazonas region by force and is expected to march upon the city today. I hope to find refuge for myself and three of the children in La Catredral Maria Auxiliadora. I regret to say that Fatima fell ill with fever yesterday. I felt it best to leave her with a family of my acquaintance, who I pray will love and keep her as their own. Miguel is faring well enough with the others, though he has yet to utter a word since your parting, and he rarely strays from my side.*

You may not write me back at this e-mail. Simply forward news of Miguel's location to the agency handling his adoption so they know where to find him. Perhaps they can negotiate some means to send him to you. I must strongly warn you that it is unsafe for you to fetch him in person.

I hope this note finds you well and whole in spirit, considering these unfortunate circumstances.

Yours Respectfully,
Timothy Benedict

With a cry of urgency, Jordan leapt up and riffled through her address book for the number of the agency in Venezuela handling her adoption. She dialed the international number with fingers that trembled with both relief and anxiety.

"*Corazones Internacional,*" answered a woman in Spanish.

"Señora Nuñez, this is Jordan Bliss. I've pinpointed Miguel's location," she breathlessly announced.

"Ah, Señora Bliss," said the woman carefully. "I'm glad you called again. Miguel's dossier was approved and returned to us today."

Jordan's heart gave a leap of joy. How long had she been waiting to hear those words? It couldn't have happened at a better time. "That's wonderful! I just received word that he's in Puerto Ayacucho at La Catedral Maria Auxiliadora."

A silence followed her revelation, so lengthy that Jordan thought perhaps the line had gone dead. "Señora Nuñez?" she queried.

"Yes," said the woman, faintly.

"The priest caring for him is Father Benedict," Jordan continued, sensing reluctance on the other end. "He says he'll be expecting one of your agents to collect Miguel."

The woman cut her off. "I'm sorry, señora," she said with lament. "I am truly sorry, but we cannot send any agents into Ayacucho. Rebels have stormed the city; there is fighting in the streets."

"No," said Jordan forcefully. "I know it's dangerous, but we have to get him out. He needs me. He isn't talking anymore." Her own voice cracked in distress. "Please don't back out on me now," she begged, her eyes stinging sharply. "It took a year to get his dossier approved."

"You need to be patient, señora. Wait a few weeks or months for the unrest to die down."

"In a few weeks or months, the Populists might run the government again," Jordan countered fiercely. "They had outlawed foreign adoptions before; what makes you think they'd even let Miguel leave the country? I have to get him now before the laws change!"

"I'm sorry, señora. I truly am. There's nothing we can do but keep his information here on file."

"Wait!" Jordan begged, gripping the phone so hard it bruised her palm. "What if I were to fetch him out myself? You could mail me his dossier with explicit directions. I'll take them to all the right people, and you wouldn't have to do a thing."

A compassionate sigh sounded in Jordan's ear. "It would be dangerous for you, señora. Very dangerous."

"I understand that," Jordan insisted. It was more dangerous to her emotional and mental health not to fight for Miguel. "But it can be done, right?"

Thoughtful silence followed. "I suppose it could be done," the woman carefully admitted, "if you found a lawyer to sign the papers and left him a money order for the final payoff of ten thousand American dollars, payable to us. You would then need to take Miguel to Caracas to the American embassy for the rest of the papers to be processed."

Jordan envisioned the monumental task ahead of her. She would need to free up funds, not just the money for Miguel's adoption but enough money for a flight, for both of them. "I can do it," she promised, the perspiration on her brow cooling swiftly in her air-conditioned study. "Just mail the dossier and your instructions to my home address."

"As you wish, Señora Bliss," said the woman with heavy reluctance. "You should receive it within five to ten days."

"Thank you," Jordan breathed. She hung up the phone

slowly, feeling stunned, shocked by the commitment she'd just shouldered. It was one thing to adopt a child through an agency; it was something else to wrest him from a war-torn country and battle the legal system practically alone.

A forceful knock at Jordan's front door jarred her from her troubled thoughts. The sound conjured an image of a man whose memory was driven deep in her consciousness, like a splinter. *It's not him*, she reassured herself, heading to answer the door.

Through the narrow pane that edged one side of the door, Jordan spied a little boy, about the age of her students.

Who on earth? She pulled the door open, admitting a puff of warm, summer air, and her quizzical smile fled.

"You!" she blurted, startled that her sixth sense had been so accurate. Solomon McGuire's silver gaze hit her like a punch in the gut. She could scarcely draw a full breath.

"Hello, again," he said, the sound of his voice causing the fine hairs on her body to prickle.

"What do you want?" she asked, feeling weak and shaken, especially on the heels of that phone call.

"Well, Jordan, to get right down to the point, this is my son, Silas," he said, confirming her thoughts. "It's a long story, but he's been missing for five years."

The son he'd lost in his poem? It was impossible to tell from the SEAL's expression. "Hello, Silas," she said, her gaze sliding to the boy.

Wide, mercury-colored eyes stared up at her as he shrank behind his father.

"Say hello back," Solomon prompted, pushing Silas up beside him again.

"Hello back," the boy whispered.

Jordan's lips twitched. His two top baby teeth were missing. He was too cute, even given his resemblance to Solomon McGuire. "Congratulations," she said to the man who'd ripped her from her own child. She glared at him, steeling herself from responding to his powerful torso, his muscle-corded neck, and especially those eyes that compelled—no, *commanded* her to do something.

"I need help caring for him," he added, snowing her with unexpected information. "His mother's dead. I work from dawn to dusk, and even though he'll go to school soon, he doesn't know how to read."

And this concerns me how? Jordan wanted to retort, only a glance at little Silas's expectant and innocent face had her biting back the words. A feeling like jealousy snaked through her. "I'm sorry," she said, gentling her words for Silas's sake. "I can't help you." He had to know he was grinding salt into a wound.

He narrowed his silvery gaze at her. "You're a teacher, aren't you?" he demanded.

"Yes, I am. What's that have to do with anything?"

"So, you should have the summer off."

"I'm going back to Venezuela," she retorted through her teeth. "To get *my* son."

His face reflected disbelief. "What, are you out of your mind? After everything my men and I did to get you out?" A V-shaped vein appeared on his forehead.

"I never asked to be taken out," she shot back. "But I did ask you to let me bring my son home." Physically and emotionally exhausted, with very little food in her system, she was helpless to control the quaver in her voice.

"And I'm sorry for that," he answered, gentling his tone in response to her vehemence. "I had my orders," he added, defending his actions.

"I understand. But I'm still going back."

"It's not safe," he insisted, glowering at her. Silas had stepped away to cling to the porch rail.

"You can't stop me this time," she couldn't stop herself from pointing out.

"Can't I?" An expression that struck her as starkly sexual crossed his face as he ran an assessing gaze over her. Jordan endured the frank inspection, hating that her nipples peaked beneath his scalding look, and they were clearly apparent beneath her tight-fitting top.

She flinched as Solomon lifted a hand. He merely reached into the breast pocket of his short-sleeved shirt and withdrew an expensive-looking pen and pad of Post-its. He scrawled his name and a series of directions in his old-fashioned cursive. "If you change your mind," he said, tearing off the page and thrusting it at her, "here's where you can find me. Silas, say good-bye to Miss Bliss."

"G'bye, Mith Blith," Silas whispered, lisping her name.

"Good-bye, Silas," she replied, finding that it wasn't difficult at all to smile at him. He was adorable.

His father was another story. Watching him retreat to a big, black truck, she took in the khaki shorts that clung to his narrow hips, revealing taut buttocks and powerful, hair-dusted calves. What was it about him she found so attractive? He hefted the boy into the passenger's side and rounded the truck to get in, holding her gaze captive.

"By the way, you need to get him a booster seat," Jordan called out to him. "And he's supposed to use it till he's eight years old and eighty pounds."

"What he needs is a teacher," Solomon retorted, ducking into his truck without severing eye contact. *I choose you,* said his expression.

Jordan tore her gaze away to watch Silas buckling his seat belt. He looked up and shyly waved as his father revved the engine. She found herself waving back.

Then she thought of Miguel, who also needed her, Miguel whose hope for a better future was draining away like sand through an hourglass. *I'm coming, baby. I'm coming to get you,* she thought, turning back into the house. All she needed was someone to help her come up with the money.

From one of the dozens of lounge chairs framing the kiddy pool at Ocean Breeze Water Park, Jordan watched Agatha frolic in water that went up to her knees. Graham and Cameron were off tackling the adult-sized water slides, and Jillian was enjoying a well-deserved day of rest at the ranch.

Jordan wasn't in the mood to frolic with her niece. Seated on a lounge chair in the only patch of shade at the park, she waited on pins and needles for her accountant's call.

Memories of Miguel played over and over in her mind, much like the mushroom fountain that sluiced young Agatha's slender frame as she stood beneath it.

The jangle of her cell phone had her reaching into her pool bag. "Anita," she said, recognizing her accountant's phone number. Her heart stilled with fearful anticipation.

"Okay, Jordan. I have good news and bad news. Which do you want first?"

Jordan broke out in a cold sweat. "The good news," she begged, clutching the phone tighter.

"Well, your loan's been approved. You can withdraw your money as early as Monday morning."

The tension rushed out of her on a gust of air, but then she remembered. "Then what's the bad news?"

"I could only approve twenty-five thousand dollars for you. Your debt-to-income ratio is just too high, hon. You just don't have enough equity on the condo to borrow more. This also pushes your monthly mortgage up another three hundred dollars. Are you sure you can afford that?"

Jordan swallowed hard. Twenty-five thousand dollars ought to be enough to pay for Miguel's adoption and fly her in and out of Venezuela, but on her meager teacher's salary, a mortgage that ate up two-thirds of her paycheck was absurd. "I don't have a choice," she replied, thinking she would face that challenge later, maybe rent out her condo and move in with her sister.

"Okay, then." The accountant sighed. "Swing by tomorrow, and we'll process your loan."

"Thank you, Anita." Jordan immediately dialed her travel agent. "Hi, Carol? It's Jordan. You know that flight I asked you to look into? I can pay for it now."

"Oh, great. Let me pull it up for you. Okay, I have you flying out of Norfolk on August ten into Mexico City and switching over to a Venezuelan airline, arriving at Maiquetía International the next morning. You do realize your visa's about to expire, right?"

"My visa?" Jordan hadn't given a thought to her visa.

"Yes, by the time you arrive, you'll only have five days left on it, so there isn't much time in there for red tape."

The phone went slippery. Five days! Could she jump through all the necessary hoops in just five days? "I see," she said, her stomach clenching uneasily. Encountering red tape was the norm in virtually any third-world country. "Can you get me out of the country any sooner?"

"Um, let me look." Jordan listened as the woman's fingers tap danced on the keyboard. "I can fly you out the same way on the sixth. That's in two weeks. Do you want me to book that flight?"

"Yes," Jordan confirmed, praying Miguel's dossier would arrive by then. "I'll come by the office and pay for it tomorrow."

"Okay, Jordan. See you then."

As she ended the call, a sense of foreboding sat heavily on Jordan's chest. The tickets she'd just bought were nonrefundable. Once paid for, there would be no going back, no changing her mind. She was going to risk everything to get Miguel out of Venezuela.

God help me, she thought. *'Cause nobody else will.*

Chapter Six

✦

She was almost broke.

That evening, Jordan sat in her kitchen with the scent of burned toast hanging in the air, her bills spread across the dinette table, pen bleeding ink onto her checkbook. She needed considerably more cash flow.

Being trapped in Venezuela had led her utility companies to slap late fees on all of her accounts. Apparently, they'd heard every excuse under the sun. They hadn't believed she'd been hiding from rebels in the basement of a mission in a foreign country—who would? She couldn't begin to cover all her bills, let alone start paying three hundred more per month on her mortgage.

Nor was she eating or sleeping as she should. She watched television compulsively, praying for the most up-to-date news coming out of Venezuela, but the news was sparse. Running out of money was yet one more obstacle between her and Miguel. At this rate, she was going to have a nervous breakdown.

The memory of Silas McGuire's hesitant farewell wave summoned a peculiar feeling in her. She hadn't been able to get his sweet, needy gaze out of her mind. Of course, each time she thought of the boy, she envied his father for having him back.

How much would Solomon McGuire pay her for teaching his son to read? With her trip to Venezuela just two weeks away, it wouldn't be much, but every little bit would help at this point.

Would he hire her, though, for such a short amount of time? Maybe she should keep the date of her departure to herself.

Standing up, she went to fetch the Post-it note she'd stuck onto her refrigerator. He'd scrawled the directions to his house but not a phone number, of course. He would have to make this harder on her, more humiliating.

An hour later, Jordan found herself following his instructions, driving toward Virginia Beach with the sun shining in her rearview mirror, telling herself this decision had nothing to do with the man, himself. Yes, he was attractive. A woman would have to be dead not to notice that, but he was also extremely annoying. She didn't like him enough for him to pose a threat to her carefully reconstructed heart.

Turning her Nissan into an established waterfront community, she scowled at the oaks and magnolias lining mansions on either side. If he could afford a home here, why not hire a full-time nanny, she groused, coming to a house on a cul de sac. *Follow drive to rear,* Solomon had written.

What was at the rear, she wondered, the servants' entrance?

She spied his truck parked beneath a carport and eased her car in alongside it, then followed a walkway to the rear entrance to knock and wait.

"Hello," answered a teenage boy.

"I'm looking for Solomon McGuire," Jordan said, angry that his directions weren't more explicit.

"Oh, he lives down at the dock," said the youth.

At the dock.

"Yeah, he used to live here, but now he just rents the pier."

The pier.

With rising concern, Jordan followed the walkway down the hill, away from the house, to a pier that jutted out into a glistening swathe of water, violet in hue, given the arrival of dusk. An osprey flapped into the skeletal remains of a tree. Insects chirped in the marsh grass. A fish jumped, leaving ripples on the water's still surface. Beautiful.

There, moored to the dock, was a houseboat named *Camelot*. Its surface was shiny and new, but the lines of the craft belonged to an earlier era. Lights shone warmly in the various-shaped windows.

What a shame, she'd come all this way for nothing.

She turned to leave. "Where are you going?" called a voice that made the hair on her nape prickle. She turned around and finally caught sight of him lounging behind a deck rail on a raised portion of the boat, as if awaiting her arrival.

"I don't do water," she called, turning away again.

A rustle and thud suggested that he had leapt off the boat and was coming after her. She squelched the urge to run.

"You can't leave yet," he said, catching up to her with speed that made her breathless. He caught her elbow and swung her around. "Come on, now. The boat's not going to sink."

"I get seasick," she added, unsettled by his touch.

"Do you see any waves? You won't even know you're on a boat."

She yanked free of his sure grasp. The reminder of his

physical strength made her inexplicably furious. "Where is Silas?" she gritted. He was the reason she'd come—him and the hope that she could pay off her bills.

"He's sleeping." This was said with such weary relief that her anger subsided. "Please, come in and we'll make arrangements suitable to both of us."

Jordan cocked an ear at the odd turn of phrase. She eyed the houseboat. It didn't look like it would sink, and it didn't rock at all on the placid inlet. "Fine," she agreed. "But if I start to feel sick, I'm leaving."

He preceded her down the wide dock and across a gang-plank with rails, holding out a hand to help her across. Wary of touching him, she ignored it and stepped briskly onto the boat. "What's with the name of your boat?" she asked. The deck was spotless, gleaming.

He smiled a cynical smile. "*Camelot?* Why, this is my castle, of course," he answered, pulling open a door with a stained-glass centerpiece.

Jordan edged inside and caught her breath.

The interior was a woodworker's paradise. From the paneled walls to the built-in cabinetry, every whimsical nook served some utilitarian purpose. Thick area rugs softened the gleaming wood floor. Recessed lighting lit the inviting seating areas. "Wow," Jordan breathed, noting both a hallway and a flight of steps disappearing into darkness. It was a bit of a castle, only where was Guinevere, the Queen? "Where does Silas sleep?" she asked.

"For now, in my bed," Solomon retorted, wryly. "He didn't want to sleep alone belowdecks. Can I get you something to drink?"

His presence in the cozy space abraded her senses. "Water would be nice," she said, moving to a window seat to put distance between them. "This is some library you have," she remarked, as he brought her a glass, fingers brushing in the trade-off. The contact sent a spark up her arm.

"I know," he answered, casting a pride-filled look at the crowded shelves. "I've read them all," he said matter-of-factly.

"Really." Jordan peered more closely at the dented and worn spines. "*Gulliver's Travels*?" she asked him. "*Moby Dick*?"

"Two of my favorites," he replied, lowering himself onto the sturdy coffee table by her feet.

Jordan resisted the urge to draw her knees up. There was something about this man that disturbed her—not that she thought he would hurt her physically. It went deeper than that.

"What did you think of my poem?" he asked her.

She took a quick sip of her water. "Well written," she answered, guarding how deeply the poem had touched her; how she'd sobbed into her pillow on several occasions after reading it again. "How did you lose Silas for so long?" she asked him.

"My late wife ran off with him," he answered, with a deep freeze in his voice.

Ah, thought Jordan, now having an answer to her earlier question.

"I spent five years looking for him," continued Solomon on that same cold note. "Turns out he was with his stepaunt in nowhere, Mississippi, abandoned by a mother who loved herself more than she loved her son."

There wasn't a trace of regret or grief in his expression, though she hadn't missed the fact that his Guinevere was now dead.

"So," she continued, steering the conversation back to his proposal, "what kind of suitable arrangements did you have in mind?"

Beneath the black moustache, his smile was mocking. "I'll pay you thirty dollars an hour," he added, lowering a lingering look at her breasts.

Jordan drew an uncertain breath. Was he serious or was he being deliberately crass? Thirty an hour was extremely generous, unless, of course, his bold gaze was an indication that he expected something more. That had to be it. Her blood flashed to a boil. She shot to her feet to glare down at him. "You said you needed a tutor for Silas," she reminded him accusingly. She started to stalk past him.

Fast as a trap, he snared her wrist and rolled to his feet. That put less than an inch between her heaving chest and his broad one. Jordan's head spun at the familiar, musky scent surrounding her. "What an interesting assumption," he murmured, his gaze sliding to her mouth. "Though why sell yourself short? I'm sure you'd be worth more than that."

"Oh!" she sputtered, even as liquid heat flooded her entire body. "You..." she groped for a word that captured how maddening he was. "...you jackass!"

He quirked a mocking eyebrow at the epithet, but then his expression turned serious. "I take my son's inability to read very seriously," he explained. "And I'm not above bribery to keep you in this country."

Bribery? Was that his only reason for offering her such competitive pay? Surely he didn't know how desperately she needed it. With humiliation pinching her cheeks, Jordan tugged her wrist free and carried her glass to the kitchen. "Just so you know, I still intend to leave for Venezuela sometime soon." There, she'd given him fair warning without actually telling him when.

He'd followed her and was now blocking her path to the door. "You're leaving when you can stand to make thirty an hour for the rest of the summer?"

"Yes," she retorted.

He narrowed his eyes at her. "Then you'd better start tomorrow," he recommended. "Come as early as you like."

"I can't guarantee that Silas will be reading before school starts," she said, aware that her knees were trembling.

His eyes gleamed with private thoughts. "Just do your best."

"Very well. I'll see you in the morning." She gripped the car keys in her skirt pocket. "Do you have a cell phone number in case I need to call you?"

"No," he said.

She just looked at him. "What about a house phone?"

"No again. I carry a pager for work, and that's it. If you intend to back out on me, you'll have to tell me so in person."

It dawned on Jordan that he enjoyed pushing her buttons. "I'll be here," she said, tightly. "And, now that you've got your son back, I recommend you get a cell phone as a safety precaution. Now kindly step aside," she added.

He didn't move. Her pulse jumped as he took a step closer, lifted his right hand, and captured her jaw with it. His touch electrified her. He pulled her gently to him, and she went, helplessly, as if under a spell. All she could do was stare at him as he lowered his head, parted her lips with his thumb, and silenced her belated, outraged gasp by diving inside her.

He filled her mouth with undulations of his tongue that

had her grasping his upper arms to keep from crashing to her knees.

God in heaven! He was kissing her, and she was responding like a woman who hadn't been kissed in three years, which was exactly the case. Which was the only excuse she allowed herself.

Of its own accord, one of her hands went up to sink into the short, thick strands of his hair. Her hips curved toward his. She leaned into him, overcome by the unrelenting maleness that crowded her, threatening to steal her very soul.

To her chagrin, he was the first to lift his head, to set her back on her heels. "Better go while you can," he advised her, softly. "Unless you'd like to change your mind and earn that hundred."

With an outraged cry, Jordan shoved him aside and fled to the door. She slammed it shut and scurried across the gangplank, all but running to her car.

"How much can you give me for these?" Ellie Stuart asked, sliding her wedding ring and Carl's across the pawnshop counter.

Mrs. Halliday, who ran the pawnshop, lifted the two gold bands, inspected them through the bifocals that hung from her neck by a chain, then directed her pitying gaze over them at Ellie. "Where're your boys?" she inquired, glancing behind her, as nosy as always. "Don't usually see you without 'em."

"At the Baptist church," Ellie answered. "It's mother's day out." Once a week she got two hours to herself, and the boys were assured a healthy snack.

"I heard ol' Carl ran off with a stripper, leavin' you high

and dry," Mrs. Halliday added, proving that the grapevine in Mantachie was working better than ever.

Ellie's spine stiffened. She didn't care to feed Mrs. Halliday's perverse curiosity, but given the looks and whispers that followed her everywhere she went, there wasn't much point to keeping secrets. "Cocktail waitress," she corrected, firming her lips.

"You found a new place to live yet?" persisted the crone, her bright eyes hungry for details.

"Not yet," Ellie answered on a quelling note. Unwilling to believe Carl's threat, she'd confronted Eddie Levi herself, demanding to see the bill of sale. Sure enough, the trailer she lived in would be his in a matter of days. According to their do-it-yourself divorce, Carl's property was his to do with as he pleased. Ellie hadn't cared, as long as she got custody of the children.

"Well, just so's you know," Mrs. Halliday added, leaning on the counter to impart her two cents with confidentiality, "I'm hearin' talk that the state might come and take those boys from you."

Ellie broke into a cold sweat, but her features remained unchanged. "How much can you give me for the rings?" she demanded, her knees trembling in secret.

Mrs. Halliday peered at them again. "Well, seein' as how you're down an' out right now, I'll give you two hundred for 'em," she offered.

Two hundred dollars. That was probably more than they were worth, but she wasn't going to give Mrs. Halliday more fodder for gossip by weeping with gratitude. "I'll take it," she said coolly, willing her hand to remain steady as she held it out to be paid.

Every instinct screamed at her to run. Run with the

boys, whom Carl had expressed no interest in seeing ever again. Run from the state of Mississippi, where Social Services was beginning to take note of her predicament.

But where could she go with two hundred dollars to her name and three children depending on her for food and shelter?

Solomon McGuire's check now burned a hole in her wallet. He'd invited her to find him anytime. And Silas's sudden absence had both her and the children moping about like someone had died. What she needed was a brand-new start, in a new place where no one knew her history or her humiliating circumstance. Suddenly she knew just exactly where that might be.

Murmuring her thanks, Ellie pocketed the money Mrs. Halliday doled out. If the Impala made it from Mississippi to Virginia, if they could subsist on the gas and food that two hundred dollars provided, it'd be nothing short of a miracle.

The sun was nearing its zenith, shining warmly on Jordan's shoulders as she strolled down the hill from the big house toward Solomon's houseboat. Catching sight of the SEAL, shirtless, with his back to her, she drew up short. Desire shimmered warmly through her veins and her extremities tingled.

I'm not here to see Solomon McGuire, she told herself.

But last night's kiss replayed itself in her head, as it had all night long, keeping her tossing fitfully, as she seethed with anger and shame.

How could she have let him kiss her like that? Worse yet, how could she have responded so passionately? He'd wrested her from Miguel. He'd toyed with her, letting her think that he was willing to pay her for sex. He was blunt and rude. Yet just thinking of that kiss made her thighs quiver, made her want more of the same, in spite of herself.

The jackass. Oh, yes, she'd decided that was the perfect word to describe him. It didn't help to discover now that beneath his clothing, he had a torso of highly defined muscles that rippled and flexed as he lowered his butt onto the dock. His shoulders were made to hang on. Not an ounce of fat padded his waist. His smooth-looking skin glowed with a healthy tan.

Her gaze slid to Silas, who stood beside his father, equally shirtless, equally tan, wearing tattered shorts. He was the reason she'd finally overcome the ambivalence that made her several hours late. The motherless boy needed her as much as he needed to learn to read. She could just imagine how lost he felt having been abandoned by a mother, only to be handed off to a gruff and surly stranger.

She watched him nod his head at whatever Solomon was telling him.

Hefting her picnic basket, Jordan continued toward the pair, curious to discover what they were up to. In that same instant, Solomon pushed off the dock and, with scarcely a splash, disappeared.

Leaving Silas all alone.

Jordan picked up her pace, sandals slapping her soles as she hastened toward the boy. The past flashed before her eyes, and she was eight years old again, playing by the cow pond. She remembered the horror of falling into water, feeling it fill her nose and ears as she tried to claw to the surface. In alarm, she cried out a warning to Silas who'd sidled up to the edge as if preparing to jump. "Silas, no! You need a life vest."

He glanced over his shoulder at her, but a firm command had him looking back at the water. In the next instant, he launched himself off the dock, splashing loudly.

Jordan dropped her basket and ran. Nearing the end of the pier, she spied Solomon, treading water a few yards out, but Silas was nowhere to be seen.

"Where is he?" she cried with worry, scanning the tea-colored water for any sign of him. "Silas!"

Just then, Solomon ducked under the water. He was gone for several seconds, long enough for Jordan to wring her hands together and utter a heartfelt prayer. But then he crested the surface bearing a sputtering and frightened Silas with him. The little boy coiled his sturdy arms around his father and hung on for dear life as he gasped and coughed and wiped his eyes.

"What," Jordan railed, dizzy with relief, "are you doing? You almost let him drown!" She flung her arms wide to encompass the magnitude of his crime.

"I'm teaching him how to swim," he retorted with an icy glare, "which is a job I happen to have great experience in. I do not, however, have experience in teaching a child to read. That is your job, and you're late!"

"You're teaching him to swim by letting him drown? What is that," she cried, "the Navy SEAL way?"

"It's called drown-proofing. You wouldn't understand."

"You're right. I don't understand the point of drowning a child. Obviously, you have no idea what kind of psychological impact that could have on him!" Hearing herself shout, she abruptly shut her mouth.

Silas, who witnessed their fight with increasing concern, put his face into Solomon's neck and burst into tears.

"You see?" Jordan pointed out. "You've traumatized him."

"The only thing," Solomon grated, that V-shaped vein appearing on his forehead, "that is traumatizing him is us!" he thundered quietly.

With a feeling that he'd tossed cold water at her, Jordan went quiet. He was right, damn him. The boy hadn't seemed too shaken when his father pulled him out of the water. Her righteousness subsided, replaced by humiliation for having exposed her private fears.

"You have a point," she conceded, taking a belated step from the dock's edge. "Silas, honey, we're not fighting. We just have different ideas about teaching you to swim. Your father *believes* he's an expert on the subject," she forced herself to add, "so I will leave it to him to teach you."

The little waves tossing all around her were starting to wreak havoc on her stomach. "Can I wait for you inside?" she pleaded, feeling herself pale.

"Go on in," said Solomon with a perceptive eye.

"I brought lunch for a picnic, for Silas and me," she added, excluding the SEAL. "And the food won't keep," she warned.

Turning her back on Solomon's scowl, she marched on board the boat to wait out the swimming lesson.

Carrying her basket to the kitchen, she found it neatly wiped down, dishes washed and put away. She peeked in the refrigerator, relieved to find food in the fridge and a gallon of milk beside a six-pack of beer. At least Silas wouldn't starve.

Curious to see the rest of *Camelot*, she peeked into a tiny bathroom across the hall, not surprised that even the toilet-seat lid was hand carved to resemble a bald eagle. There were cabinets and drawers everywhere she looked, even down the hallway. She opened several, finding a shell collection, a drawerful of medals and plaques, a closet of uniforms draped in plastic, even a pull-down ironing board.

The SEAL's unique scent grew stronger as she inched toward the master cabin at the bow of the boat. Three steps higher than the hallway, it took up the forward portion of the boat, with a huge captain's bed built in, more storage underneath, and four hexagonal windows. It was impossible not to be charmed.

The bed was still unmade. Rumpled sheets and two dented pillows had her picturing the SEAL and his son, sharing the space together. Her heart melted, then flooded with sorrowful envy.

Did he know how lucky he was to have his son back? She'd give anything to watch Miguel sleeping peacefully at her side. *I will soon*, she promised herself.

The thud of a door had her retreating guiltily toward the living area.

"I did it! I swam to the dock!" Silas exclaimed breathlessly as he ran in ahead of his father, towel in hand, dripping wet.

"Really!" Jordan exclaimed. "Good for you."

"In the shower," his father ordered, stepping in after him. "Go on." He nudged Silas toward the bathroom. The door thudded shut, leaving Jordan and Solomon alone. "So what do you think about my bed?" he asked, proving he'd caught her snooping. As he toweled his back, his powerful chest muscles flexed rhythmically.

She tried not to notice the black hair under his arms and between his taut, male nipples. Damp swim trunks stuck to his thighs like second skin, leaving little to the imagination.

Not that Jordan's imagination needed encouragement. With her mouth gone dry, she wasn't able to answer his question.

"Thirty an hour wouldn't come close to enough, eh?" Solomon added, goading her further, a wicked glint in his eyes.

Jordan's temper helped unhinge her jaw. "Let's get one thing straight," she snapped, propping her hands on her hips. "I am here for Silas, not for you."

His slow, wolfish smile was most maddening. "Now if you could just convince yourself of that," he mocked.

"You really are a jackass," she informed him.

"And what does that make you?" he countered, lifting a black eyebrow. "A desperate divorcée?"

Stunned by his unexpectedly hurtful words, Jordan pushed past him. "I think I'll wait out on the lawn for Silas." She snatched up the basket and was headed to the door when Solomon swung her around, a firm grip on her elbow. "Release me," she said, horrified to hear her voice wobble.

"That was a low blow, even for me," he admitted, soberly. "I apologize."

Lifting her stinging eyes, she found his expression grave, honest, humble...Perhaps he was human after all.

"I'll consider accepting it," she retorted, stiffly, annoyingly aware that he was nearly naked. She was here for Silas.

A thump and the sound of running water had Solomon stepping away to check on his son.

"I'll wait on the hill," Jordan decided, fleeing through the door, not trusting herself another moment in his presence.

Chapter Seven

✦

Solomon squinted down the pier and across the expanse of the lawn he used to mow toward the woman and child sitting on a blanket. He felt left out. Yes, there was plenty to do within the houseboat—laundry to wash, sheets to change, a deck to sweep, and an engine to prime and lube, but he'd rather watch Jordan Bliss do her thing.

There was something about her that he found immensely pleasing. Not only was she nicely put together, with full breasts and slim thighs, but beneath her prickly exterior she was as explosive as dried timber.

He had to guess from that kiss yesterday, plus the information he'd uncovered about her divorced status, that she hadn't had sex in months if not years. That telltale blush that highlighted her cheekbones when he looked at her a certain way told him she could be his with just a bit of persuasion. While an inner voice cautioned him that she was different from the women he normally pursued—sweeter, softer—he was confident his heart was safe from ever being lured toward love again.

He had to have her. That was the only way to overcome his growing obsession.

He watched for several minutes, waiting for Silas's instruction to begin. His twenty/twenty vision took inventory of the picnic she'd brought: a canteen of pink lemonade, a plastic container of tiny sandwiches, another of vegetables and diced fruit, and a can of whipped cream?

Solomon searched for a workbook or instructional slate and saw neither. He watched Silas devour four sandwiches as Jordan toyed with the carrot sticks and celery stalks, laying them in various positions on the lid of a plastic container. This went on for some time, with Silas an avid observer.

Impatient with the child's play and desiring more serious instruction, Solomon was preparing to intervene when Jordan pulled the top off the can of whipped cream. He immediately considered ways to use that can to its fullest potential.

Jordan squirted a frothy white shape onto a red paper plate, then let Silas dip his fruit in it. She then squirted out another shape—oh, wait, it was the letter B—and then a third and started pairing them together.

Perplexed, Solomon delayed his intervention. Out came several more paper plates, and Silas got to spray letters on them, his efforts far less proficient. Solomon had seen enough. Abandoning the lounge chair, he leapt over one railing and then another, and with a bound onto the pier, he stalked up the hill for a word with Miss Bliss.

"Jordan," he called, not bothering to mask his disapproval.

The engrossed pair looked up from plates that appeared to read C and L.

"Clap!" Silas piped up, still caught up in the game.

"That's right," Jordan answered warmly. She lifted a wary glare at Solomon as he cast his shadow over them. "What do you want?" she demanded.

Spying a worried crease on Silas's brow, Solomon caught himself. "Silas, I think the mailman came. Run to the head of the driveway and fetch the mail, would you? Ours is the box on the bottom."

"Okay!" said Silas, scrambling to his feet. With a toothless grin he added, "Wanna see how fast I can run?"

"I'll time you," said Solomon, glancing at his watch. And the boy took off, sprinting like a deer.

Solomon didn't have but a minute. "What is this?" he demanded, gesturing at the plates. "I'm not paying you to play with him. I want him to learn to read."

"I'm evaluating what he knows, in a format that keeps him interested," she answered frostily.

"Well, this had better not be an indication of your instructional methods," he warned.

Her eyes flashed with affront. "If this is the sort of interference I am going to have to deal with, you can find another tutor." She started stacking the cream-filled paper plates, one on top of the other, and shoved them in a white garbage bag. "I should have known you'd meddle."

"Hold on," Solomon ordered. "I'm the one paying you, remember?"

"Look," said Jordan fiercely, rolling to her feet. He took a cautionary step back as she confronted him, going nose to nose. "You were the expert at swimming lessons, right? Well, I'm the expert in my field, which is teaching children to read. Either you allow me to do this my way, or I'm out of here. Now, which is it?"

Beholding her flushed face, the defiant thrust of her chin, he completely forgot his quarrel. His gaze slid to the creamy length of her neck and the swell of her breasts beneath her peach-colored tank top. "You do have a point," he acceded. *Two of them, actually.*

"Yes, I do. I backed away on the swimming lessons. You can back away now and every lesson from here on. Do we have a deal?"

He couldn't wait to see her naked from the waist up. "Deal," he finally agreed. "Maybe you could show me a trick or two with that can of whipped cream," he added.

"Maybe I could," she agreed, with a gleam in her eye. She swiveled suddenly and snatched it up, shaking the can threateningly.

He didn't know if she would actually spray the stuff on him, but the idea was so enticing that he snared her hand under his and turned the can against her, shooting a ribbon of cream across her lips.

She gasped in shock, and with a chuckle, he took advantage of her open mouth to steal a kiss, the way he'd stolen one last night, anticipating the same explosive reaction he'd gotten then. To his delight, her mouth tasted even sweeter.

Calling him a blistering name against his lips, she gave in with a shudder, put her slender weight into him, and opened her mouth to his devouring.

Ah, yes! The grass under his feet was tipping, the world was reeling. The blood roared in his veins so loudly that he was barely cognizant of Silas tearing toward him with envelopes flapping in one hand, shouting, "How fast am I?"

He had to tear his lips from Jordan's to confer with his watch. "One minute ten seconds," he rasped.

She wanted him, there wasn't any question.

But then she stiffened and thrust herself out of his arms. He watched her totter and push a strand of reddish hair from her face. "Silas, I have to go now," she announced, disappointing him. "But I'll come back tomorrow."

Solomon's confidence returned.

"You did very well today," she added, addressing only the boy, avoiding Solomon's gaze. "I can tell you're a smart big boy."

With a proud grin, Silas thrust the mail at Solomon while Jordan hurriedly jammed her Tupperware and canteen back into the basket.

"Can I climb that tree?" Silas asked, pointing to a live oak growing near the shore.

Distracted, Solomon nodded. "Go ahead." As the boy scampered off, Jordan hefted the basket with one hand and snatched up the garbage bag with the other. "I'll take that," said Solomon, wresting it from her. He fell into step as she turned and hurried up the hill. He waited for her to say something about their obvious, sizzling chemistry.

But she said nothing, marching up the hill like he wasn't even there.

He fell back on their mutual concern for Silas. "Is he really smart, or were you just saying that?" he asked.

She cast him a harried glance. "I only had an hour with him, but I can tell he's very bright."

"Good," said Solomon, pleased to have his own opinion confirmed.

"But I can't guarantee he'll be reading before school," Jordan repeated. "Look," she added, pausing beside him as he dropped the garbage in a receptacle at the back of the big house. "I don't mean to sound rude or anything, but I think it's best if I meet with Silas in a public place, like a library or something."

He gently lowered the lid of the garbage bin. Those were not the words he'd expected. "Why?" he asked.

She colored fiercely, having difficulty holding his gaze. "I don't need to be distracted from my professional duties by your shenanigans," she replied.

"Shenanigans?" He couldn't help but appreciate her choice of words, though he resented the implication that he was solely to blame. "I didn't hear you ask me to stop kissing you, Jordan. If I remember correctly, you were the one with your tongue down my throat," he needled.

She gasped in outrage, just as he'd known she would. "I did not have my tongue—oh! You are such a pompous, swaggering oaf! I will tell you right now that unless you leave the houseboat while I'm here, I am not going to tutor Silas any longer!"

"Why don't you just admit you're tempted," he taunted, his own temper igniting.

"Tempted?" she sneered, her fist clenching as she no doubt suffered the urge to punch him. "I don't even like you!" she bit out.

Oddly, her retort hurt his feelings. He kept quiet as she yanked open her car door, tossed the basket inside, and slipped in. She started up the engine, glaring up at him. "You took my son away from me," she added with a quaver in her voice and a sheen of tears in her indigo eyes. "I don't know if I can forgive you for that."

Her honesty left him speechless. He watched her back up, executing a quick, tight turn.

As she pulled away, he read her personalized license plate: 4 MIGUEL. A knot of uncertainty twisted slowly in

Solomon's gut. He had to concede that Jordan was far more complicated than any woman he'd ever pursued before. Her burning love for an orphaned street child captivated him. Lust ached dully in his groin. Maybe he should give up this compulsion to have her. Forget he'd ever laid eyes on her or tossed her into a helicopter screaming invectives at him.

Heaving a dissatisfied sigh, he turned to plod down the hill toward Silas, who waved at him from high up in the live oak tree, crying, "Look at me!"

Miguel heard a noise on the street that he had never heard before, a rumbling that shook the earth beneath his hands and knees. Wide-eyed, he glanced up from the circle that was drawn into the dirt, holding back the marble he was supposed to toss. The high cement walls that enclosed the churchyard prevented him from seeing anything. He glanced at Raúl with a question in his eyes. *¿Qué es?*

Raúl shook his head and dropped his own marble. "*No sé*," he said, leaping to his feet with excitement. "*¡Ven!*"

Come, thought Miguel. That was the word Jordan would have used.

He trailed the older boy to the wall, and the rumbling grew louder. He could feel it through the thin soles of his shoes. It reminded him of the big bird that had taken his Jordan away, *el hélicopter.*

"*Sube el árbol,*" Raúl commanded.

Climb the tree.

Miguel was the best at climbing, but he was afraid. He shook his head.

Raúl nudged him forward, commanding him impatiently.

Fear made Miguel weak. Still, he could grip the banana tree with his knees and haul himself, bit by bit, up its slippery trunk. The rumbling grew louder. He was afraid to peer over the top of the wall, daunted by the broken shards of glass cemented there to keep bad men out.

But what if the noise was Jordan's bird bringing her back?

Craning his neck, Miguel peered over the glittering glass shards. His eyes flew wide. Through the dust rising into the air he watched enormous green vehicles roll past him, crossing in front of the cathedral where they stayed with Padre.

He froze as he watched them, mesmerized by their ominous thunder. He didn't know what it meant that they were here. He only had a feeling that they would keep his Jordan away.

"¡Niños!" Padre's worried voice called to them across the yard. "Come inside now. Hurry!" the priest called.

Miguel obediently loosed his grip, slid down the trunk, and crashed into the hard earth to land on his bottom. He couldn't move. He didn't want to.

The priest hurried over, clucking under his breath, and lifted him into his arms.

Burrowing into the comfort of Padre's arms, Miguel hid his face against the man's crisp white collar. With a wave of longing, he remembered Jordan's sweet, nurturing scent.

His heart ached anew, and tears flooded his eyes. What if she never came back?

Rafe awoke, as was his custom, when the first ray of sunlight struck the wall beside his bed. He kept his curtains open to invite it in, which it did quite early, given that he lived in a penthouse apartment overlooking the Elizabeth River. The sunrise was a reminder to him that life went on whether he wanted it to or not.

Opening his eyes to the red-washed wall, the first thought to hit him was: *Today Jillian's horses arrive.*

She had her son Graham and his friend, Cameron, to help off-load them from the trailer, to lead them to their new stalls, to brush and soothe their distress at finding themselves in an unfamiliar environment.

But what happened if an animal balked? Rafe drew a troubled breath at an image of Jillian wrestling down a beast that threatened to rear. She could seriously injure herself, not to mention the baby she carried.

The thought propelled him out of bed to the bathroom, where he stood under a scalding shower, unable to stop thinking about her.

She weighed on his conscience as he shaved his cheeks smooth. He considered what needed to be done at the office, whether it was absolutely critical.

Wearing a towel on his hips, he stepped into his walk-in closet and eyed the suits hanging very precisely on the rod, several still in dry-cleaning bags. He reached for the light gray Christian Dior he wore on Fridays, touched the silk and linen blend of the sleeve and let go. He couldn't go to work today.

Jillian needed him. That didn't mean he had to overhaul his life, but he did have to come up with a pair of jeans and work shoes.

Turning to the storage drawers at the back of his closet, he rummaged, dragging out a pair of soft jeans from Abercrombie & Fitch that he'd worn only once. On his shoe rack, he found a pair of penny loafers he'd kept, thinking he could use them as house slippers, they were so soft and broken-in.

Not owning a single T-shirt aside from those he wore beneath his dress shirts, he opted for the royal blue button-up Polo that his sister had given him two Christmases ago.

Eyeing himself in his full-length mirror, he scarcely recognized himself. His reflection made him look vulnerable, painfully human.

Today is not about me, he told himself, running his hands over the soft material of his shirt and jeans. *It's about a friend.* He turned quickly toward his efficiency kitchen so as not to see how eager he looked to be spending the day in her company.

The morning sunrise burnished the marsh grass surrounding Solomon's houseboat. Birds twittered in the trees. A pungent odor hanging in the cool air made Jordan think of how the jungle smelled at dawn when she awakened and peered lovingly down at Miguel, asleep on his pallet beside her.

But then she spied Solomon, lounging on his deck, and memories of Miguel took a backseat to present circumstances. As he eyed her approach over the rim of a coffee mug, every muscle in her body tensed with awareness, resentment, and self-blame.

If it weren't for the money he was going to pay her, she wouldn't have returned at all today. Yet seeing him now, his powerful shoulders gilded by sunlight, that small confident smile on his face, a secret part of her thrilled to see him again while her pride insisted Silas was the only reason she returned.

As she put her first foot on the pier, Solomon glanced at his watch. She dared him to say that she was late. It was only a quarter till eight.

"Eager to earn your money, are you?" he called, instead.

She drew up short, gritting her teeth against his jibe. "I have plans this afternoon. I need to get an early start."

His gaze narrowed at the word *plans*. "Silas is still sleeping," he pointed out.

"Then I'll wake him up," she said, heading for the gangplank.

"Grab some coffee and join me first," he countered. "We need to talk."

She stopped again, thoroughly annoyed by his heavy-handedness. "I've told you this before, *Mako*. I am not one of your soldiers. Try again."

A full thirty seconds elapsed before he said, tersely, "Would you like a cup of coffee first?"

"Yes, I would," she said, baring her teeth in a smile. "Thank you." Continuing across the gangplank, she let herself in.

Minutes later, she eased stiffly down on a chair across from his, took a quick sip of the mug she'd brought up, and shuddered. "How can you drink this?" she asked, steeling herself against his frank inspection and the warmth of his eyes as they rested on her bare legs. "Your coffee could be used as paint stripper."

"I like my drinks to have a kick," he replied.

"Me, too, but I'd prefer my kick with cream and

sugar." She put her mug aside. "What did you want to talk about?"

"I wanted to explain that I'm going to leave you and Silas alone this morning."

"Oh," she said, surprised and privately disappointed that he was obeying her ultimatum. "Thank you."

"I also bought a cell phone like you said I should. Take this number down," he suggested, rattling it off.

Jordan jotted the number down in the notebook taken from her tote bag. "You'll be glad you got a phone," she predicted.

"I doubt it. So, tell me, what methods are you planning to use today?" he asked, and she just knew he was remembering the whipped cream and how it tasted on her lips.

Squashing the memory of his kiss, Jordan traded the notebook for a workbook. "Well, if Silas can stand to sit still for three hours, we'll continue on through phonics," she explained, handing it to Solomon for his approval. "He's a dominantly visual learner, so he may do better with whole language, in which case, I've brought some reading material suitable for his age." She kept *that* in the bag, knowing instinctively that he shouldn't see it.

"I'll see you at noon, then," he replied, handing the workbook back. "Would you like me to bring you lunch?"

She shrugged. "Sure. Thank you. That would be nice." It would save her from having to grab fast food on the way to her sister's.

"What do you like to eat, Jordan?" he inquired. His silvery eyes seemed to darken as he focused intently on her mouth.

A blush heated Jordan's face at the shockingly lascivious image that flashed through her head. "It doesn't matter," she gritted, clinging to her forced politeness. "Whatever's easiest."

"And how would you like to be paid, Jordan?"

He had to know that it rattled her to hear her name rolled on his tongue like that.

"Day by day or week by week?" he added, helpfully.

"Every other day would be best," she answered tightly. She refused to squirm like a worm on the end of his hook. He was just a man, she told herself, a man with a secret talent for sentimental verse who, for whatever reason, made her think about sex for the first time in years, even though she hated him.

Okay, she didn't hate him, she just found him irksome.

"Well, then," he murmured, drawing her gaze to his taut abdomen as he stood up and stretched. "I'll go wake up Silas." And then he was gone, bearing his coffee mug with him.

Jordan exhaled a shaky breath. Perhaps she could handle a relationship based on physical attraction. She was human, after all, with normal human impulses. At least, he posed no threat whatsoever to her heart. He couldn't devastate her as Doug had.

With that comforting thought, she grabbed her bag and followed him inside.

As promised, Solomon returned at noon. Jordan and Silas sat in the breakfast nook, engrossed in the comic strip of Dragon Ball Z, when the front door of the houseboat opened and closed on the barest whisper of sound.

She didn't have time to shove the comic book out of sight before Solomon strode into the kitchen. He tossed a folded newspaper on top of the comic book, and demanded, "Read it."

His sudden presence was as unsettling as the agitation crackling in him. "Read what?" she asked, braced for bad news.

"This." He stabbed a finger at the article filling up the bottom of the page. **Coup in Venezuela Leads to Revolution.** He tossed a bag of Subway sandwiches onto the counter and turned to rummage in the fridge.

With Silas trying to sneak the comic book out from under the newspaper, Jordan skimmed the article, her heart frozen in fear. She'd watched the reports of fighting in southern Venezuela every night this past week. It seemed the Populists had won in the southern states, pushing the Moderate Army out of both Las Amazonas and Apure.

Her scalp prickled with apprehension. What did that mean for her? Would she have access to Puerto Ayacucho at all, or would the entire state of Las Amazonas be closed to foreigners?

"If this doesn't persuade you to stay in the States, then I don't know what will," Solomon growled, popping the top off a beer bottle.

Jordan's pulse tapped against her right temple, but she kept her own counsel.

Solomon tossed back a swig and pinned her with a narrow-eyed glare. "Surely you're not naive enough to think that you can just waltz back into the country, and no one will take notice."

Jordan squeezed Silas's wrist in a silent message to keep the comic book hidden. "If you're trying to scare me, Mako, it isn't going to work," she retorted.

He put his beer bottle down abruptly, splayed his hands upon the table, and leaned closer, his eyes like hot steel. "What would it take to scare you, I wonder?" he mused quietly, his gaze sliding downward.

Jordan looked at him sharply. "Are you threatening me?" she demanded, with growing outrage.

"I can read," Silas piped up, shattering the tense moment and wresting Solomon's gaze from hers.

"Can he?" he demanded. He looked back at Jordan for corroboration.

"He's making progress," Jordan hedged, halting Silas as he tried again to free the comic book.

"What are you reading?" his father predictably demanded.

"We'll demonstrate when he's proficient."

"Dragon Ball Z!" Silas shouted with enthusiasm.

Solomon frowned. "What is that?" he asked Jordan.

"It's a children's book."

"Cartoons!" explained Silas, with a gappy grin. "Just like on TV."

With a perceptive glance at their joined hands, Solomon snatched the newspaper off the table. There in all of its colorful glory was the comic book, depicting a battle between Gohan and Friesa. Solomon's eyes widened in horrific disbelief. "This is how you're teaching him to read?" he demanded in a soft but intimidating rumble.

"Well, how else do you expect a six-year-old to keep still for hours at a stretch?" Jordan retorted. "You do what he loves, and it just so happens that Silas loved watching Dragon Ball Z with Christopher and Caleb. Look, he read these three words by himself." She pointed to the onomatopoeic words. *Bam, Kaboom,* and *Zap.* "And he also found and circled these eight sight words—see?—so he can read them with me."

Solomon scowled down at the page, saying nothing.

"He's six years old," Jordan continued, appealing to his reason. "Even with periodic breaks, you can't expect him to work at one hundred percent for three hours straight!"

Solomon crossed his arms, still frowning as if called upon to make a life-and-death decision. Jordan was just warming up to her role as Silas's defender. "And while we're on the subject," she added, "who's going to watch Silas when I go back to Venezuela? You need to enroll him in a child-care program. You can't keep him cooped up on this boat forever." What she really meant was *I'm not going to be here forever.*

A secret gleam entered Solomon's eyes. "Who says he's cooped up?" he demanded softly. "That's the beauty of living on a houseboat. You're never tied down. Eat your sandwiches," he added tersely, turning away. "There's milk in the refrigerator."

With that, he let himself out.

"He's mad," said Silas, looking worried.

Yes, he is, Jordan thought—mad in the British sense of the word: crazy. "He'll get over it," she comforted. "Just think how proud he'll be when you can read this book out loud to him. Let's eat, and then we can finish this story."

They were halfway through their meal when the boat gave a throaty rumble, and the seat beneath her vibrated. "What's that?" Jordan jerked her head up to peer out the window. She caught sight of Solomon hauling in the gangplank. *Oh, no,* she thought. *Oh, no, no, no!*

Chapter Eight

✦

In alarm, Jordan dropped her sandwich and scooted out of the booth to race to the door. She snatched it open. With a loud revving noise, the houseboat started backing out of its berth. "Stop!" she called in panic, her voice bouncing off the water.

Solomon didn't answer. Where was he? She had to reason with him. He didn't know what this would do to her.

The boat started turning. He had to be steering from somewhere, but where?

There were metal steps that appeared to lead up to a canopied pilot room. She edged toward them, catching sight of him, at last. "What are you doing?" she yelled up, clutching the siding on the houseboat, terrified to approach the rail.

"Showing you that Silas is definitely not cooped up, as you suggested."

The boat was gliding over dancing little waves, like a skater over ice. Her stomach cramped in protest. "You can't do this! We're not wearing life vests!"

In the next instant, two orange vests came sailing down

on her head. One for her; the little one for Silas. "I get seasick!" she tried again.

"Just don't puke on deck," he shouted back, pulling on the throttle to move them forward.

"Oh, God!" Jordan cried, breaking out into a cold sweat. She eyed the brackish water in panic, unable even to bend over and pick up the life vests.

Silas stepped through the door. "Wow!" he cried in delight. "We're going out on the water!"

"S-Silas, put on a life vest," Jordan stammered, overcoming her terror long enough to snatch up the smaller life vest and thread his arms through the holes.

"Why? I can swim."

"It's the law," she insisted, at the same time wanting to slap that little smirk she just knew was on Solomon's face. No doubt he was having a grand time proving his point. She snapped her own life vest closed with fingers that shook. "Let's go back inside."

"No," cried Silas, darting under her arm to run to the back of the boat. He ran right up to the rail and looked over.

"Oh, God!" Jordan cried, following him on wobbly legs. She could feel the roll of the water beneath her feet. It wreaked havoc on her queasy stomach. "Silas, please!" she cried, collapsing on a padded box. "Sit down."

"Go faster!" Silas called, ignoring her to shout up encouragement at his father. To her horror, he ran for the front of the boat to watch the bow cut through the water as they moved forward now, heading for the mouth of the inlet toward the Chesapeake Bay.

"Silas!" Jordan tried to get up and follow him, but her legs gave out. They were tingling now, as were her hands and feet. Little black spots obstructed her vision. To her horror, she could feel the bile rising inexorably toward her esophagus.

Oh, help. The waves were getting bigger, and Silas was riding the swells, grinning like a pirate, his hair ruffling in the breeze. He had no idea that he could slip on the deck that was wet from the spray and crack his head open. He was small enough to slide right under the railing, into the swells.

The instinct to go after him battled her phobia. How big would the waves get? How long could Silas hang on before he was tossed off? With sweating, white-knuckled hands, she clung to her tenuous seat. To her horror, the black spots in her vision spread. Her mouth watered in advance warning that she was going to lose her lunch.

She had just enough time to lean out over the railing, risking death by drowning, to avoid the humility of having to clean up the deck—or worse, watch Solomon do it.

With her stomach empty, she prayed for the nausea to pass, but it didn't. Jordan collapsed back on the box, feeling like a puddle in a life vest, too weak to move or even open her eyes, bathed in a clammy sweat.

Solomon heard Silas patter up the metal steps to the pilot room. "Careful," he warned. "Hold the railing."

"Mith Jordan is pukin' her gutths out," Silas reported.

Solomon wrested his gaze from the channel markings to Silas's expectant gaze. He immediately shifted into neutral, sending the houseboat into a gliding standstill. There were no other boats in the inlet to worry about. He left the wheel to assess Jordan's condition for himself.

He found her pale-faced, eyes closed, clutching the rail

behind her like she would slip bonelessly to the deck if she let go. "Jordan," he called, patting her clammy cheek.

Her indigo eyes fluttered open, a colorful contrast to her green complexion. "Bend over and put your head between your knees," he instructed, recognizing her symptoms. "Silas, go inside and fetch a wet cloth. Walk!" he added, as Silas took off at a run.

Jordan's reddish brown hair hid her profile as it hung to the deck. Solomon gathered it in his hands, enjoying the cool, silky glide of it through his fingers as he hunkered down to assess her recovery. "Breathe through your nose, slow and steady."

"Why?" she choked out after a minute of steady breathing. "Why did you do this to me? I told you I get seasick!"

Feeling bad, he delayed an answer as he took the sodden paper towel Silas brought back and wrung it out. "Sit up," he said, patting her face with it, relieved to see some pink return to her cheeks. "I wanted to prove a point, Jordan," he admitted, causing her head to jerk back and her eyes to flash.

"What, that Silas isn't cooped up? You didn't have to be so heavy-handed about it."

"That wasn't my only point. I wanted you to know what it means to be helpless because, if my instincts are right, then you still plan to return to Venezuela, regardless of the dangers."

She could only stare at him, rigid with outrage, her stomach still roiling.

"You might reign supreme in your classroom, Miss Bliss," he continued grimly, "but the real world is a hell of a lot bigger and a hell of a lot scarier than an elementary school. You can't control it, any more than you can control this body of water."

She shook her head and closed her eyes, not wanting to hear it. "You're wasting your time."

"You can't go back," he repeated, desperate to convey what dangers awaited her. "The Populists are arresting Americans left and right," he added, pitching his voice lower so that Silas couldn't hear him. "If you disappear into a Venezuelan prison, you may never see the light of day again. You have no idea what hell an American woman might have to endure before she's blessed with the luxury of death," he added, shaken by the images he'd conjured.

She fixed him with an obstinate look he'd seen on the faces of junior SEALs. "It doesn't matter!" she whispered fiercely. "I still have to *try*. Because if I don't, and the Populists take over, then I will *never* see Miguel again. I'd rather die than lose another child!" she added, her voice cracking.

Another child? Solomon rolled back on his heels. Understanding ran him through, like a knife through his heart. Along with understanding came compassion and concern. His lips firmed with resolve. "Come on," he said, pushing to his feet and holding a hand out to her.

She stared at it mistrustfully. "Where are we going?"

"Up to the pilothouse. You're going to take us back."

"What?" she gasped.

"You want to venture into the real world, Jordan?" he demanded, showing her no more mercy than he showed his men. "Then you need to know how to think through your fear. The only way we're returning to the pier is if you take us there."

She just looked at him, her face draining of color. "I can't."

"I'll be with you this time," he promised, feeling for her. "Let's go." He held his hand out, insisting she take it.

It was her desire to get on dry land that no doubt persuaded her. Jordan slipped a clammy hand into his, and he pulled her to her feet. "You, too, Silas," he called, shepherding the two of them up the steps to the highest part of the boat, where the bobbing was most evident.

"I'm going to get sick," Jordan protested, her knees giving out at the view awaiting them.

He caught her, coiling an arm around her midsection as he positioned her before the ship's wheel. "No you're not. Think, Jordan. Think through your panic. You can trust me," he added, inhaling the fruity scent of her shampoo as he murmured into her ear. His junior SEALs didn't get that kind of sweet-talking from him. But she wasn't a SEAL. She was just your average, thirtysomething female with no survival training whatsoever, who wanted to venture into a war-torn country to wrest a little boy out of the cross fire.

And now he understood why. Because Miguel was the second child she'd loved and lost. He'd had no idea. Had the loss of that child been the reason for her failed marriage?

"Here," he said, unfurling her clenched fists to place them on the steering wheel. "Silas, sit down," he warned, shifting the throttle into gear.

With a lurch that brought Jordan's backside flush against his front, the boat started moving.

"Oh, God," she whimpered, sinking against him as her legs gave out again.

"Stand up," he urged, pulling her upright. He wished she weren't wearing the life vest, wished he could enjoy the weight of her breasts on his arm. He put his free hand over one of hers and ordered her to turn the boat around.

Her breath came in panicky little gasps; nonetheless, she steered them back the way they came.

They were headed straight toward a crab pot buoy. "Go around it," he warned. She overcorrected and the boat swung too far, prompting a squeal of fear from her.

"Relax," he murmured, bringing *Camelot* back under control. He reduced their speed to give her more reaction time. "Think with your head and your gut. Don't listen to your fear, Jordan. Fear is your enemy."

All the while that he spoke to her, encouraging in his instructions, his mind raced with deep concern. This was not a false alarm. Jordan was *hell-bent* on returning to Venezuela, more so than he'd realized. If he interfered in any way, he knew she'd never forgive him.

He would have to think of something else—some other way to snatch Miguel out of the country. If only he'd brought the boy with them the first time! It was going to take everything in his power to make up for that mistake.

"If I can do that," exclaimed Jordan, throwing herself down on the cushion next to Silas while Solomon disappeared to secure the boat to its moorings, "then you can learn to read."

Silas shot her a gamine grin. "Let's go out again."

"Oh, no, not today," said Jordan weakly. "I have to go help my sister. She's getting five new horses this afternoon for her therapy ranch."

"Real horses?"

"Really real. Would you like to come out to the ranch and see them next week?" she asked. "You could play with my niece. She's six, just like you."

"A girl?" he scoffed, wrinkling his nose.

A vibration under her feet drew Jordan's gaze toward the stairs. Solomon reappeared to press a few more buttons and extract the key from the ignition. "Well, shipmate Bliss," he said, eyeing her thoughtfully, "you're not exactly Captain Bligh, but you found your sea legs."

"I'd just as soon use them to walk on dry land, thanks," she retorted, trying to remember who Captain Bligh was. She pushed to her feet, unbuckling her life vest with hands that still shook. "You're lucky that I'm a forgiving person, Solomon," she warned, saying his name for the first time, enjoying how it felt on her lips and tongue. "You came pretty darn close to having to look for a new tutor."

Tossing the life vest at him, she descended the steps calling, "See you, Silas."

"Jordan."

She rolled her eyes at Solomon's peremptory tone and turned around inquiringly. "Yes, Solomon?"

The grave expression on his face made his eyes seem more gray than silver. "Give me time," he exhorted, "and I will find a way to get Miguel for you."

The offer took her aback. For a moment, she could only stare up at him, nonplussed. How thoughtful of him to make an offer like that! How gallant. How...unexpected. But she'd already bought her tickets; her money was spent. Besides, she didn't have the luxury of time, not with her visa expiring, with Miguel losing ground on his emotional recovery.

"Will you tutor Silas this weekend?" he added, his tone compelling.

"Do you want me to?" She could always stand to make more money.

"Aye," he said softly, and his sex appeal shot through her like a harpoon.

Slowly, surely, he was reeling her in. She wasn't sure whether to fight the tug of attraction or revel in it. After all, he wasn't a threat to her emotions. And having sexual urges just meant she was whole again, the pain of her divorce truly over. "Well, in that case, I'll see you in the afternoon on both days. I have to help my sister in the mornings."

She didn't miss the glint of curiosity in his eyes. He wanted to know what she was up to, but she just left him wondering. Their lives might have intersected at this critical time of her life, but in the long run, she'd remain independent—safe from any potential for heartache or crushing disillusionment.

So long as Miguel was in her life, she'd never be alone.

Rafe assessed Jillian's front stoop in the twilight, trying to determine the cause of its sagging as Jillian walked Jordan to her car. The quiet country air was disturbed only by the buzz of insects and the call of a whip-poor-will. The sisters' conversation came to him distinctly as he bent to examine the foundation on the side of the listing structure.

"Thank you, Jordan. You still have that special touch with animals. We couldn't have done it without you, today."

"Well, give the horses some credit. They're remarkably docile."

"That's how therapy horses are supposed to be. Still, thank you. I know you're busy tutoring that little boy."

"Family comes first," said Jordan. "I'll be back tomorrow and again on Sunday."

From the corner of his eye, Rafe watched the sisters embrace. "Boy, this baby's growing," Jordan laughed, laying a hand on Jillian's belly. "Have you picked out names yet?"

"No, not yet."

"You're, what, seven months along? When are you going to pick out names?"

"When I have the *time,*" Jillian answered with strain in her voice.

To Rafe's relief, Jordan offered her sister a second hug. "I'm right here to help," she comforted. "At least for a little while."

Jillian drew back. "What does that mean?"

"I'll tell you later," Jordan answered, glancing at Rafe. "You're keeping Rafe waiting. *Ciao!*" She ducked into her car and took off.

"I should be leaving, too," Rafe said, as Jillian made her way back to him. In the twilight, her hair shone like platinum as it cascaded over her shoulders, loosed from the ponytail she'd kept it in all day. He experienced a heightening of his senses as she stepped closer, her lavender scent stealing around him. Before she could speak, the front door flew open.

"Mommy! Can I use this jar to catch fireflies?" Agatha asked, holding up an empty pickle jar.

"Oh, sure, honey, but hold it by the bottom, so it doesn't fall and break."

"Watch this, Mr. Rafael. I'm going to catch fireflies and make a lamp!" With that, Agatha scampered past them, bearing her jar into the front yard in pursuit of the bugs that sparked here and there in the cooling air.

Rafe sent Jillian a wry look. "I guess I'd better watch for a while."

"Let's sit on the porch swing," she invited, with a smile.

"Will it hold both of us?" He wasn't so much wary of it collapsing as he was of sitting beside her. That had never been an issue back when she was married.

"I guess we'll find out. Everything around this house is falling apart. My father was too busy caring for my mother to keep things up. And then he died two months after she did."

"He must have loved her very much." He held the swing still so she could sit on one end.

"He did," she concurred, easing onto the swing with a groan of relief.

"You've been on your feet all day," he observed, sitting tentatively beside her. The chains creaked but held.

"That's nothing new."

He knew she should put her feet up. That's what Teresa had done in her third trimester. He pushed the offer nervously through his throat, afraid of where it might take them. "Why don't you put your feet up?" he offered, patting his thigh.

At her quick look of surprise, he was grateful for the shadows that hid his coloration. "A nurse should know better," he chided, to make the offer seem impersonal.

"Well, if you're sure." She kicked off her garden clogs and swung her knees sideways, lifting her calves up on his thighs. The soft, warm weight of her legs made his breath catch.

"Put this behind your back," he suggested, lifting a blanket off the back of the swing. "You must sit out here often," he added, as she stuffed it behind herself.

"I do." Her tired, husky voice washed over him. "I love the quiet of the country. Living in the city wasn't for me. You can see the stars out here, smell the soil, and hear the leaves rustle on the trees. I missed that in the city."

His palms itched to massage her calves, but that wouldn't be appropriate.

Jillian gave a groan. "I didn't realize till now how much my legs ache," she admitted. "Now they're tingling." She tried to lean over her bulging midsection to rub them.

He had no choice but to help.

"Oh, thank you," she breathed, leaning back with a sigh.

It wasn't any hardship. Not at all, except that he felt a little out of practice. How long had it been since he'd touched a woman, let alone caressed bare skin, all soft and silky?

"That feels good," she admitted with the slightest hint of her own heightened awareness.

In the twilight, they shared a long, thoughtful look, each one assessing the other in a different light.

Frightened by the direction of his thoughts, Rafe moved the conversation into safer waters. "You need to slow down," he cautioned. "You're trying to do too much."

Her smile was faintly sardonic. "Do you think I have any choice?" she countered. "I can't start this ranch up with a baby in one arm."

He sensed grief welling inside of her. "I'm sorry," he heard himself say.

She shook her head. "Don't. Don't be sorry. When I married Gary I knew what I was getting into. He needed the danger that went with being on a SWAT team. It made him feel alive, like he was making a difference. I took a chance and loved him anyway. It's all a part of being real."

He couldn't relate to what she was saying, so he kept his mouth shut.

"Did you ever read a children's story called *The Velveteen Rabbit*?"

"I don't believe I did," he answered, searching his

memory. Those days of reading bedtime stories seemed so long ago.

"It's about a toy rabbit who wants to be real. He's talking to the old Skin Horse, who says that you can only become real by being loved. Your fur will get worn and your eyes will get loose and jiggly. But once you're real nothing can take that away from you."

The night air seemed suddenly thick, hard to breathe.

"I was married to Gary for fifteen years. He made me real, and being real hurts sometimes. But I wouldn't change a thing that happened, except that it happened when my children were still young. At least I was loved."

Rafe swallowed hard. She was so much braver than he. Eight years ago he'd come home to a bloodbath. His entire family had been gunned down in retaliation for his work in putting the mob boss, Tarantello, and his right-hand man in jail for life. The night he'd found his family killed, Rafe had cut his bleeding heart from his chest and buried it with his family in the vault at St. Raymond's cemetery.

He'd never wanted to be real, to feel, again.

But what was it she'd just said? *Once you're real nothing can take that away from you.*

He felt suddenly, inexplicably panicked. "I have to go now, Jillian." He drew his hands regretfully to her ankles.

She just looked at him for a long, sad moment. "Okay," she relented. "Good night, Rafael. Thank you so much for coming." She swung her feet to the porch plank so that Rafe could stand.

"Wait!" Agatha shouted from a dark corner of the yard. She ran in their direction, bearing her glass like a trophy. "You have to see my lamp."

"Let me see," Rafe offered.

She placed the jar on the porch steps and bent over to be eye level with it. "You have to wait. I caught four of them!"

Charmed by her enthusiasm—she reminded him only a little of his daughter Serena—Rafe went down on his haunches to wait. He could feel Jillian's gaze on him as she swung herself gently back and forth, back and forth.

A burst of pure gold light illumined the glass jar, then another, and then another. "See!" Agatha exclaimed, her smile ecstatic. It shot through Rafe like a sunbeam.

"Thank you," he said, "for sharing your lamp with me." He ruffled her hair and strode quickly to his car. "Good night, Jillian," he called. He couldn't bring himself to look at her.

"Good night, Rafael."

He could tell by her tone that she understood what he was thinking. It'd been like that from the beginning of their friendship. They shared an uncanny ability to read each other's minds.

He slipped into his car and pulled away. She knew that he was running away. She probably even suspected he might never come back.

Chapter Nine

✦

Solomon met Jordan on the pier. "You'll have to tutor Silas later," he announced with a serious look. "We're going to the health clinic." Silas's wrist was imprisoned in his fist. "I want you to come with us."

A rumble of thunder warned of the approaching storm. Charcoal-colored clouds surged over the trees mirroring Jordan's sudden concern. "Is he sick?" She glanced down at Silas, who struggled against Solomon's hold, looking pale and frightened.

"Not sick," said Solomon. "He needs shots."

"I don't want shots!" Silas cried, his eyes filling with pitiful tears.

"Oh," said Jordan, putting two and two together. "He can't go to school without his third DPT."

"Not just school," Solomon replied, "day care, too. He needs four shots total."

"Four!" Jordan exclaimed, tempering her dismay for Silas's sake. He looked scared enough. "You're hurting him," she pointed out.

"I can't let go. He tried running from me once already," Solomon explained.

Jordan frowned in disapproval. "He needs reassurance, Solomon, not manhandling," she scolded. "Come here, honey," she said, bending down and holding her arms out to him.

Silas glanced at his father, who grudgingly released him. He stepped stiffly into Jordan's embrace, too proud to cling or cry, but Jordan could feel him trembling. "I'm assuming his shot record is lost," she said to Solomon.

"I kept a record of his earliest shots," he clipped. "And I'm sure that Ellie had him immunized with her other boys, but the only way to reach her is through snail mail, and I don't have time for that."

"Silas, honey," Jordan said, putting him at arm's length to give him a firm but compassionate look, "you have to cooperate and get your shots. They really don't hurt that bad. If you're a good boy, your father's going to take you to the toy store afterward and buy you whatever you want."

She glanced upward for corroboration and caught a bemused look on Solomon's face. "Won't you?" she asked him.

He hesitated only briefly. "Sure. Whatever you want, Silas."

"Okay?" she asked Silas, whose imagination was clearly working overtime.

"'Kay," he whispered.

"Within reason," Solomon added.

"Don't worry," drawled Jordan, straightening and taking Silas's hand. "He's not going to ask for a new car till he's sixteen."

Leading him off the dock, she glanced at the ominous line of clouds approaching. "Are you sure you need me to go with you?" she called, as a gusty breeze molded her skirt and blouse to her body. She glanced back, catching Solomon's appreciative regard. "You're paying me to tutor, not play nanny," she reminded him.

He jingled the keys in his pocket. "Come with us," he said with a nod.

Jordan sighed. "Use your manners, Solomon."

"Come with us, please," he bit back.

The squeeze of Silas's hand prompted her decision. "Fine," she agreed. "I'll tutor him later this evening if he's feeling up to it."

But Silas wasn't feeling up to it. By seven o'clock that evening, the injection sites on his arms and thighs were swollen and hot, and he was running a temperature. Jordan settled down with him on Solomon's reading couch and pulled a book from her bag. "This is *The Velveteen Rabbit*," she announced. "Agatha said you'd like it."

With rain drumming the boat's decks and flecking the windows and with Silas's cheek against her shoulder, his new toy in his lap—a Dragon Ball Z figurine—Jordan was sharply aware of Solomon's restlessness. He approached Silas three times in the course of the story: once to take his temperature; again to administer Tylenol that the doctor had sent home with him; then with a cool washcloth for the boy to keep against his forehead.

On his fourth approach, Jordan snatched her head up. "Solomon! He's fine. This is a normal reaction to immunizations."

"He's asleep," Solomon pointed out.

"Oh." Sure enough, Silas had nodded off against her arm.

"I'll put him in bed," he added.

Silas came awake as his father lifted him off the couch. "Jordan," he cried, reaching out a hand for her.

Touched, Jordan stood up to stroke the hair off his sweaty forehead. His fever had broken. "You rest, big guy. I'll see you tomorrow." It did not escape her notice that she and Solomon would be more or less alone once Silas was put in bed. And given the thoughtful glance he swung her way, he was realizing the same thing. She had probably better get out now while the getting out was good. Grabbing up her bag, she headed for the door.

"It's pouring out there. Why don't you wait until the rain stops?" With that suggestion, he turned and carried Silas down the hallway to his bedroom.

Jordan peeked outside to see if he was telling the truth. Sure enough, sheets of rain dimpled the surface of the inlet and obscured the shoreline. She'd be drenched by the time she got to her car. Perhaps she could afford to wait for the rain to clear.

Perhaps she didn't really want to leave. Besides, how far could Solomon take things with Silas sleeping in his bed?

Excited, terrified by the thought that she was willing to risk an encounter of the personal kind, Jordan moved away from the door toward the bookcase. Examining the vast collection, she drew out a copy of *Jane Eyre,* by Charlotte Brontë.

Solomon's voice made her jump, coming as it did from

right behind her. "Why is it you women always go for the romance novels?" he queried, his tone contemptuous.

She quelled her leaping heart, her sudden nervousness. "I take it you don't believe in love," she shot back.

"Love?" He raised a mocking eyebrow. "Love is a fabrication. To believe in it is to invite disillusionment."

She had to agree with him somewhat there. "Sometimes," she acknowledged, with a pinch of sorrow.

"We'd all be better off calling it what it is: biology," Solomon continued, his gaze sliding warmly over her as she pretended to read the back cover of the book. "The compulsion to propagate the species," he added, quietly.

That familiar, giddy warmth spread insidiously through her. "That's crass," she retorted, but she lacked the willpower to step away. Or even to leave, though the rain sounded softer.

He stepped abruptly closer, took the book from her slack hands, and laid it aside. Jordan's heart started to race. She knew what was coming next, waited for the slightest reluctance on her part, and felt nothing but tingling anticipation.

Putting his powerful arms around her, Solomon pulled her hips to his, giving her fair warning of his intentions. *He wanted all of her.*

Her blood heated instantly at the possessive gesture. She coiled an arm around his impossibly broad shoulders and crushed her breasts against his rock-hard chest, wanting desperately, ironically, to feel him deeper.

"Jordan," he murmured, lowering his head to speak against her lips. "Don't think about it," he advised. "Just feel. Let your instincts take over."

He didn't need to persuade her. Her mental processes

had all but shut down. She was a bundle of yearning, frightened by the ferocity of the desire that gripped her, that made her want to climb his body and coil her legs around him. How could she want a man who infuriated her?

Glancing down, she watched her buttons melt apart beneath his deft fingers, exposing the purple satin bra she wore, stretched taut over her peaked nipples. He bent his head, and her breath caught as he tipped her back and nuzzled her, grazing her tender flesh with his teeth.

She clung to him to keep from falling.

With a feral growl, Solomon swung her onto the sofa. He went down on his knees and divested her completely of her blouse and bra. Before she knew it, she was leaning back against the cushions completely topless, her body on fire. He put his hands on her, stroked her from her neck to her navel and back up again, cupped her breasts, lowered his mouth, and drank of her.

Oh, God. Jordan had never felt desire like this. The passion roaring through her blood was a hurricane where, in the past, she'd only experienced spring showers.

She had to get her legs apart—*now*—only her skirt was in the way. With a tug and a wriggle, she bunched it shamelessly at her waist and anchored him with her thighs to keep him close.

This is biology, she repeated to herself. Animal instinct. She hadn't had sex in so long, she was rabid with need. What else explained this compulsion to incinerate?

Leaving her nipples taut and aching, he dove into her mouth again and kissed her till she was light-headed. His eyes flashed with a predatory light as he pulled back suddenly, watching her reaction as he placed his hands on her thighs and stroked them, higher, higher.

"Say my name," he commanded.

"Solomon," she whispered, burning with ferocious desire, her eyelids so heavy she could scarcely keep them open.

He seized her knees, lifting them from his hips to his shoulders, and then he looked down at her. She followed his gaze to where the crotch of her purple panties peeked out beneath the hem of her rucked skirt, the most erotic sight she'd ever seen.

Very lightly, teasingly, he moved his thumb over the exposed mound. A satin panel was the only thing between them. Jordan swallowed a moan as liquid heat instantly dampened it.

He asked her a question so explicit that she could only tremble and nod her head. *Yes. Oh, please, yes.*

With a smile of anticipation, he drew her panties down her legs, slowly, building her excitement. He kissed her inner thighs, his lips hot and silky. He nuzzled her with his moustache, breathed deeply. "You smell so good," he muttered, and then he devoured her.

Jordan came off the cushion, then settled back down as his devouring turned into languid caresses, followed by flicks and nips that had her digging her nails into the fabric of the cushions. The room reeled, and her blood roared. An unfamiliar voice cried out and moaned before she realized it was her own.

She was at the verge of splintering into a million pieces when he suddenly stood up.

Spread-eagled, her senses too drugged to allow for self-consciousness, Jordan watched shamelessly as Solomon stripped off his shirt, exposing a chest that made her inner muscles clench with desire. He released the buckle of his belt, unzipped his jeans, and stepped out of them. Jordan forgot how to breathe. *Oh. My.*

This was her last opportunity to run. Instead, she reached for him. But he sidestepped her.

With an effortlessness that made her gasp, he hooked an arm beneath her waist and swung her lengthwise on the couch. He crawled over on top of her, his expression taut, his eyes like twin lasers.

Jordan's hands came up. With awe and just the tiniest bit intimidated, she ran her palms over his thickly corded arms to the bulging muscles of his upper chest and the mat of dark fur at the center. "Now touch me," he encouraged, roughly.

Heart pounding with discovery, she smoothed her fingertips downward, over the taut surface of his abdomen to his jutting arousal. His eyes melted shut as she closed her hands over him, marveling at the contrast of satin softness and unrelenting turgidity. An impulse compelled her to band his thickness, and he shuddered, growling low in his throat.

A moment later, he wrested her hands from him, held them against the cushions on either side of her head, and centered himself. His face was ruddy with expectancy, his gaze focused. In the next instant, he was entering with purpose, retreating, entering again—filling her, filling her, filling her, until their hips ground together. She whimpered, torn between a feeling of utter fulfillment and still wanting more.

She could feel his heart hammering against her breasts.

"Open your eyes," he softly growled. "I want you to know who's fucking you."

Shocked, her eyes flew open. He could have said making love or having sex, something a little less crude. But then again, at the moment, the man was like the act: base and instinctual, totally driven by his lust and passions. He'd pushed her so far beyond her normal impulses that she nearly reveled in his crudeness.

He thrust again, and Jordan's vision blurred. She couldn't believe this was happening; couldn't believe the intensity of the feelings crashing through her. Crude or not, what he was doing felt incredible.

He kissed her, his tongue imitating the movements of his lower body. The maddening assault made her whimper and squirm. He released her hands, giving her freedom to rake his warm shoulders with her nails, to clutch him closer, as their straining grew urgent, tempestuous.

A roaring filled her ears. Her skin was on fire.

"Look at me," Solomon commanded against her lips.

She slit her eyes open, excited beyond bearing by his insistence, frightened by the power of the release that was on the verge of detonating. "Solomon!" she cried, skewered by his silver gaze as she tensed, arched, threw her head back and screamed, overpowered by the force and magnitude of her climax.

She felt him convulse deep inside of her before pulling out on a groan. An unmistakable, wet warmth landed on her thigh as he used his own hand to finish what they'd started.

Jordan hadn't given a thought to birth control. Neither had Solomon, apparently, until it was almost over.

"Sorry," he muttered, catching her startled look. "I'll get a towel."

With a ripple of muscles, he withdrew and walked in splendid nakedness down the hall to fetch a towel. Jordan looked down at herself, disbelievingly.

Her skirt was twisted around her waist. Solomon's ejaculate glistened like pearls next to her auburn curls. Seeing it, a surge of emotion crested unexpectedly inside of her. She held in the sudden urge to weep by holding her breath.

He reappeared, towel in hand. With a hot face, she watched him wipe away all traces. He caught her eye, perhaps catching a glimpse of the unwieldy emotion she struggled to contain. "You okay?" he asked her gruffly.

"Yes. I have to go." She scooted quickly to the edge of the couch, stood, and covered herself, hunting for her clothing.

This wasn't supposed to have affected her emotions.

Solomon remained in one place, totally unself-conscious and apparently unaffected. "What's the hurry?" he finally asked.

Jordan didn't answer. With his watchful eye upon her, she couldn't begin to sort through her feelings. She needed to retreat, to ponder his power over her in private and whether she ought to be offended by his choice of words. Revealing any chink in her armor would only give him the advantage.

He tried again. "It's still raining," he said, as she slipped her feet into her sandals and reached for her bag.

"I know."

"Jordan."

She headed to the door, unwilling to look back lest he see how close she was to losing it.

"You'll be back tomorrow, won't you?"

She hesitated long enough to let him know she'd heard him. It was way too soon to know how she'd feel in the morning. Right now, tonight, all she wanted to do was to crawl into her bed at home and cry her eyes out, for reasons she didn't understand.

She slipped through the door without answering and fled into the rain, unmindful that she might trip or lose her footing on the wet pier. By luck, she made it to land, racing up the hill through the sodden grass, hot tears mingling with cool drops of rain.

On Sundays, the closest drugstore didn't open until noon. Solomon, who was still kicking himself for having unprotected sex, wanted to buy condoms. Lots and lots of condoms because, from what he could tell, it was going to take a long time to get tired of Jordan Bliss.

Sex had never been so good.

That was how he found himself in Wal-Mart at ten o'clock on a Sunday morning.

"What are those?" Silas asked as he dropped a box of #36 ribbed Trojans into his shopping basket, considered the unfathomable depth of his desire for her, and reached for a second box. "Vitamins?"

"Insurance," Solomon answered, cutting him a look that had the power to quell further comments—at least where junior SEALs were concerned.

Silas wasn't that astute. "They look like them balloons that get real big when you fill 'em up with water," said

Silas rather loudly. "Christopher got some and we filled 'em up and throwed 'em at each other."

They were getting amused looks from the pharmacist.

"You need new clothes for school," Solomon decided, propelling his son away from the family planning aisle toward Boy's Clothing. He could feel heat on his face.

This was her fault. *Jordan Bliss.* For some unknown reason, she had his thoughts in a jumble, his heart pumping too fast. He was thirty-eight years old, and he'd never, *never* been so intent on getting inside of a woman that he'd forgotten protection.

Who was she to have that kind of power over him—a warrior, a salty dog who'd seen it all, a callous lover who circled women watchfully, went in for a bite now and then, got his fill, and moved unfeelingly onward?

Jordan was his riptide.

The realization had him missing a stride as he led Silas into the racks of little boy's clothing.

Riptides could be deadly. Powerful, invisible, they sucked unsuspecting swimmers out to sea.

But he was a SEAL. He knew what to do when caught up in a riptide. Let it carry him where it would, all the while swimming parallel to the shore so that when the current finally weakened, he could break free and swim to safety.

He liked the analogy. It gave him the freedom to indulge again in mind-blowing sex while leaving an escape route.

The question now was, what would it take to convince her to *be* with him again?

Eyeing the sea of boys' clothing, he felt daunted by the prospect of shopping for a fall wardrobe. Jordan would do a better job of it, he decided, putting the chore off till later.

For now, he'd prefer to return to the houseboat, just in case she'd opted for an early start on Silas's lessons. "Jordan can take you shopping tonight," he decided, realizing at the same time that he was shamelessly using his son to keep Jordan near to him.

"Okay," said Silas, shrugging. A gleam then entered his eyes and he added, "Hey, you wanna go home and blow up them balloons?"

"Jordan, something's wrong with you," Jillian observed, propping the rake against the barn wall. "Are you going to tell me what it is, or do I need to pry it out of you?"

Hanging a horse bridle on a peg, Jordan didn't dare meet her sister's worried gaze lest she see too much. "I've got financial problems, that's all," she murmured convincingly.

"So ask Doug to give you a loan," Jillian suggested. "God knows the bastard owes you more alimony than he pays."

"No," Jordan retorted flatly. She didn't want a cent of Doug's money. "I've decided to rent my condo." She'd read a flyer that came in yesterday's mail: *Military couple seeks short-term, furnished rental.* The timing had seemed too auspicious to pass up. She'd given them a call, and they'd already made preliminary arrangements.

"Where would you live?" Jillian asked with startled concern. "With me?"

Jordan risked a peek at her. She'd been planning to, assuming all along that Jillian could use her help, but her sister sounded less than thrilled at the prospect. "No," she heard herself answer. "I'll stay in a cheap motel, or split an apartment with another teacher."

With the therapy horses nickering in their stalls, Jordan went back to sorting through riding tack, all stuffed haphazardly into a single crate. She heard Jillian push the wheelbarrow toward the exit but instead of sliding the door open to admit the hazy heat, she came back to stand in front of Jordan till she looked up.

"You've bitten off more than you can chew with this Miguel thing," Jillian conveyed with sisterly concern. "Just look at you, Jordan. You're falling apart. You look like you haven't slept in weeks, and now you're telling me that you're broke."

"I am not broke," Jordan insisted, bristling. "The money's a little tight, that's all."

"Look, I can't take care of anyone *else*," Jillian cut in, her voice wobbling. "My stress level is high enough without having to worry about you, too."

"I never asked you to worry about me," Jordan retorted, tempering her tone with compassion. "Forget I said anything, all right?" Her sister would probably pass out to know that Jordan was heading back to Venezuela in a matter of days. Was it better to forewarn her or spare her the anxiety?

The ringing of her cell phone kept her from making up her mind. She glanced at the caller's number, and her heart skipped a beat. *Solomon.* Now she regretted suggesting that he get a cell phone.

She stuffed her own phone back into her pocket.

"Who is that?" Jillian asked, astute as ever.

"Nobody." Just an annoying Navy SEAL who made

her blood flash hot, then cold, as she remembered her abandonment last night. How could she have let herself have sex with him? And not just any sex—explosive, orgasmic, earth-shattering sex, which he'd called fucking.

His crudeness appalled her, and yet—God help her—she wanted to be with him again.

Was this simple biology? He'd said so, and yet she'd never experienced anything like it—not with Doug, not with any man. Only Solomon ignited in her the irrational impulse to burn in the fire, like a moth drawn to flame.

Jillian persisted. "It's the Navy SEAL, isn't it?" she exclaimed with wonderment and delight. "You're avoiding him!"

"I really don't want to talk about it," Jordan snapped, turning away to hang another bridle.

Jillian gasped. "You slept with him!" she guessed, knowing her sister better than anyone. "Oh, honey, I'm so happy for you!"

Jordan whirled in disbelief. "Happy? You're happy that I got laid?"

Jillian winced. "Don't say it like that, Jordan. I'm happy that you've moved on, that's all. Maybe you'll realize now that not all men are like Doug. There are still some decent guys out there."

"Like Rafe Valentino," Jordan countered, turning the tables with a meaningful look.

Jillian blinked and visibly drew back. "Well, yes, I suppose," she conceded. "Just because Doug betrayed you doesn't mean that every other man out there is going to do the same thing. Maybe you need to give this guy a chance."

Jordan shivered. Giving Solomon a chance was like

trying to turn a shark into a pet fish. Her cell phone rang again, its jaunty tune rising to the barn's rafters.

"Answer him, Jordie," Jillian coaxed.

Jordan's mouth went dry.

"Maybe he's the man of your dreams. You like his son, right, little Silas? Why not be his mother instead of Miguel's?"

Jordan raised a hand to her chest. "How can you say that?" she exclaimed, wounded by the suggestion. "Like I can just substitute one child for another and never look back?"

"I'm sorry," Jillian apologized, immediately contrite. "I didn't mean that like it sounded, honey. I just worry about you." The cell phone stopped ringing. "Why can't you be content with what's in front of you? Watching you grieve for a child so far away, hearing that you're running out of money—it breaks my heart!"

Jordan's eyes stung at the honest admission. It was breaking her heart, too.

Her cell rang again. Damn the man! Why couldn't he leave her alone? She snatched it open, stewing for a fight. "What do you want?" she snapped, irately.

A sizzling silence followed her greeting. "When were you planning on coming back?" he testily inquired.

Just the sound of his voice made her knees weak and her breasts tingle. "I haven't decided yet," she replied.

"Funny, I hadn't pegged you as a coward," he taunted.

Bristling, she spun away from Jillian's watchful eye and marched toward the exit. "I am helping my sister get her new horses settled. There's a lot of work to be done," she added, thrusting her way into the sticky heat.

"Well, Silas goes to day care tomorrow morning since I'm going back to work, and he needs new clothing."

"So take him shopping," she suggested through her teeth.

"I don't know what kind of clothes to buy him. You're the teacher."

She threw her free hand into the air. He knew just what buttons to push, damn him. He certainly couldn't send Silas to day care in the ragged shorts and T-shirts he currently owned. "Fine," she conceded, for Silas's sake. "I'll take him shopping this evening, *if* I have the time."

"The mall closes at six," he pointed out. "And I want him in bed by seven. He's getting up with me at four in the morning."

"Four in the morning? You can't wake him up at four in the morning."

"Why not? The child-care center's open."

Jordan sputtered, "It's inhumane to drag a child out of bed when it's still dark outside!"

"Well, what else do you suggest, Miss Bliss?" Solomon demanded, sounding frustrated.

She realized, too late, that she was setting herself up. "You need a nanny," she gritted, "and, no, I'm not volunteering my services. I'm leaving the country, remember?"

"Not if I find another way to get Miguel out."

"Solomon." She sighed, kicking the ground with her booted heel. "You know that's not going to work."

"Don't underestimate me, Jordan," he retorted. "I have a lot of contacts. There's bound to be a way."

For a second she let herself hope for a miracle. If Solomon did that, she would owe him her eternal gratitude. She wasn't sure she liked that idea.

"Listen," he added, his voice turning low and seductive. "I have a thought. Why don't you spend the night on the houseboat? You could sleep in one of the bunks downstairs with Silas."

"No," she said, quickly cutting him off.

"This isn't for me," he insisted. "It's for Silas. That way I wouldn't have to wake him up so early like you said. You could tutor him, take him shopping, get him ready for school."

And she could rent her condo to that couple that so desperately needed it.

"No," she repeated, but it made too much sense. She could even pay her bills off with their first month's rent and deposit.

"Jordan, I won't pressure you to sleep with me if that's what you want to hear," he surprised her by adding.

She frowned, sensing a trap. "Really," she scoffed.

"I promise," he purred with far too much confidence.

He thinks I'll cave in to my desire and beg for it, she realized. Well, wouldn't it be a blow to his ego to call his bluff?

God, she couldn't believe she was actually considering living on a houseboat!

"I'll think about it," she relented, withholding her final answer. "Right now my sister needs me, and family comes first."

She got deep satisfaction out of hanging up on him.

Chapter Ten

✦

The sun was dropping fast behind the big house, casting cool shadows on the hill, when Jordan made her descent to the houseboat. Spying Solomon on the foredeck, standing over a smoking grill, she suffered a moment's doubt. Her tug on the heavy suitcase, as she rolled it through the thick grass, flagged. It didn't help matters that she could see his self-satisfied smirk beneath the lift of his moustache, visible even from a distance.

"Took you long enough," Solomon called down as she stepped onto the pier. His gaze slid to the enormous suitcase. Every personal item she owned was stuffed inside of it. The couple renting her condo would be moving in tomorrow.

Jordan didn't deign to answer. She hauled her bag along the planks, making as much noise as a freight train till Solomon met her at the gangplank and took it from her, swinging it aboard effortlessly.

Silas stood at the doorway grinning. "Hi, Jordan," he said. "You're going to spend the night!"

Jordan's stomach cramped uncertainly. She didn't

know if she could actually *sleep* on the water. "That's right."

Solomon disappeared down the steps with her suitcase, appearing to keep his end of the bargain that he wouldn't pressure her for sex. When he returned, he sent her an innocent look, and asked, "Are you hungry?"

She was ravenous. "Yes."

"Good." He went to fetch the burgers off the grill.

They all sat in the cozy nook in the kitchen and gorged themselves.

Jordan's heightened awareness and her innate distrust of Solomon's motives kept her edgy. This was clearly an arrangement that would take some getting used to, on everyone's part.

"I'll get the dishes," she volunteered, when Solomon stated that he needed to run Silas a bath.

"No need," he argued. "You're the guest."

"No," she corrected him. "I'm not."

"Then what are you?" he asked her with that infuriating look of his.

Was there a right and a wrong answer to that question? "I'm...an employee," she said, sensing a trap. "As such, I'm earning my keep by cleaning up the dishes."

"Ah," he said, with a gleam in his eyes. "Are there other ways you intend to earn your keep?" he innocently inquired.

"Stow it, Solomon," she warned, flicking an uncomfortable glance at Silas.

With a chuckle, Solomon stood and ruffled his son's hair. "Come on then, tadpole. It's time for your bath."

Once Silas was scrubbed and dressed in hand-me-down pajamas, Solomon asked Jordan with that same bland smile and laughing eyes, "Would you like to see where you are going to sleep?"

She trailed the two males down the steps to the bunk-room in the boat's belly. Silas had already chosen which bed was his. Jordan elected to sleep across from him, on the lower bunk. Once they made up their beds with linens neatly folded in a closet, Silas clambered into his bunk and Solomon opened a worn copy of *Treasure Island,* in what was clearly their established, nightly routine. With a shoulder propped against Silas's bunk, he began to read.

Jordan kicked off her shoes and squeezed into her bunk to listen. Solomon's rough baritone, his intonation and quaint pronunciations captivated her. As he lost himself in the story—one he'd professed to reading dozens of times as a child—his dialect grew more distinct.

She envisioned what he must have looked like—just like Silas, probably, minus the sweet disposition. Who were his parents? she wondered. Did he still have family in New England? And how had he become a man of both brawn and intellect?

Realizing the magnitude of her curiosity, she shut down her thoughts and rolled out of her bunk. To know Solomon any better was asking for heartache, certainly.

Snatching her own pajamas from her bag, Jordan slipped away beneath Solomon's watchful regard. "Good night, Silas. I'm going to take a shower so I can sleep with you," she interjected into the story.

"'Kay."

She scuttled up the stairs and showered briskly, drop-ping the bar of soap, her fingers clumsy. It was only eight o'clock at night. Would Solomon really let her get away with going to bed so early? Or would he entice her in some way to stay up with him? His bed, she couldn't help but recall, was at their full disposal.

The water's spray caressed her sensitized skin, heightening her awareness. How had she gone from a divorcée with no sexual urges at all to a liberated woman with the sexual appetites of a twenty-year-old?

It had to be Solomon's fault. With his mesmerizing eyes and seductive, raspy voice, he'd brought out latent desires she had no business feeling.

If only she could be sure her desire was based just on biology, then she'd indulge again. God knew she wanted Solomon again—in every possible position, for as long as she could stand it.

But biology wouldn't give rise to confusion afterward, not to mention regret, and a feeling of stark emptiness, every bit as frightening as the feelings she was left with in the wake of her divorce.

God forbid she might do the stupidest thing she could ever do and fall in love with a heartless man, a man who didn't even believe in love!

It wasn't beyond the realm of possibility. She'd loved Doug at one time, despite his wandering eye. Solomon McGuire was crude and forceful. But she'd seen another side of him—the side that had written that poem; the side of him that made him tender with Silas. That side of Solomon scared her more than the rebel army had.

Emerging from the bathroom in her nightclothes, her teeth scrubbed and her hair damp, Jordan drew up short to find the object of her obsession lounging right outside the door. For a heart-thudding moment, she wavered at the invitation in his eyes. Her body clamored for his possession, her skin felt flushed. "I'm going to sleep," she announced, in an unconvincing voice.

His gaze drifted downward to where her nipples poked out the fabric of her tank top. "If that's your choice," he said, his low voice giving rise to goose bumps that chased up and down her thighs.

"Yes," she whispered. Her insides clutched with yearning and regret, and her feet seemed pegged to the floor.

He gestured toward the stairs. "Sweet dreams, then."

That prompted her to turn away, but not before glancing longingly down the hallway toward the inviting expanse of his captain's bed. "Good night."

Following the tiny lights inset into the floor, Jordan found her way to her bunk, tossed her old clothes alongside her suitcase, and squirmed between the sheets. Silas was already sleeping, his soft snores a balm to her fraying nerves.

With the blanket pulled to her chin, she listened to Solomon's stealthy tread as he moved around the living area, extinguishing the lights. She listened to the water sloshing against the hull, separated by mere inches of steel and wood. Dear God. However would she sleep like this?

She heard Solomon retreat to his bedroom and envisioned him stripping down to nothing. He struck her as the type to sleep nude. She gave a faint moan at the thought. But pride and self-preservation kept her back against the mattress. In just one week—provided Miguel's dossier arrived on time—she'd be gone, and Solomon wouldn't have the power to tempt her or to trample her fragile heart.

Squeezing her eyes shut, she practiced breathing in and out, in and out, in a vain attempt to relax her body and cool her overheated imagination.

It was going to be an impossibly long night.

*   *   *

Father Timothy Benedict waited for Miguel to fall asleep before attempting to slip out of the cathedral's rear exit. He'd been called to administer last rites to Fatima, who lay so ill with fever that the family keeping her was certain she would die.

Heart heavy with the task before him, Timothy was halfway up the steps that gave access to the rear gardens when the door yawned open behind him. He turned to see Miguel dashing up the steps in his wake, his face a reflection of terror.

"Ah, my boy," Timothy crooned with frustration and lament as Miguel threw skinny arms about his thighs and clung to him for dear life. "Now, you can't come with me," he explained, lowering himself on the topmost step to reason with the mute child. It was then that he felt Miguel quaking.

He pulled him to his chest, knowing he took comfort in the sound of a beating heart. He sighed as he stroked Miguel's silky, black hair. "Well, why not?" he added, knowing full well the boy would shriek and scream and eventually waken the others if he were left behind.

Timothy stood, lifting Miguel into his arms. The home where he'd left Fatima stood less than two blocks away. The sun had set hours ago, and with a curfew imposed after sunset, it was imperative for the priest to keep out of sight.

He unlocked the gate from within, peeked out upon a deserted street, and ventured forth warily, keeping to the shadows that shrouded the walled residences, many of which had been abandoned, some now occupied by Populists.

In the terrifying days following their invasion, they'd slaughtered Moderate supporters and left bodies rotting in the streets as examples of what others could expect.

Timothy was a servant of God; he trusted the Lord to keep him safe. At the same time, he was practical enough to keep his footfalls quiet on the cracked cement. As he stole along the cinder-block and stucco walls, he cocked his ears to noises other than the buzzing of insects and the ever-rushing waters of the Orinoco River. Miguel's head lolled drowsily upon his shoulder.

A volley of gunfire lent speed to his gait as he hastened across a narrow street. He rounded the corner with only one block to go when two young men thrust themselves out of the alcove, drawing Timothy to a stop. "*Alto,*" cried the first, aiming his pistol straight at Timothy's chest. "Where do you think you're going?" he demanded.

Miguel startled awake.

"To the house of a sick girl," Timothy explained, patting the boy, hushing him in his ear.

His accent betrayed him. "You're North American," the second one accused. "Show us your passport."

"I'm British," Timothy corrected him. He put Miguel on his feet, putting him at arm's distance as he fished for identification. "Let's see here," he stalled, his heartbeat swift but steady. He'd been taught in seminary to turn the other cheek, to remain passive in a violent confrontation. But if something were to happen to him, what would become of Miguel?

Only one of the two men had a gun.

And Timothy had been a mercenary long before he'd converted to the Faith.

Pulling his passport from his pocket, he made to hand it over, then tossed it instead. Both men turned, following its flight. Timothy kicked the pistol, which flew into the darkness, clattered and rolled.

The young men bared their teeth and attacked him with bare hands. Within seconds, both of them lay on the street, moaning and injured.

Timothy bent to retrieve his passport. Slipping it into his pocket, he held a hand out for Miguel, who stood with his back to the wall, gaping down at the soldiers in disbelief.

"Come, my boy," Timothy urged, holding out a hand insistently. "I'm sorry you had to see that." But he was heartened by the flash of approval in Miguel's eyes before the boy launched himself into his arms.

With the child clinging to him, he took off at a run. This night's business was likely to be unpleasant enough without having to worry about reprisal.

He was the only white priest in the city. It wouldn't take the Populists long to find him.

Jordan sipped her strawberry smoothie through a straw and eyed Silas thoughtfully. "Are you happy, Silas?" she asked on impulse. They sat outside the entrance to the ice-cream parlor under the protection of a patio umbrella, enjoying a well-deserved reprieve from morning lessons.

"Yep," he said, making loud sucking noises with his straw.

"You don't mind sleeping with me instead of your father?"

"Nope. I used to sleep with Chris'pher an' Caleb," he added. Almost immediately, his little face clouded over.

"You really miss them, huh?" she prompted.

"An' baby Colton, too," he admitted thickly. "Aun' Ellie, too." As he stared down the inside of his straw, his brow wrinkled in a way that reminded her of Solomon. "I can't even 'member her face."

Jordan felt for him. "Maybe they could come visit you," she suggested.

He shook his head. "Naw. Her ol' car would never make it."

She loved his backwater drawl. "Tell you what," she said, wanting to stroke the cowlick that stuck out on the top of his head but knowing he wouldn't appreciate it. "Tomorrow I'll take you out to my sister's ranch so you can play with Agatha and see the horses."

He lifted a considering look at her. "How big are them horses?" he wanted to know. "Bigger'n my daddy?"

With a start, Jordan realized this was the first she'd ever heard Silas call his father *Daddy*. "Even bigger," she replied, happy for Solomon, who would melt the first time he heard it. But then with a stab of longing, she thought of Miguel. "Just wait and see."

Silas's sorrow gave way to a grin of anticipation.

Jordan smiled back but then her smile faded. Oh, dear, who was going to care for Silas when she left for Venezuela?

She supposed he'd have to go to day care at four in the morning, after all.

*   *   *

Solomon was relieved not to find Jordan and Silas at the houseboat when he returned from work. The last thing he wanted was for them to see him in such a shitty mood.

He popped the top off a beer bottle and drained it in five swigs.

The Elite Guard whom he and his platoon had trained on behalf of the Moderate government of Venezuela had just switched allegiance to the Populists. It was all the talk at Spec Ops today.

Solomon seethed with resentment every time he thought about it. He'd worked one-on-one with dozens of those young, Venezuelan men, believing all the while that they were committed soldiers of Democracy. And now they were backing the fucking rebels!

And Jordan thought she was going to waltz back into that country to pluck little Miguel out of the fray. Over his dead body.

Too frustrated to eat, with enough testosterone in him to fuel a tanker truck, Solomon paced the circumference of his boat, thinking. He went up on his deck, to nurse a second beer and settle his agitation.

Half an hour later, he spied Jordan and Silas moving jauntily down the hill, chased by their shadows, and a familiar tingling centered at his loins. Her slender thighs, the way her hair swung around her shoulders, the watchful quality in her eyes as she looked up at him, elevated his desire to nearly unmanageable proportions.

If she didn't come to him soon of her own will there was no telling what he might do.

"I rode on a horse!" Silas shouted as he galloped onto the pier, imaginary gelding between his legs. "Agatha let me ride with her."

"Who's Agatha?" Solomon called down, as Jordan approached the gangplank.

"My niece. She's six, like Silas."

"You put two six-year-olds on the back of a horse?" he asked, wanting clarification.

"I knew you'd have something sarcastic to say," she snapped, glaring up at him. "How about, thank you, Jordan, for giving my son a unique experience? I'm sure he wouldn't get that much sitting in a day-care facility." Her spark of temper made him realize she'd probably slept as little as he had last night. They were both stewing for a fight. Lovely.

"Thank you," he growled.

She remained stiffly where she stood. At last she showed him the plastic bag in her hands. "We ate at my sister's, but she sent home leftovers for you. Fried catfish."

His stomach rumbled. "I'll be right down."

After wolfing down his dinner, Solomon felt moderately less savage. He joined the twosome in the living room, throwing himself down on the sofa to watch their game of checkers. Jordan lay on her stomach on the rug. Solomon's gaze settled on the lush curve of her bottom and remained there.

Silas trounced Jordan three times in a row. It was entirely possible that she let him win, although she stifled several enormous yawns. Her heavy-lidded gaze, when she finally deigned to look up at him, snatched his attention from her backside.

"What has gotten into you?" she finally demanded. "You're brooding like a bear."

Silas giggled.

Solomon considered whether to tell her or not. Maybe

the news was daunting enough to give her a reality check. "The soldiers I trained in Venezuela have transferred their loyalty to the Populists," he announced, watching her face carefully.

Her expression didn't change, although some secret thought seemed to scurry behind the indigo-blue of her eyes. "Are you being called upon to do something about that?" she asked carefully.

"No," he answered. "Not yet, anyway. But this will make it harder for me to find someone to get Miguel out."

"I see," she said, not sounding terribly disappointed.

He eyed her more closely. Her creased brow reflected concern, and concern was certainly merited, but he expected something more.

"I hope you're not still thinking of going back, yourself," he warned, speaking softly so as not to alarm Silas. The boy watched them worriedly, dividing his attention between them.

Jordan didn't say anything. She wouldn't even look at him.

Solomon's concern spiked to new heights. "Jordan," he said firmly. "With the Elite Guard backing the ex-president, there's no stopping the Populists. Do you understand?"

She finally looked at him, her eyes flashing with hurt and outrage. "I'm not stupid, Solomon," she replied. Color suffused her face and her eyes grew bright.

"I wasn't implying that you were," he said, gentling his tone. "I just want you to realize that you can't do this by yourself. I'm going to help you. I just need time."

"I don't have time!" she cried, startling all of them.

She leapt to her feet. "I'm sorry, Silas, I can't play anymore," she apologized hoarsely. She walked quickly into the bathroom, shut and locked the door.

"*Damn it,*" Solomon growled, aware that Silas was looking at him with big, wide eyes. He drew a steadying breath and, with forced pleasantness, asked his son, "Would you like me to play with you?"

Silas's dismay evaporated. "Sure," he answered with delight.

Solomon went down on the rug, which was still warm from Jordan's skin. He arranged his checker pieces with one ear cocked to the sounds in the bathroom. Other than the shower running, he couldn't hear a thing, and yet he knew she was in there, pining for Miguel. Her heart ached, and there was nothing he could do about it—except move mountains to make her smile again.

That thought brought him up short. He postponed his move on the checkerboard, pretending to ponder the results of his actions as he asked himself why Jordan's emotional state meant anything to him.

Was it merely that his conscience bothered him, since he was the reason she'd become separated from Miguel in the first place?

Or was it more than that? Something that had to do with who she was, how she made him feel?

He swallowed heavily, thrusting aside the terrifying thought that Jordan was carrying his heart out to sea, and he could no longer even see the shoreline.

With four days to go before her scheduled flight, Jordan swung by her condominium to check her mailbox.

If Miguel's dossier did not arrive on time, all her plans would have to be scrapped.

Licking tiny beads of sweat off her upper lip, she inserted her key into one of the many cubicles, whispered a prayer, and slowly opened it.

A thick envelope took up most of the space inside.

With a cry of relief, she pulled it out and glanced at the return address. Then she clutched it to her heart and let tears of both joy and regret fill her closed eyes, careful not to let Silas see them as he sat in her air-conditioned car.

She'd waited a year for this packet to be ready. And now that it was in her hands, she savored the possibility that soon Miguel would be in her arms, also, where he belonged—*if* she could actually pull his adoption off the way she planned.

With trembling fingers, she tore the envelope open and riffled through the contents. At the top were Señora Muñoz's instructions, carefully typed in less-than-proper English for her to follow. As she skimmed them, her mouth went dry.

Once in the country, make your way to Puerto Ayacucho using any means of transportation available. They will be limited. She'd typed the number of a lawyer by the name of Lorenzo. *He lives in Puerto Ayacucho and has agreed to meet you at La Catedral Maria Auxiliadora. Once he has received your check and signed his portion of the paperwork, you must make your way with the boy to Caracas, where the immigration office at the U.S. embassy will sign the immigration forms. Only then will the airlines allow Miguel to leave the country with you.*

This might have been easy a year ago, considered Jordan. But Solomon's disheartening news the other night filled her with cold foreboding. Bringing home Miguel in the limited time allowed by her visa was going to be a serious test of her resolve.

Sliding the dossier back in its envelope, she carried her mail to the car and slipped it under the driver's seat, so that Silas, who sat in back on a booster, didn't see it.

What would Solomon do if he found out she was going through with her plans, regardless? Would he even forgive her for leaving him and Silas in the lurch? And why, damn it, did it matter to her if he forgave her or not?

"Mornin', Jordan!" Silas's cheery greeting roused Jordan from a night of terrifying dreams in which she and Miguel had been chased by soldiers while trying to escape Venezuela. With a groan, she came to one elbow to wipe sleep from her aching eyes.

The knowledge that she was leaving soon had driven her anxiety to unprecedented levels. It filled her with mixed regret, dread, and—yes—fragile hope.

With rain coming down in sheets outside the octagonal window and Silas squirming through his lessons, Jordan gave in to her scattered thoughts and took him to the movies.

By the time she and Silas stepped aboard the boathouse that afternoon, soaking wet from their dash through the rain, she wanted nothing more than to crawl back in her bunk and sleep. She'd even gotten used to the sound of sloshing water.

But Solomon was home from work and apparently in a cheerful mood. "Let's go out," he suggested, with a look that saw more than she wanted him to. "I want to take Silas to the aquarium."

All Jordan wanted was to put her face in a pillow and forget the daunting task ahead of her. "I'll stay here," she said. "Go ahead and take Silas."

"But I want you to come," Silas protested. He slipped his hand into hers and tugged her toward the door.

Guilt nipped Jordan's conscience. She felt like she was abandoning Silas to get to Miguel. Her day was a wash anyway. Not even Solomon could make it any worse.

But, surprisingly, he made it better. Jordan spent the next three hours watching in amazement as the surly senior chief became a lighthearted companion and father. He and Silas laughed at the otters in the tank outside the aquarium. Once inside, he whisked Silas past the marsh exhibits straight to the big tank full of sharks and fishes.

A great white drifted past the glass, making Silas squeal. They watched in glee as it gobbled up a smaller fish. Jordan found herself smiling wryly.

Silas begged to pet the baby stingrays. For forty-five minutes, he watched them slip fluidly under his palm.

"Are you sure this is safe?" Jordan asked, mistrustful of the little critters.

"They clip their barbs," Solomon assured her. He stepped behind her and surreptitiously pinched her nipple. "Like this."

She gasped and swung around to elbow him, but with a boyish grin, he dodged her reprisal.

The grin left her reeling. Who'd have guessed that Solomon had a playful side? The last thing she needed was for him to appeal to her on another level. Her desire for him was enough of a distraction.

They wandered to the next exhibit to watch a documentary on sharks. It was dark. With no seats in the room, they had to stand. Silas's gaze was glued to the revolving screen and the mako shark circling them. "Makos are the only species of shark that are warm-blooded," announced the narrator. "This allows them to live in arctic waters."

Who'd have guessed? thought Jordan, waiting for her chance to get even. As the shark opened his mouth to attack, she pinched Solomon—hard—right where a love handle would have been, if he had one. He snared her wrist before she had a chance to pull her hand back and hauled her to him, locking her against his bigger body. Jordan, privately pleased to be his prisoner, pretended to struggle.

His smile flashed in the darkness. "You shouldn't tease a shark," he whispered.

"Let me go," she hissed back, shoving him halfheartedly. His rock-solid frame, that unique musky scent of his, made her heat with desire. Oddly, the day's stressors seemed to augment her sexual appetite.

She crowded helplessly closer, pressing herself against the solid length of his thigh, gasping with delight as his hand came up and covered her right breast. Relying on the shadows and his averted face to conceal his actions, Solomon fondled her. Jordan shivered. Her nipple swelled and peaked, jutting toward his palm with secret abandon.

For the next ten minutes, he treated her to a massage, from her shoulders to her buttocks, kneading and molding away the tension until she was little more than a puddle of longing—and his for the taking.

When the movie ended, he released her, adjusting himself with a crooked smile. He left her swaying on her feet as he moved away to collect Silas.

By the time they returned to the houseboat, Jordan's worries about traveling to Venezuela had faded behind the realization that she and Solomon were going to have sex tonight. There was no ignoring the signs. He'd made his intentions perfectly clear, and she lacked any willpower to deny him.

Tonight she would be a creature of instinct and compulsion. What did it matter when, within days, she might be dead?

While Solomon read *Treasure Island* and tucked Silas in, she showered and dressed as usual. She descended briefly to kiss the boy good night. "I'll see you upstairs," she informed his father breezily.

The scorching look that followed her had her prickling with anticipation. She found she couldn't just sit and wait in the living area. Crawling into his bed was just too obvious. So, she slipped outside to cool her overheated skin.

Chapter Eleven

♦

The summer rainstorm had departed, yet the air remained saturated with the scent of wet leaves. Jordan approached the rail to eye the waxing moon. A hoot owl loosed a hopeful call, and far away, another answered.

A chorus of frogs and insects serenaded Jordan's stroll to the rear of the boat. The wide inlet reminded her of how Solomon had taught her to think through her fear. She had a sinking feeling that lesson would come in handy very soon now.

She found herself climbing the metal steps that zig-zagged up to the pilot's station—the bridge, Solomon called it. There, the view was intoxicating, especially when she heard Solomon's muffled footfalls pursuing her.

She whirled to face him, and his gaze pinned her to the ship's wheel as he gained the last few steps.

"I don't know what I'm doing here," she stalled, her heartbeat accelerating. His naked chest, awash with moonlight, made him look like the god Poseidon. He wore only soft gray sweatpants, and nothing, she would wager, underneath.

He stalked her, and her breath backed up in her lungs as he tipped her chin up. "Waiting for me," he guessed, searching her face. "Am I right?"

She touched the tip of her tongue to her upper lip. "Yes," she admitted.

With a brief, triumphant smile, he lowered his head and kissed her.

Whimpering with what sounded like relief, Jordan threw her arms around him, surrendering to the tide of passion that rose up and engulfed them.

He drew her fiercely into his embrace, and she coiled one leg around him, then the other, supported by the ship's wheel at her back.

"Say it, Jordan," Solomon exhorted between deep, hungry kisses.

"Say what?" she asked, trembling uncontrollably.

"Tell me that you want me," he added, nudging her just where she wanted him most.

"I want you," she repeated, but her heart froze in dismay as she realized it was more than that. This wasn't about the compulsion to procreate the species. "Right here, right now," she added helplessly.

She could feel his heart thundering beneath her palm as he whisked off her tank top. His eyes blazed for a moment, then he bent down to nuzzle her. With movements that were both possessive and gentle, he drew her deep into his mouth. His hands dove beneath the waistband of her pajama bottoms, pulling her off the ship's wheel in order to undress her completely.

In a single, sweeping motion, he exposed her to the moon's regard and the wind's caress.

Come what may, she was going to let this happen, Jordan realized. And in the morning, once the yearning was fulfilled, she could only hope that her heart would still be wholly hers.

His hands cradling her face brought her eyes open.

"You're so damn beautiful," he murmured, catching her off guard with his romantic-sounding utterance. His taut, admiring gaze made her feel exotic, slightly endangered, and wickedly alluring.

She surprised herself by sinking gracefully to her knees, dragging down his sweatpants.

The need to consume him had her circling him with one hand, cupping him below, and driving her lips as far down him as she could. He whispered an archaic-sounding curse and fisted her hair with hands that trembled. Jordan smiled.

If she was going to lose control then, by God, so was he. She would not be alone in this risky venture.

She repeated the assault until he stayed her movements, dragging her up with a plea for mercy. He swung her around, so that her backside fit against the curve of his hips. His breath rasped in her ear as he gave his hands freedom to roam over her body, his desire burning like a brand between them.

Reaching around her, his fingers slipped between her legs. He stroked her, attentive to what pleased her, pausing with each clenching of her innermost muscles to thrust a finger into her wet warmth.

"Tell me what you want, Jordan," he whispered, as she arched against his hand, clamoring for more.

"You," she panted.

"You want me to what?" The smooth head of his erection nudged her opening. "Say it."

Shaking with the force of her need, craving the feel of him inside her, she whispered what he wanted to hear.

But in her heart of hearts, she knew she wanted more.

She shied away from analyzing just how much, concentrating instead on the feel of him surging and retreating, stroking and seeking. He drove into her, deeper and deeper, clasping her hip with one hand, her breast with another, fiercely enough to let her know he suffered the same irrational compulsion to burn in the flame as she did.

The realization made her climax. Stars exploded behind her eyelids as the sweetest, keenest sensations wrung her womb. If not for Solomon holding her up, muffling groans against her neck, she would have crumpled.

They remained locked together, their gusting breaths subsiding. Jordan's heart beat heavily against the palm that cupped her breast. Too weak to pull away, she relied on the wall of his body to remain standing, gazed up at the stars pulsing in the cobalt sky. *Don't let it end,* a part of her whispered, as she reveled in the ripples that resonated in the aftermath.

She clutched him in remembered pleasure, wringing another groan from him. He remained where he was, buried deep inside, in no more of a hurry, apparently, than she was to separate.

"Jordan," he finally murmured in her ear. "Come to bed with me." He gave a thrust that rekindled her yearning. "Say, yes," he urged, his voice as much a persuasion as the fact that he was swelling again, reawakening her desire.

She resisted his propensity to take control. She had to believe she could navigate these waters and still come out whole. No man would ever make a fool of her again. But, for now, desire outweighed the considerations of her heart.

* * *

Reality doused Solomon the instant he pushed into the houseboat's dark interior. He'd forgotten to use a condom—again! He had sixty-four of them beside his bed, but he hadn't thought to bring a single one along when he'd joined Jordan on the deck. That meant they'd had unprotected sex two times now.

He pulled up short beside the bathroom door. "You want to shower first?" he asked, not knowing if it would help. It couldn't hurt.

She glanced at him and shrugged. "Okay."

He placed their clothing on the back of the toilet, turned on the water, and then hit the light switch, using the dimmer to conceal his sudden concern. He didn't fool her, though. She was looking at him intently.

"If you're worried about the lack of protection," she said, reading his mind, "you don't have to be. I can't get pregnant the normal way."

His gaze slid curiously to her soft-curving hips. She looked perfectly equipped to him. "What's wrong with you?"

She flinched at his tactlessness and dove behind the shower curtain.

Kicking himself, he followed more slowly. "What I mean is, you look perfectly good to me," he amended, joining her.

"I had endometriosis when I was younger," she explained, her voice muffled as she bent over to reach for the soap.

"But...you implied that you'd been pregnant before." The day she'd driven the boat, she'd mentioned something like that.

"I was. But it took the help of a fertility specialist," she admitted, averting her face. "I had to stay in bed most of the time, and I still lost the baby."

The wobble in her voice had him reaching for her. He wanted to chase off hurtful memories, yet all he could do was pull her water-slick body close and hold her tight. She held herself stiffly, at first, but then softened in his arms as the shower's spray sluiced over them.

To Solomon's consternation, protective and tender emotions held him in thrall. He wondered at the reason for them. Just how far out to sea was Jordan carrying him that he no longer cared about the shoreline? He cautioned himself to break free of her before he found himself disillusioned.

Not that Jordan was like Candace, a woman too self-absorbed to be content with one man. Jordan would be faithful, no question, as long as her man treated her well. For a brief instant, Solomon pictured himself in that role. Silas would have a mother and a father, perhaps even a sibling if Miguel's adoption went through.

He jerked his imaginings to a halt. Love was a fabrication. He'd proved that time and time again, leaving his lovers without a backward glance, relieved to be free of them. The same thing would happen when his lust for Jordan subsided. And when that time came, he'd be the one to end their affair, keeping his heart safely intact.

"Tell me about your childhood, Solomon," Jordan whispered hours later, as they lay in his captain's bed, limbs entwined, sheets smelling of shared passion.

He grunted noncommittally. "It's not a happy story."

She had sensed that already. "Tell me," she urged.

He heaved a sigh and rolled toward her so that they lay hip to hip, nose to nose.

"My father was a fisherman. He fished off the coast for mackerel, mostly, and he was gone a great deal. My mother was an English teacher. She loved the Romantic Period, best of all. She read me books while we waited for my father to return from his work. Only, one winter, he didn't come back."

"How old were you then?" Jordan whispered.

"Eight. My mother pined for him. She went slowly mad."

"You mean, she lost her mind?"

"Aye."

"Oh, Solomon." She envisioned him, looking much like Silas. He must have felt orphaned, like he'd lost both parents. "What happened to her?"

"She overdosed on Valium," he said flatly.

"Oh, no." She put an arm around him, surprised when he willingly accepted her gesture of comfort.

"My grandparents took me in," he continued after a moment. "They owned a store in Camden, and from that day on I worked after school, stocking shelves, sweeping. I had to sneak away to read my books, which they considered a waste of time. And I swam," he recollected. "I swam in water so cold it made the Bay of Coronado feel like a bathtub."

"Isn't that in California?"

"Where I did my SEAL training," he corroborated. "I was a soft intellectual trying to make it through the most rigorous selection process in the world. The one thing I had going for me was my swimming. I excelled in exercises in the water. The rest I had to work for."

She squeezed the dense muscle of his upper arm. "It feels like you worked pretty hard."

"Aye," he said. "Don't you think it's ironic?" he added.

"What is?"

"That my strength is your weakness. You're afraid of water," he pointed out.

"I almost drowned," she admitted. "In a cow pond of all things, so shallow that I could've stood up if I hadn't panicked. My sister pulled me out, and I wasn't even breathing. She gave me mouth-to-mouth, and then I threw up on her."

He grunted in amusement. "This is the sister who owns the horse ranch?"

"Jillian. I worry about her," Jordan reflected. "She's widowed with two children and a baby on the way. I wish I were more of a help to her."

"We all do what we can," he murmured sleepily.

Wasn't that the truth, Jordan considered, her heart weighted by the many hurdles before them. Jillian faced starting up a business and giving birth to a baby, all without a man at her side. Rafael Valentino had made himself scarce, lately. And she, Jordan, faced even more menacing obstacles in her bid to rescue Miguel from a country torn by revolution.

Lying in Solomon's arms, she suffered the impulse to unburden herself, to tell him of her plans because backing out now might mean never seeing Miguel again. She opened her mouth to broach the subject, only to be cut off by his soft snore.

Another time, perhaps.

Perhaps not.

Emotional intimacy was not supposed to follow their earthy, physical union. She might just regret telling him her plans lest he find some way to frustrate them. "Good night," she whispered, kissing his shoulder lightly before yielding to the pull of exhaustion.

Ellie divided a panicked glance between the road signs bisecting the dark highway up ahead. *Which way do I go?*

"Christopher," she called, careful not to wake up the baby and Caleb, both asleep in the backseat. "Christopher!"

But her ten-year-old navigator was sound asleep.

Hitting her directional signal, Ellie guided her car into the breakdown lane. The instant her tires dropped onto the rougher pavement, steam bloomed out from under her hood to cloak her windshield. She braked abruptly, terrified of striking the guardrail that divided the highway from a copse of trees.

The car came to a shuddering halt. As the steam rose and thinned, Ellie found herself pinned between a forest and intermittent but fast-moving cars.

Releasing her held breath, she unfurled her white-knuckled fingers from the steering wheel and glanced at the boys to find them still asleep. Then she eased from her seat to round the steaming hood. It wasn't like she could fix her engine in the dark, even if she had the right parts.

God, you've got to help me, she thought, lifting eyes that burned with exhaustion toward the starry sky. She had thirty-eight dollars in her pocket and miles to go before she could let her guard down—if ever.

But how was she going to get her family to Virginia if her car broke down?

The sharp snapping of a stick and the sound of something

rustling through the woods had Ellie dashing for her door. She jumped inside, locking it behind her. With her heart beating fast, she peered through the beams of her headlights, waiting fearfully.

But nothing happened. She felt foolish for being so afraid. She'd lived in the country, knew what kind of critters lurked in the woods. Regretfully, she turned off the ignition, not knowing if her car would even start come daylight.

The quiet that enveloped them was stifling. She cracked her window to let in the warm summer air, the sound of chirping crickets. It wasn't safe to remain in the vehicle, right there on the side of the highway, but what could she do—haul three sleeping children out to sleep in the wet ditch?

Wriggling across the front seat, she put an arm around her eldest son, fighting the urge to cling to him. With her cheek on the headrest, she closed her eyes. A car roared by, and her eyes sprang open.

This, thought Ellie, *is bound to be the longest night of my life.*

Awakened by a silvering sky, Solomon opened his eyes to the vision of a woman in his bed.

An extraordinary woman.

Jordan's hair lay like a russet scarf across his arm. Her full, pale breasts brushed his chest with every rise and fall of her chest. His gaze lingered on the curve of her jaw, the soft fullness of her lower lip, and memories of her passionate nature had an immediate, physical effect on him.

What if it was more than physical?

He tried to dislodge the uncomfortable question from

his mind. But from last night to this morning, with each shared word, each tender caress, Jordan seemed to sink inside of him to a place where no woman but Candace had ever been. How had she done it, breaching the cold fortress he'd built to protect himself?

It wasn't as if she'd set about seducing him. She, more than he, had resisted their magnetic attraction, only it had overpowered them both. And now it was steamrolling his defenses; he could feel the walls crumbling just looking at her.

He had to protect himself, but how?

What did he fear most about Jordan? It was her fierce independence, her private determination to adopt Miguel in the face of ever-growing odds. She was keeping secrets from him; he could sense it. She had plans, plans that would put her in danger; plans that might ultimately destroy this beautiful intimacy they enjoyed.

The only way for Solomon to ease his fears was to address them. Today he would find someone, a third party, to retrieve Miguel, so that Jordan could remain safely here, in his bed, in his life where she belonged.

Until, of course, he was done with her.

Jordan plucked a gallon of milk off the shelf in the grocery store and froze in alarm. The milk expired on August 8, Jillian's birthday. She, Jordan, would be three days out of the country by then. She would miss Jillian's thirty-fifth birthday.

Oh, dear. And Jillian had hinted heavily that she would enjoy a dinner at Waterside, Norfolk's waterfront. Graham's gift to his mother was to babysit his little sister.

I'll be in the doghouse forever, thought Jordan, placing the milk in her grocery cart. Silas seized her momentary distraction to slip a box of Popsicles in beside it. Would Jillian ever forgive her?

She would have to do something to make it up to her.

Half an hour later as she stocked Solomon's refrigerator with nutritious snacks and meals appealing to a six-year-old, the answer came to her. If she could convince Rafael Valentino to take her sister out to dinner, then Jillian would surely forgive her.

And it was just Jordan's luck that the agent had handed her his business card the day he'd retrieved her in Curaçao. She'd stuck it in her passport, which she kept in her purse.

With one eye trained on Silas, who sat on the pier licking his Popsicle, Jordan dialed the agent's number.

He answered the phone after three rings. "Special Agent Valentino."

"Rafael?"

Silence.

"This is Jordan. Jordan Bliss."

"Oh, Jordan. How are you? Is everything all right?"

"Yes, I found your business card in my passport," she explained. "I'm heading out of the country soon, and I realized that I won't be here for Jillian's birthday. I was hoping you could do me a favor."

"What kind of favor?" he inquired warily.

"Well, I was supposed to take Jillian to Waterside for dinner to celebrate. I don't suppose I could talk you into doing that for me?"

"What does your sister say?"

"She has no idea. I don't want her to know, actually. She would try to talk me out of leaving."

"I see." A long, thoughtful silence ensued. "It really isn't safe for you to return to Venezuela," the agent warned, guessing her destination with accuracy.

"I know. I'll only be there five days. Please?" She went straight to groveling. "This is something that I have to do, for myself and for Miguel. But I love Jillian, too, and I don't want her to be sad on her birthday."

He heaved a long sigh. "What time should I pick her up?" he asked, sounding resigned.

"Oh, thank you! Like six o'clock?" she answered. "It won't take her long to guess why you're there instead of me, so...try to cheer her up, okay?"

He whispered something in Italian.

"I know," she commiserated, though she had no idea what he'd just said. "I'm going to owe you for the rest of my life. And just for the record, I hope I know you that long."

She hung up quickly before he could change his mind. *Oh, please, let that situation work out for the best,* she prayed, slipping his business card into her pocket.

Grabbing a Popsicle out of the freezer, she stepped outside to join Silas on the pier.

"You're awfully quiet," Solomon commented the following night as they lay back to front in his bed, a waning moon visible through one octagonal window. Jordan's body felt sated and content, yet the reality of her impending departure kept her eyes open, her mouth shut. "What are you thinking?" he asked.

"Nothing." She looked over her shoulder to send him a forced smile.

His eyes narrowed. He shifted, rolling her onto her back and leaning over her. "Jordan," he growled, lowering his forehead till they were eye to eye. "I hope you're not making plans and keeping them to yourself," he warned.

Her heart beat faster. She was certain he could tell, too. He knew her body all too well.

"The atmosphere in Venezuela is volatile," he explained, his voice flat and gravely serious. "The Populists are marching toward Caracas as we speak. You're an American, the enemy. You're also a woman. That makes you doubly vulnerable. Now swear to me, you're not planning anything behind my back."

Behind my back. Words like that made her sound like Candace. They also conveyed the full fragility of his trust.

She swallowed against a dry throat, stricken by both guilt and fear. "I'm sorry, Solomon, but I can't promise you that," she whispered.

He seized her shoulders, his grip tight as he all but shook her. "Jordan," he thundered quietly. "Why do you have to be so goddamn stubborn?"

"I have to go back for my child," she retorted, tears overflowing her eyes.

"No, you don't," he insisted, his tone gentling. "Sweetheart, I've looked into this. As long as Miguel's paperwork is complete, any U.S. citizen can bring him home. I've made inquiries, Jordan. I'll find someone there to bring him back. All you would need to do is to pay for his ticket."

Both the offer and the unexpected endearment sounded

too good to be true. It couldn't be that easy for a stranger to bring Miguel home, not when she possessed the dossier, when a lawyer named Lorenzo was expecting her check. "Miguel would be terrified to have a stranger pick him up," she argued, tucking the word *sweetheart* away, to be pondered later. "You don't know how traumatized he is already. He needs *me,* not a stranger."

"But what if he was told that he was being brought to you?" Solomon persisted.

Jordan shook her head, wishing with all her heart it was as simple as he made it sound. But it wasn't. Her tickets were nonrefundable. She'd gone into debt to secure them. And more than that, with mere days remaining on her visa, she couldn't afford to delay her departure in the hopes that someone else might take her place. "You can try, Solomon," was all she could tell him.

He closed his eyes and put his forehead to hers with a long, heartfelt sigh. "Jordan," he rasped. She sensed him struggling for words. "I'm going to find someone," he finally swore. "Just, please, don't go."

Guilt and regret strangled her vocal cords. How she wished she could tell him the truth—that she was leaving in just three days. Only, she feared he would try to stop her, abduct her and carry her out to sea—anything to keep her from getting on her flight.

No. She couldn't say anything.

With a gentle kiss, Solomon shifted over to settle in beside her. He kept one arm securely about her waist, as if that would keep her bound to him. Within seconds, his soft snores sounded in Jordan's ear.

With fear and guilt chasing each other's tails about her brain, Jordan knew her own sleep would remain elusive.

Chapter Twelve

◆

The sound of footsteps on the pier and a woman's voice issuing a firm command drew Jordan and Silas's noses out of the comic book they were reading. "Who could that be?" Jordan wondered aloud.

Silas shot to his knees to peer out the window. His jaw dropped open as he gasped in delight. "It's Aunt Ellie, an' Chris'pher, an' Caleb, an' Baby Colton!" he shouted, stepping across her lap to get out of his seat.

"Easy," Jordan cautioned, following his breakneck sprint to the door.

Silas unlocked it and threw it open, startling the woman who was about to knock. With a baby on one hip and her knuckles raised, she looked down and smiled, visibly wilting with relief. "Silas!" she cried.

Silas rushed into her arms, and she nearly toppled over at his fervent embrace, covering up her collapse by kissing the top of his head.

"You came!" Silas marveled, grinning up at her. "I wished it on a falling star, and it came true!" He squirmed out of her embrace to hurdle the gangplank, racing up the pier toward Christopher and Caleb, who'd been instructed, apparently, to wait.

"Careful!" called Ellie, gripping the doorframe as she called out with worry.

"He can swim now," Jordan reassured her.

She found herself the focus of wary, gray-blue eyes and the baby's sparkling blue ones. The young mother didn't look a day over twenty-five, but the furrow on her forehead and the wisps of hair escaping her long braids made her look careworn and weary. The smudges under her eyes and wilting posture bespoke of exhaustion.

"You must be Ellie," Jordan surmised, with a warm smile. "Silas talks about you and his cousins all the time. I'm Jordan," she added, "his tutor."

"Nice to meet you." Ellie spared a glance for the boys, who were already tussling and rolling like puppies on the hill. "I was hoping to speak to Solomon," she added, with a hint of strain in her voice and a blush of what looked like humiliation.

Jordan had never heard another woman call Solomon by his first name. "He's at work until five o'clock or so," she said, surprised to feel a pinch of jealousy.

"Of course." Ellie hitched the baby higher. Given her exhaustion, his weight was probably too much for her.

"Would you like to come in?" Jordan offered, sympathetically. "Silas could show the boys around."

The furrow on Ellie's brow deepened. "Oh, I wouldn't want to impose," she said.

"Please." Jordan opened the door wider. "You came all this way; you can't leave now. I was just about to warm up some chicken noodle soup. I have plenty, and I'm sure your boys would like something to eat."

At the mention of soup, Ellie's brow cleared. "Thank you," she decided, shifting the baby to her other hip. "Boys!" she called. "Come on down here, but stay in the middle of the dock and don't fall in."

With a noisy tromping of feet, the trio stampeded toward the boat, grinning ear to ear, grass in their hair, talking excitedly.

Jordan and Ellie shared a wry smile. "Boys will be boys," Jordan murmured.

"Ain't that the truth," said Ellie, wearily.

By the time Solomon arrived from work, Jordan had convinced Ellie to nap with Colton in one of the bunks downstairs while she watched the boys. It took some heavy-handed persuasion as Ellie initially refused, but Jordan, who recognized mental and emotional fatigue when she saw it, persisted. At last, with the boys settled down watching a video of Dragon Ball Z, Ellie took the baby belowdecks for some badly needed rest.

Solomon stepped aboard soon after. Jordan had called his cell phone, giving him advance warning of their guests. As was his custom, he sought Silas out first, ruffling the hair on his head, asking him about his day. He then cornered Jordan, kissing her long and leisurely. Today he didn't have the luxury to get carried away.

"Where is Ellie?" he asked, his lips lingering over hers.

"Resting downstairs," Jordan answered. "She's exhausted. I think she might have driven all the way here without stopping."

"I'm surprised that old clunker even made it," Solomon marveled. "Did she tell you what she wants?"

"Not a handout," Jordan surmised, quietly. "But I think her situation's pretty bleak."

As if on cue, the door to the steps yawned open, and Ellie stood there, her braids even more disheveled, her eyes now bloodshot. Baby Colton, on the other hand, looked entirely alert. "I thought I heard you," she said, directing her gaze at Solomon.

With a sweeping look that saw everything, he stepped closer and plucked the baby out of her arms. "Good to see you again," he said, concern evident on his handsome face. "I'm glad you came."

In that instant, Jordan was struck by a feeling of pride. Solomon was a good man.

Ellie drew a shaky breath and looked down at the carpet. "The boys and I missed Silas," she admitted huskily. "Here's your check," she added, pulling it from the pocket of her shorts. She held it out until he took it. "I don't want charity, just a little help."

Reading pride and defeat in the lines of Ellie's willowy frame, Jordan felt an instant kinship with her.

"Well," said Solomon, gruffly, as he patted the baby's back. "You've come to the right place."

Ellie dragged a comb through the wet snarls of her freshly washed hair and pricked an ear to the conversation in the houseboat's living area. The stranger's voice was like dark molasses, especially when he laughed. He had to be Solomon's SEAL buddy, the one who fixed up houses and rented them out. He'd helped Solomon build this boat.

Gazing at her dazed reflection, Ellie had to admit she looked as old and tired as she felt. Carl's last words to her still echoed in her head. *Go ahead,* he'd taunted when she'd told him she was leaving. *Make yourself someone else's problem.*

With a sharp breath, she put the comb down.

She would never burden Solomon or any man with her situation. *She* was the one who'd made mistakes, marrying young, thinking Carl was her ticket out of foster care. Whatever it took to get a fresh start, to give her children what they deserved, she would do, even if it meant working her fingers down to nubs to pay back Solomon for the first month's rent.

With her heart pumping fast, Ellie eased from the bathroom, flinching as three boys thundered past her, down into the bunk area. Solomon, who held Colton in one arm, swung around at her approach, and Ellie's gaze flew to his guest, a bald, muscular man in his early thirties. He rolled respectfully to his feet.

"Here she is," said Solomon, waving her forward. "Ellie Stuart, this is Chief Sean Harlan. Harley, meet Ellie."

The impact of Harley's smile combined with his frank, blue gaze caught Ellie off guard. He reminded her of Mr. Clean—not quite as tall but every bit as muscular. Thrusting out a hand, he left her with no choice but to take it.

"Nice to meet you," she murmured, shocked by the warmth and pressure of his fingertips.

"Pleasure's mine," he drawled, sliding an appreciative gaze down her body.

Ellie snatched the baby from Solomon and used him as a shield.

"Sean says he's got a house for you," Solomon announced.

"Well, if you don't mind the fact that it's not quite finished," the younger SEAL apologized in his easy drawl. "I still have to put a deck on the back and steps up to the front door. The interior isn't even painted yet."

"I'm sure it's fine," said Ellie, whose head spun at the thought of living in a real home and not a trailer. "How much is the rent?" she asked, bracing herself.

"How about five hundred a month?" he offered, his blue eyes watchful.

She tried not to blanch. Five hundred was a lot more money than she'd seen in a long time. Still, for a house, it was a mighty fine deal. "How many bedrooms?" she asked, like she was in any position to turn it down.

"Two and a half," the SEAL answered. "Third bedroom's more like a closet," he admitted, shifting closer to stroke the baby's cheek. "But you don't care, do you, little fella?" he asked Colton.

A citruslike scent wafted into Ellie's nostrils. The man not only looked incredible, he smelled delicious. She stepped back, wary of her attraction.

"You want to see it?" he added unexpectedly. "I got nothin' else to do right now. I could drive you over, let you take a look."

His enthusiasm stole over her, chasing away her exhaustion. The offer, like the man, looked and sounded too good to be true. *Better watch this one,* she thought. She looked at Solomon and Jordan to gauge their opinion.

"We'll watch the boys for you," Jordan offered.

"Oh, no," Harley protested. "They'll want to see it, too. Bring 'em all. I got plenty of room in my truck, even for a car seat."

There had to be catch. "If you're sure," Ellie hedged, alarmed by his mounting appeal. He even liked kids.

"Sure I'm sure," he answered with a grin. "Bring 'em on."

Jordan had already crossed the stairs to call the boys up.

"I hear you're from Mississippi," Harley said to Ellie, his smile drawing her attention to his mouth. "I grew up on the Mississippi River, myself, in Cape Girardeau, Missouri. Ever heard of it?"

She was ashamed to admit she hadn't.

She dragged her attention to the boys who tumbled out of the stairwell. Putting a hand on Christopher's shoulder, she informed them all that they were going to look at a house. "And you'll be on your best behavior," she warned, raking them with a firm look, "or else."

"Yes, ma'am!" they chorused, a squirming mass of expectancy.

The SEAL quirked his reddish blond eyebrows. "Well, all right," he said, his tone redolent with respect. "Let's git 'r done."

As they marched for the door, Ellie sent Solomon a grateful grimace. She accepted the bottle of apple juice Jordan had poured into the baby's bottle. With fullness pressuring her chest, she managed to choke out a word of thanks.

Either she'd died and gone to heaven, or life was finally taking a turn for the better.

A light tap on his office door drew Solomon's gaze up.

Second Lieutenant James Augustus Atwater III, who had come from Afghanistan three months ago, hovered at the open door.

"Come on in, sir," said Solomon, giving the young officer the respect due to him but not bothering to stand. He jotted a final note in the training plans he was working on, making the junior SEAL wait. "How can I help you?" he asked, at last, putting his pencil down.

Gus's caramel brown eyes were inscrutable. He didn't speak much, just watched how things were done and imitated with competence. He came from wealthy Rhode Island stock and held a master's degree from MIT, but other than that, Solomon didn't know much about him.

"I'm here about the Interteam memo you put out yesterday asking if anyone had contacts still remaining in Caracas."

Solomon sat up straighter. "You have a contact?" he asked hopefully.

"I might," the younger man conceded. "I went to college with a Lucy Donovan. She's a secretary at the embassy in Caracas, I believe."

Solomon's heart sank. "No, I need a man for this job. It's too dangerous for a woman."

"You don't know Lucy Donovan," Gus said without blinking.

Solomon tapped his fingertips on the surface of his desk. "You think she could pick up a young child in Puerto Ayacucho, which is currently occupied by the Populists, and escort him stateside?" he inquired, dubiously.

"Certainly," said Gus.

Solomon liked his succinct and articulate use of language.

"I looked up her e-mail address," the lieutenant added, handing him a square of paper with an address jotted down.

Solomon took the note and glanced down at it, praying he'd stumbled on the solution to keeping Jordan from leaving the country. "Thank you, sir," he murmured to the young officer.

"You're welcome, Senior Chief." Swiveling on the heels of his polished boots, Gus Atwater walked soundlessly out of the room.

Silas squirmed with anticipation and craned his neck to see over the backseat and out the front window, thrilled to be visiting his cousins in their new house. It was, in reality, an older home, built in the 1950s, gutted and restored by the fabulously talented Chief Harlan.

"Here we are," said Jordan, turning into the third driveway on the right. Silas had been here before, but this was Jordan's first time. The little white bungalow was set in a deep yard backed by oaks and flanked by houses identical in size and vintage. Unlike the neighboring houses, it boasted vinyl siding, new windows, and a brand-new door. The steps to that door were only partially finished though, with boards laid in a makeshift ramp to provide access.

Silas was out of the car and up that ramp, pounding on the door, before Jordan could call him back. She rounded her Nissan to pop the trunk, which was filled with household goods. Sean had mentioned to Solomon that Ellie had nothing, save for a few personal items, to put in her house.

Jordan grabbed the box of chinaware, purchased at a secondhand store, and followed Silas to the door. He was already inside, greeting his aunt, who hushed him with a warning that the baby was sleeping.

Jordan noted that Ellie looked slightly more rested than yesterday, her hair loose and tumbling down her back as she held the door open. Eyeing the box in Jordan's arms, she stiffened suspiciously.

"This comes with a price," Jordan quickly emphasized, not wanting to offend her. "I have to ask you a favor."

"Come on in," Ellie offered. "What's in it?"

"Dishes," said Jordan.

"Kitchen's back here." Ellie preceded Jordan through a big, empty living area toward a small kitchen, updated with new appliances.

As Jordan slid the box on the brand-new counter, she breathed the smell of fresh-cut lumber and new linoleum. "This place is perfect," she offered, taking it in.

"Sure is," Ellie agreed with a fervent nod. "So what's the favor?" she prompted.

Jordan stepped closer and pitched her voice low. "I need you to watch Silas for me," she admitted, swallowing down her jitters. "But you can't tell Solomon or even Silas. I'm leaving for Venezuela tomorrow to pick up the little boy I'm adopting."

Ellie gave her a long, searching look. "He's going to be mad at both of us," she guessed, referring to Solomon.

Jordan winced. "I know. I'm sorry, but I really have no choice, and I can't tell him, or he'll try to stop me. Don't worry," she added, reassuringly, "he won't blame you. I'm the one he'll be mad at."

"I'm happy to watch Silas," said Ellie, with a grave look that saw more than Jordan wanted to show. "Just be careful," she added with concern. "I've heard about Venezuela on the radio."

Jordan's heart palpitated at the reminder of the dangers awaiting her. "I will," she promised. "Let me get the other boxes from my car."

* * *

Jordan couldn't sleep. Thoughts of her impending departure kept her mind churning, evoking terrifying visions of being detained by soldiers, questioned, incarcerated, and locked in a dark dungeon forever. She snuggled closer to Solomon, seeking solace in his warmth and strength.

With a sleepy murmur, he hooked an arm around her and pulled her closer. "Forgot to tell you," he said, rousing for a moment. "I found a woman at the embassy in Caracas who says she can fetch Miguel for you."

Jordan's heart stopped, then resumed an erratic beat. "What? She will? When?"

"Don't know. But she says he can leave the country with the remaining Americans if and when the embassy's evacuated."

Jordan pictured Miguel's terror at finding himself with a total stranger while being evacuated at the last, harrowing hour.

She turned her head to make out Solomon's shadowed features. His rugged, handsome face tugged at her heartstrings. With a sharp stab of regret, she realized she would miss him—more thoroughly than she ever would have guessed. "Thank you," she whispered, lifting a hand to his cheek and then his chest, burrowing her fingers into the crisp hair there. *Thank you, but it's too late,* she wanted to add. *I'm leaving tomorrow. This has got to be done right, and I'm the only one to do it.*

Had there really been a time when she considered Solomon unfeeling? His love for Silas and his generosity with Ellie made it plainly clear that beneath his tough facade, he was every bit as romantic as his mother. No wonder Candace had so easily crushed his faith in love.

She, too, had sworn never to harbor tender feelings for a man, to give another human being power over her heart. And yet, this emotion that made her chest hurt felt an awful lot like love.

The other night he'd called her *sweetheart*. Did that mean he reciprocated her feelings? Or did it even matter? She didn't have the leisure to dream beyond the next harrowing days. Miguel was her priority, first and foremost. If she managed to bring him home, and Solomon deigned to speak to her again, then she would know what *sweetheart* really meant to him.

A sudden yearning to connect physically with him, just one more time, overcame her.

Her palm drifted downward, over the hair-roughened plane of his abdomen, lower still to cup and stroke him. They'd made love earlier that day, but it had been a race to abate the tension that crackled the minute Solomon walked through the door. And with Silas dawdling in the kitchen over his pudding, they hadn't had much time.

But given the possibility that she might never make love to Solomon again, Jordan wanted one more memory to carry with her. She pushed to her knees and ducked her head beneath the covers, noting that he'd slit his eyes open. His low growl was all the encouragement she needed.

"Damn, woman," he said on a ragged whisper, sifting his fingers through her hair.

Eventually, she climbed over the top of him and filled herself, slowly and steadily, savoring the heady fullness, the thrill of him inside of her. His hands branded her hips, her breasts, her neck and lips as she undulated around him, lingeringly, tenderly, in no hurry to seek completion.

What if he won't forgive me? she wondered, drawing a

breath at the feeling of loss that enveloped her. *What if he refuses to see me again?* Tears pressured her eyes even as the pleasure in her womb approached crisis.

A sob escaped her, and Solomon mistook it for a plea for intervention. He stroked his hands up her thighs and delved his thumbs into the moist alcove between, impelling Jordan into the current of her release.

She resisted for as long as she was able, putting off good-bye, but it tugged her under, smothering her in poignant rapture for the last time. Solomon was with her, clutching her fiercely, shuddering as his pleasure spilled into hers.

With their bodies still joined, they fell together, limply intertwined. Jordan buried her face into his neck so he wouldn't see the tears brimming her eyes. She was certain he could sense the fullness in her chest.

"If I knew you'd thank me like that," he murmured, stroking her hair, "I'd have told you earlier," he said, mistaking the reason for her expressiveness.

She had to smile at his self-satisfaction. "You're awfully thoughtful for a cold-blooded shark," she replied.

"Makos are warm-blooded, remember?"

"Oh, that's right," she murmured, recalling what she'd learned at the aquarium. She'd misjudged him entirely. But would he be warm-hearted enough to forgive her, she wondered, when he discovered that she'd left despite his efforts?

Solomon's sixth sense had given him hell all day. Something was wrong; he didn't know what. At the office, all his business was in order. The men had passed their physical readiness tests. All weapons and ammunition were operational and accounted for. Lucy Donovan had even advised him via e-mail that she would undertake her objective sometime this week. Everything at Spec Ops was shipshape.

It had to be something at the home front that had his antennae twitching, though he couldn't imagine what. Silas had learned over one hundred fifty sight words. He couldn't be any happier with his cousins now living in close proximity. And then there was Jordan...

Solomon savored the memory of her sweet, passionate nature. He'd never had a lover who satisfied him so thoroughly, so honestly. Perhaps she was just grateful for his help in securing Miguel, but there'd been a suggestion of desperation in her touch last night.

He'd mulled over it all day, unable to shake the feeling that he'd overlooked something.

The first thing he noted as he parked his truck beneath the carport by the big house was that Jordan's car was missing. He shrugged his concern aside with the reassurance that she'd soon be back and headed down the dappled hill toward the houseboat. A breeze ruffled the leaves overhead. A distant roll of thunder stirred the uneasiness in his gut. His sixth sense was at it again.

He stalked on board and let himself inside, greeted by deafening quiet. Five steps into the houseboat, he spied the note stuck with a magnet to the refrigerator.

Premonition chilled his blood as he approached to read it.

Dear Solomon, I hope you will eventually forgive me but I left for Venezuela this morning. Silas is with Ellie, who has agreed to watch him in my place. I'll be back in five days with Miguel.

Take care,
Jordan

"No!" Solomon shouted, yanking the note off the fridge and crumpling it in his hands. He swiveled in fury and helplessness and pounded his fist on the counter. "Damn it, Jordan!" he railed, unwrinkling the message to read it one more time. How could she do this to him? He'd made it perfectly clear that her life could be at stake, that others could bring Miguel stateside, and Jordan wouldn't have to step foot outside the country.

She hadn't listened to a word he'd said. Like Candace, all she'd thought about was herself, leaving without any word of her intentions. An awful but familiar betrayal bubbled within him.

Snatching up his keys, he stalked back outside, into the impossibly muggy heat to fetch his son. He drove like a demon toward Ellie's cottage, cutting off cars, blaring his horn. He roared into the driveway and braked abruptly.

Sean Harlan looked up from the bricks he was laying to make front steps. As Solomon jumped out of his truck and slammed the door shut, Sean put his trowel down and stood up, blocking his trajectory to the door.

"The boy's inside," he said, in his low easygoing lilt, "and he's fine."

Solomon met Harley's watchful blue gaze with disbelief. "You know about this?" he demanded.

"All I know," said the chief in that same calming voice, "is that Miz Stuart is watching Silas for you now. She's concerned that you would be upset about that."

"Damn right, I'm upset. Do you realize where the fuck Jordan went?"

"Back to Venezuela," Sean replied. "Take a deep breath, Mako, and don't even think about taking that tone with Miz Stuart. You know this wouldn't be happening if you'd let Jordan bring that little boy back."

Solomon heard something in his head pop. He turned around and walked away. It was either that or plow his fist into Sean Harlan's belly. With a pulse thrumming at his temple, he dropped the tailgate on his truck and planted his butt on it. He ground his teeth together and willed himself to calm down.

Sean approached him, crossed his arms over his chest, and waited.

"Women," Solomon said, choking out the word with venom, "are senseless. Does she really think she's going to waltz into a hot zone and pick up that boy and fly out with him again?"

"She'll do anything to get him back. You should've realized that."

Solomon glared at him. "Fuck you. Instead of taking her side, why don't you help me think of a way to protect her?" he growled.

"Okay," Sean conceded, with a shrug. He stroked his square, shaven jaw. "Who do we know that would help?"

"No one," Solomon growled. "Because the soldiers we trained are now backing the fucking Populists."

"Someone at our embassy, then."

Solomon thought of Lucy Donovan. Sending one woman to help another was, in Solomon's mind, like asking the blind to lead the blind, but Lucy was bound to have contacts. "I know where to start," he said, slipping off his tailgate and shutting it. "Now. Let me get my boy. I promise to be nice," he added with a snarl.

* * *

Three hours later, Solomon stepped aboard his houseboat all alone. With Jordan's protest echoing in his ears—*You can't wake up a child at four in the morning!*—he'd ended up asking Ellie to watch Silas in his stead. No doubt that was what Jordan had intended all along.

Shutting himself inside, Solomon listened to the downpour that had left him wet and chilled. Silence coiled around him, surrounding him in solitude and loneliness, reminding him of the night he'd returned from Iraq to find his wife and son missing.

Jordan had betrayed him. She'd left.

But not the way Candace had, he admitted. She'd left him a note. She hadn't stolen Silas away. She'd even said good-bye, he realized belatedly. That was what his intuition had been trying to tell him all day long—that Jordan's sweet possession of him last night had been her farewell.

"Damn me for being a blind idiot," he growled, his back to the door, his face in his hands. If something happened to her, he had only himself to blame. With a shuddering breath, he dropped his hands, squared his shoulders and pushed away from the door.

He needed to contact Lucy Donovan, ASAP.

Chapter Thirteen

Jordan eased out of the taxi on knees that jittered. A wind-tossed, two-seater plane piloted by an amateur had been the only transportation she could find from Maiquetía International to the rebel-occupied state of Las Amazonas. From the tiny airstrip outside of Puerto Ayacucho, she'd been lucky to find a taxi. And, now, by the grace of God, she was here, closer to Miguel than she'd been in weeks.

She was tempted to pinch herself. She had dreamed so many times that she was back. Yet the scent of the soil was distinct enough to assure her this was real.

This city had sprung out of a trading post set beneath the rapids of the Orinoco River. Built on black granite, surrounded by jungle-shrouded, flat-topped mountains called *tepuis,* it now housed more than seventy thousand souls, including those of mixed race, but also tribal natives who, fifty years ago, had never seen a white face.

The city looked just as it had earlier this summer: a sprawling and unwieldy conglomerate of buildings, from ramshackle huts to skyscrapers lost in the mist that seeped out of the surrounding jungle. There was only one difference: the presence of armed soldiers standing on every street corner and armored vehicles parked everywhere she looked.

Pulling down the brim of her baseball cap, Jordan darted from the taxi to the cathedral across the street. Ignoring the curious gazes of two soldiers standing nearby, she darted up the cathedral steps and tugged on the cathedral doors. They were locked. With her heart jumping up her throat, she knocked briskly on the dense wood. "Hurry, please!" she begged, as the soldiers started to approach her.

They were almost upon her when a window set into the bigger door slid open, revealing the face of Father Benedict. "Jordan!" he exclaimed, glancing behind her. With a scrape, the big door swung open. The priest yanked her inside and slammed the door shut, sliding a bar across the threshold.

"Jordan," he said again, "What are you doing here?" His face struck her as pale in the gloomy antechamber.

"I've come for Miguel, of course."

"Miguel? But—"

"But, what?" Her pitch rose with alarm.

"A woman from the American embassy was just here this morning," he announced in bewilderment. "She showed me a note explaining that she was having Miguel escorted home to you."

The floor of the musty space seemed to perform a slow turn. The woman in question had to be Solomon's contact, the one who'd said she would have Miguel evacuated with the embassy workers. "No," Jordan cried, so profoundly disappointed that she would have collapsed if the priest hadn't caught her.

A rapping at the door startled them both. "They won't dare breach the door," he whispered with confidence, drawing her deeper into the nave. "Come inside, and we'll talk about this situation."

"But I have to go after Miguel," Jordan protested.

"That may not be possible," he retorted grimly.

The pounding at the door had ceased. The light of the stained-glass windows bathed the priest's robes as they paused in the sanctuary.

"The woman who came this morning—Lucy Donovan—didn't know if she could get back into the city. The Populists are marching on Caracas as we speak."

More bad news. "But I have to get Miguel. I have forms that need to be signed in his presence. I have the money to pay for him!"

The priest startled her by pulling her into his embrace. "Peace, Jordan," he murmured, fiercely. "We must think prayerfully about your next move. God got you this far. He'll see you through," he promised.

Jordan swallowed heavily. *Okay,* she thought, *but does God know that I only have four days left on my visa?*

Within the next six hours, Father Benedict summoned Señor Lorenzo, the lawyer, to the cathedral to receive Jordan's payment. The lawyer secured a seat for her on a public bus bound for Caracas. He even agreed to escort her to the bus terminal.

Jordan bid a sorrowful farewell to the priest, not knowing if she would ever see him again.

"I'm sorry I can't go with you to the terminal," he

apologized. "I'm a wanted man out there," he added with a mocking smile.

"Thank you for everything and for taking care of Miguel."

"The pleasure was all mine, Jordan. Now, go. Be safe."

At the bus terminal, Jordan waited in the lawyer's car until the last possible moment. As a result, she got the only seat remaining, between an open window and a woman holding a pig. She took it gratefully, pulled her cap down over her eyes, and tried to sleep. She had many long hours ahead of her.

But the pig squirmed continuously, and the bus hit potholes that slammed Jordan's temple against the window, startling her from shallow slumber. The occasional volley of gunfire in the distance had her snatching the hat out of her eyes in fear.

It was just as Solomon had predicted, Jordan thought with a frozen heart: Venezuela's bid for democracy was doomed. Would she even be able to get Miguel out before the Populists took complete control?

Afternoon dragged into evening. A tangerine sunset drew Jordan's gaze to the rolling western plains. The wild rugged beauty of untamed land made her think of Solomon. Regret lanced her heart, followed by an aching emptiness. He and Silas seemed so far away.

Her consolation was Miguel—*if* she found him. *If* she got him out in time.

The sun dropped from sight, drawing darkness behind it. Exhausted, Jordan closed her eyes and lost herself to dreams in which Solomon held her close, murmuring assurances that Miguel would be all right.

The realization that the bus had stopped awakened her abruptly. It was past midnight, she saw, pressing the light on her wristwatch. The low murmuring of passengers infused the idling bus with tension. "What's going on?" she asked the woman beside her.

Speaking in rapid Spanish in a dialect difficult to understand, the woman said something about a road block.

Jordan peered fearfully up the length of the bus. At first, the glare of lights ahead suggested traffic backed up on the highway. But then, with a shiver of dread, she made out the shapes of tanks, parked sideways to prevent the passing of vehicles. Soldiers were leaning into cars, speaking to the drivers, then waving them on.

Jordan swallowed against a dry mouth. She carried both her passport and her visa in her backpack. She wasn't in the country illegally, and yet Father Benedict had warned her that Americans were being picked up and questioned, and those believed to be supporters of the Moderate government were not released. With just four days left on her visa, she could not afford delay of any kind.

"Do you know where we are?" she asked her companion, her pulse accelerating with fear and desperation.

"Just outside of Caracas," the woman replied.

Jordan sought landmarks beyond the glare of the blockade. She made out a forested hill dotted with lights that signified buildings, civilization. "I need to get off the bus," she said out loud.

The woman whispered something to her husband who sat across the aisle. She then turned back to Jordan. "Use the door at the back," she suggested. "Perhaps the soldiers won't see you."

"Thank you," said Jordan, patting the pig's head as she

squeezed out of her seat. Considering that Venezuela's poorest supported the Populist coup, she was lucky they weren't grabbing hold of her.

The latch on the emergency exit was stuck. With escalating panic, Jordan jiggled it. The old man sitting closest to the door offered assistance. The latch yielded with a squeak. Jordan croaked out a word of thanks, eased the door open and jumped out. She shut it quietly, unwilling to draw attention to herself.

The bus's fumes filled her nostrils as she peered toward the blockade, measuring her ability to vault the low wall at the edge of the roadway without being seen. *Solomon could do it,* she thought, tightening the straps on her backpack.

Without warning, the bus moved forward, leaving Jordan no choice but to sprint out of the traffic. With her heart in her throat, she raced toward the wall, bounding upward and bruising her knees.

A warning shout sounded over the rumble of engines. In the next instant, gunfire cracked the air. A bullet whistled past her head. On hands and knees, Jordan scrambled toward the vegetation growing on the hillside.

Oh, Jesus! The metallic taste of fear filled her mouth. *She'd been shot at. She could've been killed!*

Raised voices and the beam of a powerful spotlight warned her that they were coming after her. She commanded herself to rise on rubbery legs and run. But the incline was nearly vertical. Grasping the limbs and branches she could now see because of the light shining up at her, she hauled herself upward, weighted by sudden terror and the pull of gravity.

The vegetation thinned and then there was a guard

rail. Vaulting it, she found herself on a street above the highway. Spying an alley, Jordan sprinted pell-mell into its welcoming darkness, putting distance between herself and the sound of pursuit.

She had covered four blocks at a dead run before the stitch in her side forced her to a gasping halt. She stood by an abandoned factory, utterly lost, shaking from head to toe, trying to catch her breath. A car cruised by, and she shrank back into the shadows.

What now? she thought, digging in her backpack for her cell phone. It hadn't worked at all in Puerto Ayacucho, but perhaps it would here, in this modern city.

With trembling hands, she eyed the digital display and quickly silenced the ringer that indicated a new message.

Solomon had called her.

Putting her back to the wall, her heart racing to see what he'd had to say, she played his message back, closing her eyes as the rumble of his voice filled her ears.

"Jordan," he said on a note that brought goose bumps to her skin and tears to her eyes, "if you have any sense whatsoever, you will get in touch with Lucy Donovan. I'm going to read you her cell phone number."

Relief made Jordan's knees tremble. Solomon had thrown her a lifeline, giving her hope that he hadn't cut her out of his life forever. She memorized the number, and whispering it over and over to herself, she dialed Lucy Donovan with fingers that shook so badly, she could scarcely accomplish the feat.

Lucy Donovan had instructed Jordan to look for a silver Hummer with tinted windows. When a vehicle fitting that description squeezed into the alleyway heading toward their designated rendezvous point, Jordan first thought it was a tank.

She pressed herself against a cinder-block wall, cringing as it approached her, but then a beam of light glinted on the silver fender wall, and she realized this was Lucy, who, despite Jordan's sketchy description of where she was, had found her within an hour of her call.

Jordan darted over to the waiting vehicle and pulled the door open.

"Hurry," said the woman at the wheel. "There's a curfew."

Jordan climbed into the leather seat, shut the door, and grappled for her seat belt. The SUV took off, turned a sharp corner, and headed up a hill.

There was no sign of Miguel in the car, only a shovel on the floor of the seat behind her. "Where's my son?" Jordan asked.

"Safe," said the woman. "You'll see him soon."

The interior of the vehicle was dark, but Jordan could tell that Lucy Donovan was younger than she would have thought, her dark hair caught up in a ponytail. She wore black clothing, and there was a dirt stain on her right cheek, evidence that she'd been using that shovel a short while ago. What on earth for?

The woman flicked a glance at her and then at her rearview mirror. She turned abruptly left. "You are either extremely brave," she said in a cool voice, "or extremely naive."

Jordan stiffened. "How is Miguel?" she asked, choosing to ignore the comment. The woman was going well out of her way for her.

"He's fine," she answered with certainty. "He'll be glad to see you."

"I went all the way to Puerto Ayacucho, and he wasn't there," Jordan quietly accused.

Lucy flexed her fingers on the steering wheel. "You shouldn't have come into Venezuela in the first place," she opined. "The airport is being overtaken as we speak. Everyone but DEA agents, hard-core military attachés, and code clerks have left the country."

Jordan's heart stopped, then started again. How would she get out of the country with the airport closed? "I need someone at the embassy to sign the adoption papers," she said, deciding she would face that obstacle later.

"It's a little late for that," said the woman quietly.

"But the embassy isn't evacuated yet," Jordan pointed out.

"I just told you most of the personnel have already left the embassy."

"But someone could sign his papers," Jordan insisted.

Lucy thinned her lips. "We'll see," she said without optimism.

As if on cue, light flared in the night sky, and the sound of an explosion vibrated the shell of the SUV. Jordan gripped the armrest, her heart in her throat.

"That came from the airport," Lucy informed her. "The few workers remaining at the embassy will be evacuated soon. You can leave with them."

"Only if Miguel comes with me," Jordan replied. "I won't leave again without him."

Lucy Donovan cut her a reflective glance. Silence filled the vehicle as she switched into a lower gear, and they ascended yet another steep, narrow road, seemingly bound for the top of the mountain where high-rise apartments loomed toward a starry sky.

"Thank you for coming to get me," Jordan added. Better to be with fellow Americans than lost and alone.

"You're welcome," Lucy said, matter-of-factly.

Her earlier words, *You can leave with them,* echoed in Jordan's head. "Aren't you leaving the country also?" she asked.

"Eventually," Lucy replied.

The vague answer made Jordan curious, but she had worries of her own to preoccupy her—like whether Miguel would be able to come with her this time. The memory of her last evacuation filled her with premonition.

What if the powers that be refused to evacuate Miguel? She couldn't remain in Venezuela indefinitely, hiding from persecution, while managing to care for him.

Oh, Solomon, she thought with a heavy heart, *maybe you were right. I should have let Lucy handle this all along.*

Lucy Donovan lived in a high-security, high-rise apartment building. A keycard and a code punched into the alarm system admitted them into the parking garage. An elevator bore then to the very top floor, where Lucy entered a second code that released the door to the penthouse suite. There, a panoramic view of the city of Caracas filled the wall of windows.

Jordan wasn't as enthralled with the view as she was with the realization that Miguel was somewhere inside this modern, impersonalized apartment.

"*Gracias,* Julieta," Lucy said, dismissing the maid who slept on the couch, awaiting her return.

With a bob and a good night murmur, the maid left the apartment. Lucy slipped off her muddy boots, leaving them beside the door. "Are you hungry?" she asked, striding in socks to the kitchen and flooding it with lights. Jordan glanced at the modern amenities and graphite counters. "I have beer and pizza," said Lucy, opening the refrigerator.

Jordan took stock of her. Wearing a black halter and leggings over her trim, athletic frame, Lucy Donovan looked like Lara Croft from *Tomb Raider*.

"No thank you. I'm not hungry. Where's Miguel?" she asked, dying to reunite with him.

"In the guest room down the hall," said Lucy, glancing at her with light green eyes. "It has its own bathroom," she added. "Help yourself to anything you need."

"Thank you so much," Jordan answered, turning and hurrying down the short hallway.

As she pushed through the closed door, her gaze flew to the small lump huddled under the blanket on the king-size bed. She turned on the bedside lamp, needing to see him, to reassure herself that Miguel was really here.

As she pulled the edge of the sheet from his cheek, he startled awake and drew back with a cry.

"Miguel," she said, removing her baseball cap. "It's me, sweetheart."

For one awful second, he didn't seem to recognize her, but then his big, dark eyes filled with tears, and he launched himself at her, clinging so tightly that she could barely breathe.

"I missed you, too, baby," she choked, as tears of exhaustion and happiness flooded her eyes. "I came a long way to get you back," she crooned, rocking him as he continued to hold on. Running a hand up and down his narrow back, she could tell that he'd been fed, but he clearly hadn't had much of an appetite.

"Do you remember your English words?" she asked, when he didn't speak. She held her breath, hoping he would speak for her, as he had in the past.

"Yes," he said with hesitation.

"I'm going to take you home with me," she told him. "This time I won't let you go. Do you understand?"

He searched her face, his eyes wide and filled with far too much sorrow for a boy of four years. He didn't answer. She suffered the feeling that he didn't believe her, though he should. Nothing short of hell and high water could separate them ever again.

Ah, here she is, Jillian thought, hearing the crush of gravel under the tires of an approaching car. She secured her second earring, stepped into sandals too tight for her swollen feet, and reached for her matching handbag. She hadn't even been sure that Jordan would show up tonight. She'd been trying to reach her sister for two days now to firm up their plans.

"Graham," Jillian called at the top of the stairs. "Aunt Jordan's here. I'm leaving now."

"Okay," said Graham, who was in his bedroom.

"That means you need to get off the computer and play with Agatha," Jillian reminded him. "Make her a ham and cheese sandwich and don't let her out of your sight."

Graham appeared suddenly at his bedroom door with a

sneer on his face. "If Aunt Jordan is taking you out, then why is that FBI guy coming to the door?" he demanded.

"He is?" Jillian hadn't even thought to look out the window; she'd just assumed it was Jordan. "Oh, dear."

Beset with suspicions and fears, Jillian hurried down the steps. The heel of her right sandal wobbled, and she stumbled suddenly, clattering down several steps before catching herself with one hand on the rail, the other on a step behind her.

"Mom!" Graham called, thundering down the steps in her wake. "Are you okay?"

"I'm fine," said Jillian, though her ankle and one wrist were now both tender. She felt a tightening in her womb that she attributed to a Braxton Hicks contraction. They happened regularly, now. "Get the door, honey."

With a returning scowl, Graham brushed past her to open the door. Jillian stood up, feeling flustered and ungainly. As the door swung open, Rafe's midnight gaze impaled her. "Did you just fall down the stairs?" he asked, looking impossibly handsome in a black suit and crisp, white shirt, though his complexion seemed pale.

"I just slipped a few steps. I'm fine. What's going on?" she asked, descending more carefully to approach the door.

He looked her over, his gaze still worried. "Are you sure you're all right?"

"I'm fine. Why are you here?"

He drew a deep breath. "Jordan sent me here tonight to take you out to dinner. She's out of the country," he announced.

"Oh, my God." Jillian wilted against the door, beset by

shock. "I had a bad feeling when I couldn't get in touch with her," she admitted.

"I warned her not to go," Rafe added somberly. "There's a coup occurring in Caracas as we speak."

Jillian couldn't speak. She closed her eyes and shook her head. The news left her cold and weak. "Graham, go find Agatha." She could sense Graham hovering right behind her. He turned and stalked away.

"You look pale, Jillian," said Rafael, who still stood on the welcome mat. "Come sit with me out here." With a warm, gentle grasp, he drew her outside and helped her ease onto the porch swing. He sat gracefully beside her, his sidelong gaze like a blanket. "I'm sure she has the sense to retreat to the American embassy," he comforted.

"Does she?" Jillian tossed back. "Does she have any sense whatsoever returning to that country? It took a platoon of Navy SEALs to get her out the last time, Rafael. What's it going to take now?"

"She's living her life," he pointed out gently. "The little boy she's trying to adopt must mean the world to her."

"I hope she doesn't get killed trying to get him out," Jillian retorted. She tried to cling to her anger, but guilt and fear won out, and her eyes filled abruptly with tears. She looked away, not wanting Rafael to see them.

He started to rock the swing, ever so gently, while she blinked back her tears and briskly wiped the corner of her eye. "It's your birthday," he pointed out, kindly.

With a sniff, she glanced at him and mustered a smile. "Yes, it is."

His gaze drifted downward, over the cream-colored crocheted sundress she wore, the matching sandals, and the handbag in her lap. "You look beautiful."

She'd twisted her long, gold hair into a French knot, dabbed on perfume, a little makeup. She had thought, looking critically into the mirror earlier, that she looked fat, overly ripe, but his appreciative gaze didn't make her feel that way.

"I'll understand if you don't wish to go out still," he continued, a little self-consciously.

"Oh, I do." She cut him off before he had the chance to back out. "Yes, I realize Jordan's in a very dangerous place right now, and something terrible could happen to her. But until and unless something does, I'm going to enjoy my birthday because it's the last time I'll ever be this age."

Rafael eyed her with what was clearly mixed respect and wariness. "Very well," he conceded with his self-mocking smile. "We have reservations for seven-fifteen at Waterside."

"Let me say good-bye to Graham and Agatha, and I'll be ready."

She didn't invite Rafael inside for a reason. Graham stood over two halves of a ham and cheese sandwich, mutilating the bread with his vicious strokes as he slathered on the condiments.

"But I don't like mustard," Agatha whined, watching him.

"Tough," he retorted. "You don't always get what you want."

"Graham, Agatha, I'll be home around ten o'clock," Jillian casually announced. "Rafael is going to take me out in Jordan's place."

Graham froze and glared up at her. "You're dating already?" he accused.

"I'm going out to dinner for my birthday," Jillian answered, meeting his glare. "I think I deserve a couple of hours to enjoy my life, don't you?"

Graham was the first to look away. He screwed the lid down without answering the question.

"Can I come?" Agatha pleaded. "I promise I'll be good."

"Not tonight, honey," said Jillian, giving her a hug. "You and Graham are going to watch *Flicka* on DVD, remember?"

She brightened considerably. "Oh, yay!"

"Call my cell phone if there's an emergency," Jillian said to Graham, kissing his cheek. "And you can still go to Cameron's when I get back." That was how she'd bribed him to babysit. "See you soon." She headed for the door.

"Mom."

She paused and looked back. "Yes, honey."

"Have fun," he said, grudgingly.

"Thank you," she said, recognizing the effort it took for him to say that. "I hope you'll have fun with Agatha, too."

"Yeah, right." He slid the sandwich toward his sister.

Chapter Fourteen

✦

With a groan for her aching feet and a little laugh at the recollection of Rafael's disco-era moves on the dance floor, Jillian eased back the leather seat of his sleek black Lexus and sighed. "That was so much fun," she admitted, chuckling again. "I had no idea you could dance like that."

"Neither did I," he replied drolly, as he sped her back to her home.

They were more than an hour late. To give Graham credit, he hadn't called to complain yet. "Oh, come on. Tell the truth, now. You were a party animal in your youth, living it up in the city that never sleeps."

A reflective silence filled the sedan. "No, actually," he refuted.

Jillian slit her eyes and turned her head to admire his Mediterranean profile. "What were you like?" she asked, utterly drawn to who he was, both then and now.

He sighed. "Studious," he admitted. "Diligent. In high school I had dreams of going to college and graduate school, but—" He shrugged.

"But what?" she pressed gently.

"I got my girlfriend pregnant. So I married her."

Jillian regarded him in surprise. She'd assumed he'd married Teresa out of love, the way she'd married Gary. "You never told me that," she accused. During his recovery at St. John's two years ago, they'd talked about almost everything.

"By day, I beat the streets as a rookie cop. At night I went to school," he confessed. "It took me eight years to earn a B.S."

He fell suddenly quiet, and the only sound in the car was a haunting aria sung by a lyrical soprano. Jillian sensed a sudden darkening of Rafe's mood. Earlier that evening he'd gone to great lengths to keep her thoughts off Jordan and her spirits lifted. He'd treated her to dinner at one of Waterside's finest restaurants, distracted her with stimulating conversation, and taken her on a stroll along the river, afterward, her arm in his.

It had been Jillian's idea to slip into the dance club that pulsed with an enticing beat. She'd known a devilish urge to loosen Rafe's tightly bound self-control by drawing him onto the dance floor. If she could dance in her third trimester, he could take his jacket off and join her.

He'd done more than that. For one wild and wonderful moment, he'd become spontaneous, fun-loving, happy. Earlier he'd apologized for not buying her a gift. He didn't even realize that his kindness, his companionship, and his playfulness were gifts in themselves.

But now, with conversation turning back the hands of time, she could feel him retreating into his shell. She turned onto her left hip and placed a hand on his arm, a friendly and affectionate gesture. She felt him flex, and her pulse leapt. He'd mentioned once that he worked out at the gym at FBI Headquarters. Given the rock-hard bulge beneath her palm, he worked out religiously. The woman in her delighted in her discovery.

"Did you love her, Rafael?" she heard herself ask. She longed to know him even better than before—intimately, soul to soul. He had mentioned Teresa only fleetingly in the past, preferring to dwell on memories of his children, Tito, Serena, and the baby, Emanuel.

"Of course," he said, vaguely.

"As a lover, as a soul mate?" she pressed. "Or as the mother of your children?" Why, she wondered, was it suddenly so important for her to know?

He was quiet so long that she could feel heat building in her cheeks. The last thing she wanted was to compromise their friendship.

"As the mother of my children," he finally replied, his voice more ragged than ever. He stared dead ahead, two hands on the wheel.

Her heart felt curiously buoyant. At the same time, she felt sad, sad that he'd never truly been in love, never truly real. No wonder he was content to work day after day in a relentless pursuit for justice, putting aside his own needs and desires, scarcely even alive.

"You deserve so much more than that," she lamented.

"I've gotten what I deserve," he countered flatly.

"Oh, no you haven't," she insisted. She lifted her hand from his shoulder to his cheek, where she breathlessly stroked the hint of stubble and the hard line of his jaw, pleased to hear his indrawn breath, to see the rise and fall of his chest. "You deserve joy, Rafael. Joy and passion," she added, savoring the heightening of her senses as desire flooded her, as intoxicating as it was unexpected. "I wish..." She caught herself, measuring the words that teetered on the tip of her tongue. "I wish you trusted me to show you what you've missed."

"Jillian," he said, with as much reluctance as doubt, "I can't be what you need."

His words were meant to push her away, but she refused to hear them because his body was telling her a different message. She could feel the tension in him as she drew her hand slowly down his arm to his thigh. It wasn't self-doubt that made his muscles flex. He was as aroused by the possibility of a connection between them as she was.

"You already are," she told him, unperturbed, but drawing back before she took her discovery too far. "You're exactly what I need," she said, turning her gaze out the window as they crossed a high, arched bridge. Stars winked in the sky as if privy to her personal satisfaction. "Thank you for a wonderful night," she added. "I almost forgot all about Jordan."

Her stomach clenched with renewed dread as she thought of her sister so very far away.

To her deep gratification, Rafe placed his hand over hers, and their fingers twined together. Desire rose up again, just as abruptly, and Jillian opened her hand to draw him closer. Their bond became fervent, almost desperate. Jillian's heart pounded, her ears rang. "Would you stay with me tonight?" she heard herself beg.

"I don't know if that's a good idea," he said, shakily.

"If it's my pregnancy that disturbs you, then I understand," she began, wetting lips that felt suddenly dry. Was she really going to say this? "But if it's because you're afraid to really live, to feel things the way other human beings feel them, then I think it's time you forgave yourself for what happened to your family."

The silence following her words was deafening. Rafael slowly removed his hand from hers. She turned her head to look at him, and the cold mask he'd donned made her heart sink. But she would not apologize for telling the truth. She gazed out the window at the cars they passed as Rafe sped along the freeway.

Not another word was spoken. Jillian's cell phone rang, and she spent a moment drawing answers out of Graham about his and Agatha's evening. "I'll be home in about five minutes," she promised, hanging up.

She slipped the phone in her bag and sighed. "I know you don't like what I said," she told Rafael, "but please think about it."

His only acknowledgment was a brief nod. With a despairing sigh, Jillian looked out the window again as he peeled off the highway on the exit to her ranch.

Short moments later, they were crawling up the long gravel driveway. Jillian dug deep for the courage to end the evening on a positive note. As he threw the car into park, she seized his arm to prevent him from getting out. "I'll get my own door," she told him. "Good night, Rafael. Thank you for the dinner and the company. But the best gift was seeing you dance." He sat in stoic silence as she rolled up on one hip to kiss his cheek. He didn't take advantage, but when she drew back, she saw that he'd closed his eyes.

"Good night, Jillian," he rasped as she pushed her door open and got out.

She headed toward her house. A horse nickered, reminding her that tomorrow would bring her first patients, one paraplegic and two amputees, all looking to regain their grace and balance.

Aren't we all? she thought with a wistful smile.

She stepped onto the porch that sagged worse than ever, put her key into a door that needed painting. The pressures of single parenthood nudged aside the pleasantness that had enveloped her until now. Her belly contracted fiercely, almost painfully, as she pushed her way inside.

Jordan awoke to a small hand stroking her face. Her first thought was of Silas, but then she cracked her eyes and recognized Miguel, his blue-black hair reflecting the sunlight that framed the heavily curtained windows. It was morning.

Pulling him into her arms with a happy cry, she savored the familiar feel of his body pressed to hers. *My child,* she thought, eyes stinging with emotion and lingering exhaustion. Oddly, though, thoughts of Silas and Solomon pressed closer, and her heart ached with loss.

Pulling back, she inspected him. Balling up a hand, she asked, "Remember the game we played? Rock, paper, scissors." She spread two fingers to represent scissors, and he tapped them with his fist. "Rock beats scissors, that's right." It thrilled her that he remembered, though they hadn't played that game since before they'd hidden in the cellar. "I love you," she said, stroking his cheek. "*Te amo mucho.*"

He hugged her again, as sweetly affectionate as she remembered. She wished he could articulate his experiences and fears. For now, they remained locked within his mind until his fluency developed enough to share them.

A distant rumbling followed by the clatter of gunfire snatched Jordan's thoughts to the situation outside. She rolled from the bed, hefting Miguel in her arms as she crossed to the window and drew the curtain back.

The bright morning haze made her blink. Plumes of smoke billowed in the distance, in the direction of the airport at Maiquetía. Squinting down at the crush of smaller buildings, she caught sight of people running, carrying guns and throwing rocks. The sound of gunfire came again, then again and again, drawing nearer.

There was fighting in the streets! How was she supposed to get Miguel out of the country in this mess?

"Help me, Solomon," she heard herself whisper. He'd thrown her a lifeline in the form of Lucy Donovan. Perhaps that was all he could or would do for her; he'd told her not to come here.

A knock at the door preceded its abrupt opening. "We need to leave here in five minutes," said her hostess, her tone calm but grave. "Come grab a bite to eat."

Jordan stuffed Miguel's change of clothes into her backpack, then led him into the kitchen, where she set him on a stool and tempted him with bread and goat cheese. When he would only take a token nibble, she wrapped the rest in a napkin and jammed it into her backpack.

Lucy Donovan reappeared in camouflage slacks, a gray T-shirt, with a handgun holstered under her left arm. Miguel reached mistrustfully for Jordan.

"Don't worry, Little Guy, I'm on your side," Lucy reassured him, even as she strapped a webbed belt loaded with paraphernalia to her waist. Dragging a rucksack from a closet, she swung it onto her back. "Ready to go?" she asked Jordan.

"Yes," said Jordan. The bread she'd just swallowed felt like it was stuck in her throat.

She would have to trust GI Jane, here, to get her to the embassy alive. But what would happen to her and Miguel after that?

"Damn," swore Lucy Donovan, braking to a halt. They'd driven straight into a mass riot outside the walls of what had to be the U.S. embassy.

Lucy threw the SUV into reverse and stepped on the accelerator. Jordan, who clung to Miguel in the backseat, lurched forward as the tires squealed. Lucy backed up into an alley, flinging the occupants of her vehicle forward as she sped away from the crowd.

"There's another way in, right?" Jordan asked, swallowing down her sudden queasiness.

The mirror on the passenger's side shattered with a loud pop. Lucy gunned the engine. The Hummer roared and flew. Jordan shrank lower in her seat, shielding Miguel with her body. "Was that a bullet?" she squeaked.

Lucy didn't answer. She swung a sharp right up a road that appeared deserted. She whipped into an open gate to park on someone's driveway, hidden behind their walls, and whipped out her cell phone.

Jordan watched and waited, her heart thumping. Miguel twisted in her lap and pushed his face against her breasts. "Hush, sweetheart. I'll protect you," she whispered.

"Hey, Tommy," Lucy said in a voice that didn't even waver. "It's Lucy. Are you inside the embassy?"

"Yes"—Jordan could discern the faint thread of his voice on the other end—"hell are you?"

"Six blocks away. When are you planning to exfiltrate?"

"We can't," said Tommy. "The insurgents...every major road in the city blocked. We've locked ourselves in...burning the files."

"Damn," Lucy swore again, and this time, Jordon could hear the stress in her voice. "I've got an American woman with me and her adopted son, a small boy."

Tommy presumably chastised Lucy for not reporting in last night.

"I was busy picking up the woman and kid," Lucy replied.

Actually, thought Jordan, she'd been out digging a hole somewhere with the shovel still under her feet.

"I don't know what to tell you," said Tommy, his voice suddenly audible as Lucy switched ears. "Go back to your apartment and lock your doors. Try to stay safe, and when we're evac'ed out of here, I'll make sure someone comes for you."

"Will do," said Lucy, but Jordan could tell by her voice that she had no intention of waiting out the coup in her high-rise apartment. "'Bye, Tommy."

"Take care, Hot Shot."

Lucy grimaced as she severed the call. She put an elbow on the back of her seat, preparing to back out. Meeting Jordan's gaze, she hesitated. "Listen," she said, with resolution in her light green eyes, "I'm going to get you out of the city and head for the coast. But I have something important to do along the way, and you two are just going to have to sit tight and wait."

"You're not really an embassy worker, are you?" Jordan replied, her limbs filmed in cold sweat.

Lucy didn't answer. Instead, she floored the Hummer, ejecting it from its hiding space. In the next instant, they were roaring down streets that seemed too narrow for the broad, American SUV to navigate. They came upon a wave of protesters, ordinary citizens of Caracas, pouring out of their shops and hovels to welcome the ex-president back into the city.

Venezuela's poorest were convinced that the bones the Populists tossed them would change their lives for the better. From their perspective, it meant nothing that the Populists opened their doors to terrorists.

"Keep your head down," Lucy advised, jamming a Kevlar helmet on her own head as she drove the Hummer straight into the crowd.

Angry fists beat on the reinforced steel and tinted windows. The protesters couldn't see inside, but government plates made it apparent to those who could read that they weren't locals. To Jordon's horror, two men leapt aboard the moving vehicle.

Lucy accelerated, then braked abruptly, shaking the hitchhikers like a couple of annoying flies. She kept driving, turning into alleys and unpaved roads rutted with potholes and hemmed in by houses made of cardboard, leftover lumber, tin cans.

The rumbling of tanks grew more distinct. As they crested a hilltop, bouncing onto a paved street from an unpaved alleyway, Jordan got her first good look at the Populist Army.

A line of tanks at least a mile long cruised ominously up the thoroughfare and then diverged, tanks splintering off in three different directions. Citizens of Indian descent ran alongside the convoys, cheering, waving them on.

"Hold on," said Lucy.

They shot across Avenida Sucre, driving into the yards that separated dilapidated row houses. Clotheslines snapped. Trash cans and boxes flew. They bounced into a public park, scattering pigeons. Not a soul got in their way.

Jordan willed her tense muscles to relax. Miguel was trembling. She'd be lucky if he didn't wet them both. Even she had to pee, but Lucy obviously knew what she was doing. Provided they could get away from the troops and out of the city, they'd all be fine.

Or so she hoped. The alternative was way too scary to think about.

At CIA headquarters in Langley, Virginia, SIS Gordon Banks waited politely for the director, John Hurley, to give him his undivided attention. Hurley skimmed the remaining documents in the folder Gordon had given him, then flipped back to Lucy's photo on the first page. "Where is she now?" he asked.

"According to the GPS on her cell phone, she's heading out of Caracas toward Maiquetía."

"That's not the evacuation port," Hurley pointed out.

"No, it's not."

"Why the hell is she going that way? The Populists seized the airport last night."

"There's a warehouse there, sir, that she was scrutinizing when we told her to bury her intel gear and pull out. I have a hunch she's going back there."

"In other words, she's ignoring orders to go on ice."

Gordon hesitated. He didn't want to see a good case officer get sacked. "Obviously she thinks she's got a target that's more important to U.S. security than her career," he replied, defending her.

Hurley sent him a wry grimace. "Look, I'm not out to hammer this girl. She's extremely promising. I just want her kept safe. Who's getting the rest of our people out of the embassy?"

"Er," Gordon conferred with the memo in his hand. "SEAL Team Twelve, sir."

"Twelve?" Hurley perked up. "I think we've trained at least one member of that team—fellow by the name of Atwater. He was detailed to us in Afghanistan last year. Go ask the CNO if the Navy will loan him to us for a week or so to find Lucy Donovan and bring her home."

"Will do, sir," Gordon replied. Relief left his shirt sticking to his back. "Good day, sir."

He hastened back to his office to call the Chief of Naval Operations on the green line.

Solomon felt sick to his stomach. His commander couldn't tell him if Jordan was among the nine Americans stuck inside the embassy in Caracas or not. He supposed he should be grateful that Team Twelve, having just been in Venezuela, was the team selected to extract the remaining Americans. He just wished he knew whether Jordan was among them.

"We don't have a roster of who's inside," Joe Montgomery had said earlier, before the meeting started.

Echo Platoon now sat around the circular table in the

Briefing Room, brainstorming. That was standard operating procedure, and every man from the lowliest petty officer to the CO himself got to give his input, though it was the operations officer, Lieutenant Lindstrom, who, with the CO's blessing, got the final say.

"I think this calls for a surprise helo extract with gunship support," Lieutenant Lindstrom said, opening the mission up for discussion.

Everyone but Vinny agreed. He wanted to infiltrate via submarine and slip in to the embassy compound by foot. "What if they have RPGs?" he pointed out.

Rocket-propelled grenades were a serious concern. "It takes a clear shot plus time to arm, aim, and fire a stinger," retorted Harley. "Chances are they'd miss."

"We're not taking chances," Lieutenant Commander Montgomery interrupted. "We'll stage a diversion."

"There's an ammo dump on the northwest side of the city, not far from the airport," Lieutenant Lindstrom reported. "A big enough explosion should persuade the enemy to pull some firepower out of the city. If we come in fast and low, suppressing whatever fire they direct at us, we should be fine."

"We get all the Americans in the embassy to gather in one place," suggested the only African-American SEAL in the platoon, Teddy Brewbaker. "That way we're in and out in under five minutes."

"We'll need two Cobras or Blackhawk gunships for support and four MH-60s," the lieutenant agreed.

The men fell silent as they envisioned the high-risk mission. Solomon wiped moist palms on his pant legs and swallowed down the acid creeping up his throat.

"You're awfully quiet there, Senior Chief." Commander Montgomery's thoughtful gaze focused on Solomon.

He didn't know where to start; didn't know if Lucy Donovan had managed to stow Jordan and Miguel safely in the embassy. Last he'd heard from her, she'd had them both at her apartment, but now the city was being besieged. "If there's a woman at the embassy," he said, measuring his words with care, "with a little native boy that she's trying to adopt, I want both of them pulled out and brought stateside."

The commander narrowed his eyes. "Who's this woman?" he asked.

"Jordan Bliss. We extracted her from a mission in the jungle a few weeks back."

"Ah, the one you had to tranquilize," said the CO, sitting back and crossing his arms. "Now you're suggesting we evacuate a non–U.S. citizen?"

"Jordan Bliss wouldn't be in Venezuela right now if I'd let her bring the kid home with her."

Joe Montgomery narrowed his eyes. "Sounds like you've been beating yourself up, Senior Chief. You were following orders."

"To hell with orders. I want both of them brought home this time."

A startled and uneasy silence hovered over the round table. Something flickered in the CO's eyes as he stared hard at Solomon. "The rest of you are dismissed," he said, quietly.

The legs of chairs scraped the floor as six men got up silently and headed for the door.

"Sir," murmured Gus Atwater as he passed the CO, "I need to speak to you when you get a second."

Joe Montgomery looked at Gus, seemed to remember something, and nodded. "Come to my office in ten minutes," he suggested.

"Aye, sir."

The room emptied in record time. Solomon swallowed hard. The CO could doom his career with the stroke of a pen. He probably hadn't forgotten that Solomon had fondled his bride-to-be in his hot tub last November, either. But that was then. Having met Jordan, having made love to her, tasting both heaven and hell, it seemed like a lifetime ago.

"Talk to me, Solomon," invited the CO, surprising him. He put his elbows on the table and leaned in, signaling that he was all ears.

Solomon cleared his throat. "It's like this, sir. Jordan Bliss needs Miguel in her life like she needs air in her lungs. She's taken all the right measures to adopt this kid, and she's risking her life, again, to get him out of the country. Either we respect that effort, or I quit the teams."

The commander's eyebrows shot up. He sat back into his chair. "Well, well," he murmured, his lips twitching toward what appeared to be a smile. "You just surprised the hell out of me, Solomon," he admitted.

"How's that, sir?" growled Solomon, chagrined by the level of passion he'd just exhibited, though he'd meant every word.

The CO spread his fingers to suggest that it was obvious. "You're in love," he stated, his dark eyes dancing with private glee. "I never thought I'd see the day."

The word *love* shocked Solomon into silence.

Impossible. He'd sworn he'd never love another woman in this lifetime. Love was an illusion, a well of misery and torment that took years to climb out of. He broke out in a panicky sweat just thinking about it.

But hearing the CO say it, he had to admit there wasn't any other *word* that described his feelings better. Jordan had caught him hook, line, and sinker. He was a doomed man.

And now there was nothing left to do but protect his heart from inevitable despair, and the only way to do that was to protect Jordan herself. "Damn it," he rasped.

"Are you going to be able to do your job, Solomon?" the commander demanded, all hint of humor fleeing. "Love has a way of clouding a man's judgment, you know."

Solomon marshaled his careening emotions. He met the CO's gaze with a challenging glare. "Oh, I'll do my job, sir," he said quietly.

The CO gave a grudging nod. "Glad to hear that. In answer to your question about the boy—by all means, bring him home if that's what it's going to take to keep you in the teams."

"Yes, sir. Thank you, sir," Solomon growled, fighting to contain his relief.

"You're welcome," said the CO with warmth creeping into his tone. "And you're dismissed," he added wryly.

Solomon was already halfway out the door.

Rafe awoke, alone as usual, in his impersonal, high-rise apartment to peach-hued sunrise filling the open window. Memories of the night before flooded warmly through his mind. He relived the feeling of Jillian's soft hand straying toward his thigh, at her invitation to stay. His morning erection felt exquisitely sensitive as he stretched beneath the sheet.

He felt so alive!

The sensation was as disturbing as it was exhilarating, yet there was nothing sudden about it. The first stirring had begun two years ago, when he and Jillian first met. It had been as subtle then as the beating of a butterfly's wings.

This morning, there was nothing subtle about it. His heart pounded with the yearning to rise and to live, and yet he still lay in limbo, impaled by memories of the past.

I think it's time you forgave yourself for what happened to your family. Jillian's soft suggestion replayed itself.

He dared to look back, felt his horror take hold.

Had he punished himself sufficiently for not protecting them? Eight years of solitary confinement was a long time.

Not that he'd locked himself away in jail. But spiritually, emotionally, and sexually, yes. He'd been merciless in his punishment.

Perhaps it was time to forgive, to let himself truly live again.

With a cry of relief, Rafe threw back the sheet that covered him and leapt out of bed.

Chapter Fifteen

✦

The odor of horses, leather, manure, and grass mingled in an earthy bouquet as Rafe cut through the barn and out the rear doors to the riding ring. His gaze went straight to Jillian as she encouraged the amputated vet to ride a chestnut mare one more time around the ring. Sweat stains gave testament to the young man's efforts to keep his seat. But Rafe's concern was for Jillian, who held her belly as she hurried to keep pace with the horse and patient.

As the riding session wound to a close, a burly aide assisted the veteran off the horse and into a wheelchair. They reconfirmed their next visit, and Rafe and Jillian were left alone.

"Rafael," she called, smiling her pleasure as she hurried over, sunlight sparkling in her hair.

Her beauty dazzled him. He found himself reaching for her, loving the feel of her hands in his.

"Why aren't you at work?" she asked, her gaze delving his.

"I took the day off. Where are the children?"

"Grief camp, for children who've lost family members," she explained. "It's being hosted by the church down the road."

"Ah." His pulse quickened at the realization that they were truly alone.

"I had to threaten to take Graham's computer from him in order to get him to go," she admitted. "Of course, Agatha was delighted to be with other kids all day. My afternoon patient has canceled," she added, the pink in her cheeks growing more distinct, "so you couldn't have picked a better time to visit."

His heart beat faster. So, they were alone *and* they had time. There was no mistaking what she was telling him. But then he noticed the dark circles under her eyes and tendrils of moist hair that stuck to her neck. She looked to be exhausted already.

He reluctantly set his yearnings on the back burner. What Jillian needed most was to rest.

Ensconced in her bathtub, with her feet elevated and bubbles popping around her bulging midsection, Jillian felt like a beached whale. No wonder Rafael hadn't pressed her for sex. Instead, he'd suggested a bath and even run the water for her himself. She could hear him in her room now, acquainting himself politely with her private sanctuary.

At this rate, I'm going to have to seduce him, Jillian thought, questioning herself one last time. She felt admittedly nervous, having only ever been with Gary. She searched herself for guilt, for the least indication that her heart still belonged to her dead husband, and found none. What they'd had would always be theirs, but it belonged in the past.

With her toes, she pulled the chain on the plug in the antique tub and let the water drain out of it. Then she heaved herself up on her aching feet, stepped out, and toweled herself dry.

If she could only fit into one of her old nightgowns. But the terry-cloth robe was the only garment big enough to encircle her midsection. With a wry smile, she slipped it on and cracked the door to peek into her bedroom.

She found Rafe plumping the pillows on her bed. Her lace curtains had been lowered, though they did little to filter the noontime sun. He turned his head, meeting her gaze with a cautious smile. "Come lie down," he offered, patting the mattress. "I'll massage your feet."

Jillian didn't want a foot massage. With a shrug of her shoulders, she let the robe slide down her arms and crumple behind her. His stunned gaze took in the shapely fullness of her body as she rounded the bed and slowly approached him.

Seduction, under the circumstances, wouldn't be an easy feat.

She lifted her arms to encircle his neck. Her bare belly touched the belt at his waist, but he didn't seem to notice. His onyx eyes were riveted on her face. A hint of dull color highlighted his cheekbones. She stroked one hand into the crisp black waves of his hair and pulled his head down to kiss him.

His lips felt and tasted exactly as she'd known they would. As their mouths merged and their tongues twined, she knew the exact moment that he surrendered his noble intentions. The tremor in his hands as he lifted them to caress the length of her spine told her plainly that he wanted all of her.

As the kiss deepened and gained momentum, he

gently cupped her full breasts, bent his head, and reverently kissed them. Jillian reached for the buttons of his dress shirt, undoing them with less and less efficiency as he continued to explore her body, stroking her hips, her thighs, with hands that were amazingly gentle.

She craved his touch, wanting more, but his clothes and her belly remained between them. At last, he stepped back to unbutton the rest of his shirt, shaking it off impatiently. His crisp white T-shirt was quick to follow, disappearing in one fluid movement. Jillian tackled his belt, loving the way his flat abdomen clenched as she brushed his hot skin. He wriggled out of his jeans, the same pair he'd worn the other day. And then he was as naked as she was.

Golden brown, from his shoulders to the tips of his toes, Jillian feasted her gaze on him.

"Look in the mirror." He encouraged her to turn toward her dressing table.

Her gaze locked on their reflection. Backdropped by his darker, bigger frame, she looked surprisingly slim and fair, aside from fullness of her breasts and belly. With her bottom pressed to his hips, he nuzzled her neck and stroked a hand over her unborn baby, awakening a tenderness that brought moisture to her eyes.

"You're so lovely, Jillian," he rasped in her ear. "I don't want to hurt you. Please tell me if I do, and I'll stop."

"You won't," she replied with certainty. She watched him touch her, lingeringly, sparking magical sensations between her thighs.

It was a struggle to keep her eyes open. Reaching back, Jillian touched him in turn, marveling at his velvet texture, letting him know by her touch that she was ready for more.

He sat on the edge of her bed and gently lowered her onto him. Jillian gripped the bedpost as he filled her. "Oh, God," she breathed, enthralled with the view, with his tenderness, with the pleasure building inside of her.

She felt him shudder as he thrust gently deeper. The hands stroking her breasts, her throat, her lips, trembled with the effort it took to restrain himself. She caught his fingers in her mouth and sucked them. The sweetness was too much to bear.

She convulsed around him, drenching him in passion too long withheld. He muffled a cry against her shoulder, biting her gently as he pumped himself into her.

A spell of dizziness assaulted Jillian. A ringing filled her ears. She felt herself tipping over, and he caught her, swinging her onto the bed to gaze down at her with real concern. "Jillian! What happened? Did you faint?"

She offered him a weak smile. "I'm okay. All the blood rushed out of my head, that's all."

"Don't scare me like that."

He sounded truly shaken. She lifted a hand to his cheek. "I'm fine, Rafael. There's a phrase in French for that phenomenon, *La Petite Morte*. You should be flattered that you had that effect on me."

He searched her face. Emotion, stark and unexpected transformed his features for a moment, making him look younger, more vulnerable. "I really couldn't stand it if something happened to you," he admitted, roughly.

"Nothing's going to happen," she reassured him, touched by his fears, understanding the cause for them.

He closed his eyes and dropped his face in the curve of her neck.

"It's going to be okay," she murmured, stroking his

short, crisp hair. With a dart of fear, she remembered her sister. "It's all going to be okay," she insisted.

Despite the falling temperatures outside, the air in the Hummer was sticky and hot—more so with Miguel slumped against her, fast asleep. Jordan longed to lower a window, but Lucy had taken the car keys with her. She'd also instructed Jordan not to open any doors, for any reason, and Jordan wasn't eager to test her luck.

Skirting major roadways earlier and four-wheeling through the countryside, they'd left Caracas for the portside city of Maiquetía, skirting Simón Bolívar International Airport. It looked like they were headed straight toward the source of the explosions that lit the darkening sky like a fireworks display, when Lucy pulled into an industrial area, past a warehouse, and into a yard of abandoned railcars.

She'd parked the Hummer between two rusting shells. "Help yourself to the food in my rucksack," she'd offered, checking her pistol and pulling the brim of her camouflaged hat over her eyes. "I should be back before daylight."

"You'll be gone all night?"

"Stay in the vehicle," she'd continued, deaf to Jordan's dismay. "If you have to go to the bathroom, stay close to the vehicle and shut the door quietly."

That had been hours ago. Jordan's stomach rumbled. She was tired but not able to sleep as she puzzled over Lucy's purpose here. Did she have to go skulking like this, with Jordan and Miguel's future at stake, so close to the source of explosions that rent the nighttime quiet and shook the ground beneath the SUV's tires?

So far, Lucy had proved capable of keeping them safe,

but could she be relied upon to get them out of the country when her personal agenda was so obviously different from theirs?

In the dark, stuffy car, in an alien location with strange creaking noises being emitted from the corpses of rail-cars, Jordan's panic would not subside. Her stomach was empty. The enormous responsibility of Miguel's safety weighted her down.

She shouldn't just sit here, relying on Lucy to get them out of the country. Perhaps she could try to contact Solomon.

Fumbling in her backpack, Jordan pulled out her cell phone and eyed the black screen with dismay. She hadn't remembered to charge it.

Lucy had a cell phone. Had she taken it with her?

Wriggling to the edge of her seat, Jordan found Lucy's cell phone in the compartment between the seats, powered off.

Turning it on, she located Solomon's cell phone number, preprogrammed with the international prefix, in Lucy's address book. Her heart hammered expectantly as she pressed the TALK button. Clicking sounds gave way to ringing. Her mouth went dry. She realized she would give anything to hear his voice right now. Only he didn't answer. Disappointed, she was forced to leave a message.

"Solomon? It's me. If you get this message, please help me. We couldn't get into the embassy in time." *Kaboom!* An explosion rent the night air, rocking the SUV. "Lucy's going to take us to the evacuation port," she added, speaking louder, "but we've stopped at a warehouse near the airport. She's doing something; I don't know what." *Kaboom!* "I'm scared, Solomon. And I'm sorry that I didn't listen to you. You were right. It's really not safe here. But at least I've got Miguel. He's sleeping now—" The line went suddenly dead. She tried again and again, only to discover that the call would not go through.

Loath to drain Lucy's battery, Jordan powered the phone down. She put it back in the compartment, slid back in her seat, and adjusted Miguel's head on her shoulder.

Exhaustion claimed her briefly. But then a brisk knock on the door snatched her awake. With her adrenaline spiking, she detected male voices conferring. The beam of a penlight punctured the tinted window. A shadowed face was pressed against the glass as a man peered in.

"Oh, God!" Jordan whispered, shrinking down into the seat, trying to hide in the car's shadows. But she was spotted.

"*¡Abre la puerta!*" commanded the man peering in. He hammered on the door more loudly.

What do I do? Jordan asked herself, clutching Miguel against her. Amazingly, he continued to sleep.

The man at the door pressed an object to the window. Jordan recognized the outline of a gun. "No! Don't shoot!" she cried. She scooted to the door and reluctantly unlocked it, her mouth as dry as dust.

With a wail of disorientation, Miguel awoke and, seeing a stranger, shrieked and buried his face in her chest.

The door was wrenched ajar. Two soldiers, dressed in black, with some kind of fancy insignia on their arms, leaned in, pinning the occupants in the glare of their penlights. Jordan was barraged with questions that came too quickly to answer.

One of the soldiers opened the front door, seizing Lucy's rucksack. He rummaged through it, noting the government-issue, ready-to-eat meal packs. More questions were fired at her.

Jordan reached for the passport in her backpack, and they pointed a gun at her. "*Mi pasaporte,*" she explained.

They snatched the backpack out of her hands.

"You're from the United States," accused the bigger man, beetling his brow at her.

"Yes, I'm adopting this little boy. I'm trying to leave the country, but I got lost," she replied, floundering in fear, her Spanish less than fluent.

"She's lying. She works for her government."

"No, this...this isn't my car. I took it."

"Why are you here? Why are you parked like this?"

"I told you. I'm lost."

"Get out of the car."

She knew she was doomed. They were going to drag her off. She'd get thrown into a Venezuelan prison and never be seen again. "Please," she cried, "all I want is to take Miguel home with me."

Tears gushed from her eyes. She had thought there was nothing in the world worse than being separated from Miguel that morning Solomon forced her onto the helicopter. She'd thought wrong.

Deaf to her pleas, they seized her, dragging her out of the vehicle. They grabbed up her backpack and Lucy's rucksack. For Miguel's sake, Jordan fought to remain calm. He was wailing in fright, clinging to her like a cat up a tree.

"Walk," they commanded, ordering her at gunpoint to precede them.

Jordan risked one look back. She could only hope that Lucy would realize that they'd been nabbed by Populist soldiers and that she'd find a way to rescue them.

Chapter Sixteen

✦

Solomon intended to be the first SEAL to jump from one of the four UH-60s onto the roof of the American embassy. The helos rose into choppy air off the aircraft carrier in the south Caribbean, accompanied by two Cobra gunships, both armed to the teeth.

In the waters far below, Gibbons and Teddy were withdrawing from the port city of Maiquetía, slipping away in an SDV, a tiny submarine. They'd reported the successful arming of explosives at the ammo dump, setting off a chain reaction. The result had been just what the SEALs had hoped: A contingent of Populist troops had pulled out of Caracas to investigate, leaving it marginally safer to swoop down on the embassy and pluck the Americans free.

But Solomon had been a SEAL long enough to know that even the best-planned missions could turn into clusterfucks.

Not a soul, for instance, had expected bad weather. The pilots had advised that the mission be delayed, but pressure from the White House saw it ordered, anyway.

As they bumped through the unstable atmosphere, Solomon eyed his men in the glow of the helo's interior lighting. Only Harley looked perfectly at ease, lolling on the bench across from him, his eyes half-closed.

He envied the sniper's laid-back attitude. Then again, as far as he could tell Harley'd never been in love—not the way Solomon was. Now that he'd admitted to his condition, he would stop at nothing to ensure things worked out right. How would he react upon coming face-to-face with Jordan? Would he kiss the shit out of her or throw her over his shoulder and run like hell? He'd have to carry Miguel if he did that, of course. He knew for a fact that Jordan wasn't going to let go of the boy.

Not after all she'd done to get him back.

Within the warehouse's central office, Lucy slipped an empty CD into the server's X-drive and saved the documents she'd been viewing. The information was a detailed accounting of the weapons stored in this warehouse and where they'd come from. It was all she needed to prove that a Shia splinter cell called The Party of Liberation was arming the Populists and helping them take back the country.

Replacing the first CD with a backup copy, Lucy saved the information a second time. She then snapped both CDs in fireproof, shatterproof cases, slipped them into a wide pocket on her pant leg, and erased her activities from the computer log.

Pulling out a wad of bills, she tucked it in a prearranged location for the janitor—a local groomed by the CIA to serve as informant—to find tomorrow. She checked her watch.

Her quest had eaten up four hours—far more time than she'd anticipated, no thanks to the two guards whom she'd had to incapacitate, bind, gag, and drag into an abandoned railcar, clear across the parking lot.

Leaning over to power down the server, Lucy detected a wail that made the hairs on the back of her neck prickle. That wasn't a child's cry, was it?

She dove for the floor and listened. It came again, accompanied by the intimidating sound of tramping boots. She crawled briskly toward the office door, keeping her head below the windows overlooking the interior of the warehouse.

A loud crash signaled the arrival of interlopers. Lucy leapt to her feet and, keeping low, raced toward the stairs, along the elevated metal walkway that ran the circumference of the building.

It was too late now to take the stairs. She'd be seen if she tried.

Putting her back to the wall, her heart beating fast, she peered toward the bay doors, which were being wrestled open.

Bright, halogen lights flickered on, and Lucy shrank back farther. *Damn it!*

A dozen soldiers, dressed in the uniform of the Elite Guard, swarmed into the building toting submachine guns. Lucy shuddered with frustration. If the Elite Guard, trained by U.S. Navy SEALs, hadn't betrayed the Moderate government, these would be the good guys securing a warehouse belonging to the Populists and stocked by terrorists. Instead, they were probably here to arm themselves. Given their shouts and orders, she could tell they were looking for someone—probably her, since Jordan stumbled suddenly into view, as pale as a ghost and fiercely clutching a wailing Miguel.

Shit! Shit! Shit! Lucy thought, figuring her odds. With the lights on and the soldiers splitting off to search the warehouse, it was only a matter of time before they caught her. She had to get rid of the CDs before that happened.

She inched along the wall, searching for someplace, anyplace, to stow the cases.

The elevated walkway was riveted to solid, vertical beams. Feeling a space between the beams and the wall of corrugated metal, she wedged the CD cases in the crevice. Then she marked the beam with a line of chalk she always carried in her pocket.

With the CDs hidden, she counted to three, prayed she wouldn't get shot, and made a run for the exit.

Of course, she never made it. She hadn't expected to.

"*¡Alto!*" yelled a voice, and she froze, putting her hands high in the air. The next moment, she was being divested of her weapon, manhandled, and forced to march into the center of the warehouse, where Jordan looked up from the crate she was sitting on, still cradling Miguel.

The reproach in Jordan's eyes hit Lucy like a punch in the gut. "Sorry," Lucy muttered.

Jordan was not among the ten or so Americans being herded up the steps to the embassy rooftop. Solomon seized the nearest embassy worker by his shirt collar. "Where is Lucy Donovan?" he yelled, in order to be heard over the thundering rotors of four helicopters and the firepower of two Cobra gunships raining bullets onto the streets surrounding the compound.

"She's not here," the man shouted back. "She never made it in. I told her to go back to her apartment."

Solomon roared out a swearword. "Did she say anything about a woman with her?" he asked, catching the man before he headed up the stairs.

"Er—" The man had to think. "Yeah, actually. She had an American woman and a kid with her."

Solomon cut a look at Gus, who stood at the bottom of the steps urging the civilians to move out briskly. "Atwater," he growled over the interteam radio. He'd counted on Jordan to be here, but she was still with Lucy—*God damn it!*

"Senior Chief?"

"I'm going with you to find Lucy Donovan. Don't disappear without me."

According to the CO, Lieutenant Atwater had orders from the Chief of Naval Operations himself to find Lucy Donovan and bring her home. Either the woman had relatives in high places, or she was more than just a secretary.

Gus just narrowed his eyes.

Solomon turned and hustled the last civilian out the rooftop door, into the gale-force winds of the MH-60s. The 20mm Gatling gun spewed fire from the Cobra gunships to create a deafening roar.

"Twenty seconds to lift off," Solomon shouted into his mouthpiece. "Echo Platoon, pull back."

Eight SEALs darted out of the shadows from their various positions to scramble back into the helos.

Solomon opened his mouth to tell Harley that he was staying behind, when Gus jumped into the helicopter.

"Aren't you staying?" Solomon asked him.

"Negative. New orders," he said, patting the satellite phone strapped to his chest.

Solomon's stress level soared. He wanted to remain and find Jordan, only they didn't have time for a leisurely conversation. With two thumbs up to the pilots, he jumped aboard and closed the hatch.

The men held a collective breath until the four helos were safely out of range of any stingers. Solomon snatched off his helmet and moved closer to Gus, so the others wouldn't hear. "What the hell is going on?"

"Just got a call," said Gus gravely. "Lucy used her cell phone two hours ago. The GPS in her phone puts her location in Maiquetía, close to the ammo dump."

Solomon gaped in horror. "Jesus," he whispered, envisioning what that meant. Populist troops were descending on Maiquetía in great force, thanks to the explosions Gibbons and Teddy had set off. "We've got to get them out."

Gus was reaching for the ICS headset. "Trident Actual, this is Trident 1," he barked into the ICS, using the call sign for the Command HQ. "Request in-extremis redirect for Trident 1 and 2 to GPS coordinate 10 degrees, 36 minutes North, 66 degrees, 58 minutes West. Over."

"Trident 1, this is Trident Actual," the reply came through crisply, but with hesitancy in the CO's voice. "State your intentions. Over."

"Trident Actual, this is Trident 1. Purpose is to retrieve my recovery target, who was not at the embassy, over."

A lengthy silence followed Gus's request. The commander's reply came with hesitancy. "Trident 1, we have an AWAC over those coordinates reporting a large hostile presence. Use alternate LZ. Trident 2, return with birds 3 and 4 to rendezvous. Over."

"Will do. Over." Gus took off the ICS headset and shared a grim look with Solomon.

"What the fuck is Lucy Donovan doing in Maiquetía?" Solomon demanded. Not expecting an answer, he turned toward the other three SEALs: Harley, Haiku, and Vinny. "Change of plans, gentlemen," he announced. "We're going to take a detour."

Even with a bruised and swollen lip and a rib that hurt when she breathed, Jordan found something to be grateful for: Miguel wasn't witnessing her interrogation.

Perhaps because he was Venezuelan, the soldiers had spoken to him gently. They had tempted him with chocolate and carried him off, calling out for her. He was somewhere in the building, but his cries had subsided. She was certain he would not be harmed.

But she and Lucy were a different story.

The soldiers had separated them, dragging Lucy up the stairs to a glassed-in office. Jordan's wrists were bound. She was made to sit on a crate that left splinters in her thighs. Fearing for her life, she did her best to answer the questions fired at her by the wiry, thick-mustachioed *capitán*. He seemed like a reasonable soldier, refined, with a dignified air about him. Surely she could convince him of her innocence.

But as the harassment dragged on, she realized with dismay that her answers weren't sticking. He didn't believe her. Shock and exhaustion numbed her thoughts, and she started to stammer. An unexpected slap left her ears ringing and her heart frozen in disbelief.

This can't be happening to me.

"Explain again. Why are you in Maiquetía?" he demanded. She viewed his lean, handsome features in a different light. He was a ruthless killer.

"We were headed to the port, to get on a boat," she whispered, horrified.

"But you were sitting in a parked car," he pointed out.

"Waiting for my friend," she insisted, hoarsely, "to get directions." That had been her story from the first: that she and Lucy were Americans fleeing the country. They'd gotten lost and stopped to ask the way.

"Speak up!" he snapped, popping her on the mouth so hard that her teeth cut her upper lip.

"Please," she begged, tasting blood, "I'm telling the truth. All I want is to adopt Miguel."

"Tell me what your friend was doing here, and I'll release you."

"I don't know!" she cried.

"You're lying." He slammed his knee into her ribs and turned away, snatching up her backpack. Fear gripped Jordan's vocal cords as he drew out Miguel's dossier. She gasped for breath, dreading the possibility that he might destroy it. Then all her work, all her efforts, would be for nothing—no thanks to Lucy, who'd put them in this position. Damn her!

Yet, as furious with Lucy as she might be, Jordan was terrified for her. She couldn't see what was happening to the woman behind the glare on the office glass, but the officer questioning Lucy had stepped out for water, and there'd been blood on his knuckles.

The wiry officer hunkered suddenly by Jordan's knees and yanked her hair, pulling her chin up. "Tell me your true purpose here," he threatened, predictably, "or I'll destroy these papers."

Fury exploded within Jordan. With a roar of maternal rage, she attacked him, striking out with her feet. She kicked viciously, spilling him onto his backside. Then she leapt up and kicked him again, as hard as she could, payback for her bruised rib.

But he was a trained fighter. In one deft move, he swept her feet out from under her, sending her somersaulting.

Jordan's head struck the cement floor, so hard it sounded like a gunshot.

They'd found the chalk in Lucy's pocket.

"What is this for?" demanded the barrel-chested officer grilling her. He held it up to her face, so close that she could smell it, mingling with the copper scent of her own blood, even without cracking her one good eye. The other was swollen shut.

He yanked her ponytail, causing her scalp to burn, when she didn't immediately answer. "What's this for?"

"Playing hopscotch," Lucy retorted, wincing inwardly at the unlikely excuse. It was the first thing to pop into her head.

"Hopscotch?" he scoffed.

"With Miguel."

The answer made him pause. "Go ask the kid if he played hopscotch with this woman."

"Yes, sir," said the second soldier, slipping out.

The lieutenant leaned over Lucy, expelling his foul

breath across her face as he murmured, "I will enjoy hurting you when I hear that you are lying to me."

"I'm sure you will," she retorted, inviting a vicious slap. It was nothing compared to what he was going to do once he realized she was lying.

Swimming in a cold sweat, she remembered the line she'd drawn to mark the spot where she'd hidden the discs. What were the odds that they'd see that thin, pink line?

Please, God, don't let them see it. As long as the CDs remained hidden—as long as she remained alive to retrieve them—this punishment was worth the cost.

The office door reopened. Lucy swallowed down the sour taste of dread in her mouth.

"The boy says she plays hopscotch with him," volunteered the soldier, shrugging.

Lucy glanced at him in amazement. Either Miguel was inventing fantasies—*and* talking, which he'd refused to do for her, or the soldier was taking pity on her. He was younger than his superior officer, quiet and watchful. The name stitched above his pocket read SANTIAGO.

The lieutenant sounded put out. "Are you certain?"

"Positive," said Santiago, avoiding Lucy's gaze. "He even mentioned the chalk in her pocket. I think she's telling us the truth."

Praise be to God, she had an ally! Was that enough to keep her alive, though?

The officer shook his head. "No," he said, folding his arms across his chest. "There's more going on here than she's admitting. Don't worry," he boasted to the soldier, "she will tell us the truth. I'll see to that."

The grin splitting his wide, square face made Lucy's

gut clench. He reached for the buckle on his belt, and she snapped her good eye shut. Oh, no. Maybe she ought to have listened to her father and joined the FBI, instead.

Trident 1's pilot, wary of missile launchers, dropped all five SEALs off on a deserted strip of beach, four miles up the coast from where Lucy's phone had last been used. The second their boots hit the sand, Solomon led them in a stealthy jog.

The scenery through his NVGs was like a slide show, going from bad to worse. First there were mountainous sand dunes that sucked at their boots, then a chain-link fence, topped with barbed wire. They climbed the fence, snipped the barbed wire.

The explosions that Teddy and Gibbons had instigated lit the open terrain in glaring light, forcing the SEALs to hit the dirt more than once as they crossed the near end of the airport's runway. The ground beneath them shook. Once past the airport, they headed straight into a caravan of tanks and armored cars heading toward the ammo dump.

They waited for what seemed like a lifetime for the Populist Army to roll past.

The SEALs then consulted their compasses and fanned out. It was Vinny who discovered what had to be Lucy Donovan's vehicle, parked in a graveyard for railroad cars, not far from a warehouse that was buzzing with activity, military jeeps coming and going, men shouting.

Rallying up, the SEALs searched the Hummer silently. Solomon pulled Lucy's cell phone from between the seats.

He powered it up and discovered that—Jesus—he'd been the last person Lucy had called.

So where were she and Jordan and Miguel? Foreboding spread like ice water through his veins.

"What the hell is this shovel for?" Haiku whispered, his head buried under the backseat.

No one answered him. Gus's head came up suddenly. "Did you hear that?"

They found two men, security guards, on the other side of the lot, bound and gagged, kicking the inner walls of an abandoned railroad car.

"Lucy did this," Gus decided, taking one look at the cuffs that bound them. "Vinny, put them to sleep," he added, and the corpsman reached for his syringes.

"Lucy's in the warehouse," Gus guessed, as the SEALs brainstormed in the shadows of rusting boxcars.

"Then where are the other two?" Solomon asked, dreading corroboration of his fears, grinding his molars to keep from howling at the dark, smoky sky.

"Maybe she left them somewhere safe," said Gus, but tension in his voice told Solomon that they shared the same concern.

"What's inside?" Solomon snapped, eyeing the vast, metal structure. The corrugated walls rippled and groaned in the offshore breeze. Another explosion turned night into day, and the SEALs hit the ground again.

"I'm not sure," Gus admitted, spitting dirt from his mouth. "But Lucy wouldn't be taking chances like this if it wasn't important."

Solomon swallowed a virulent curse. There was nothing in the world more important to him than Jordan and Miguel's safety. As he pictured them inside that warehouse, held against their will, he clawed the loose earth beneath his fingers. What would he and Silas do without Jordan? Oh, why hadn't he let her keep Miguel the first time? "Let's get this the fuck over with," he pleaded, pushing off the ground.

"Slow down there, Senior Chief," Gus advised, with authority that Solomon had only sensed in him before but never heard. "We're going to do this my way."

With a shuddering breath, Solomon reined himself in. The only reason they were here at all was because Gus had orders from the CNO.

Gus signaled to the other men to surround the building, wait, watch, and report. In classic hostage-rescue situations, the observation period averaged forty-eight hours, with the SEALs noting routines, shift changes, mealtimes, et cetera.

The prospect of inaction made Solomon's stomach churn. It was necessary, of course it was, especially when the odds were five to what looked to be a dozen or more. But just suspecting Jordan was inside, probably scared out of her mind, made cerebral, tactical planning virtually impossible. His commander had been right to ask whether his feelings would interfere with the objective. He wanted to smash into the warehouse with guns blazing, pluck Jordan, Lucy, and Miguel free, and prove himself the hero of the day.

The possibility that it might really be too late for that lodged very uncomfortably in his mind.

Lucy had been trained to cope with rape. Cope, as in keep from spilling the truth, scurry into the corner of her mind where nothing could touch her, and not go stark, raving mad. But her training at The Farm, however realistic, hadn't involved an actual, physical rape, just a mauling that she'd handled like a champ because she'd known her instructor wouldn't really hurt her.

She didn't know if she could actually cope with the real deal.

The lieutenant had his fly unzipped, and he was gaining the upper hand on her determination to remain clothed.

She craned her neck to send a pleading look at the junior officer. Santiago stood way back in the shadows by the door. *Please,* she begged him silently, keeping her jaw clamped shut. Begging out loud would only goad the lieutenant, who was muttering crudities under his breath as, inch by inch, he exposed her lower half.

He didn't hear the junior officer slip soundlessly out of the office.

There was nothing she could do to stop this. Lucy squeezed her good eye shut and sought that elusive corner in her mind to hide in. But her brain was a maze, and she scurried like a frightened mouse as the lieutenant hauled her to her feet, spun her around, and shoved her facedown on a work table.

With her cheek ground into the desk's surface and her hipbones bruised against the table's edge, she dove into pleasant memories of the past, into her first two years in college, when the world seemed like a great place to be. She tried to block all feelings from the neck down, but her tears seeped from her eyes as he positioned himself behind her.

The room flooded abruptly with lights. An authoritative

voice from the doorway barked, "Back away, Lieutenant! You do not have the authority to degrade our captives."

The lieutenant responded like a petulant child. He seized Lucy by the waist and flung her across the room. With her ankles bound, she plowed headfirst into a metal file cabinet, her forehead slicing open as it struck a pull handle.

The lieutenant and captain commenced to sharing heated words. Santiago crossed wordlessly to Lucy, pulled her clothing up over her hips, and helped her back into the chair. Her head throbbed and burned. Blood slipped warmly down one side of her nose.

"What has she told you?" the *capitán* demanded.

"Nothing," snapped the lieutenant.

"We've wasted enough time questioning them," decided his superior. "Bring the other woman up here. The child will come with us. Tie them up. We have work to do."

"And then what?" demanded the lieutenant. "We can't just leave them here. They're spies. It's obvious."

"I have orders to destroy the building. They won't live to tell any tales," added the *capitán,* meaningfully.

Lucy's skin shrank. They were going to blow up the building? Dear God! She'd seen what explosions did to the human body. The roadside bomb that had killed three friends in Valencia during her junior year abroad was the main reason she'd joined the CIA: to stop terrorism.

This was not the way she envisioned her own demise.

"No," she croaked, but the lieutenant had already turned to bark at the junior officer. "Santiago, bring the other woman up here and secure them tightly."

"Yes, sir!"

Blinking through the blood that ran into her good eye, Lucy watched him leave. The other two ignored her as they discussed which of the crates to load and which to leave. Missile launchers and submachine guns were their first priority. "If we have room for rifles and ammunition, we'll take those, too. What's left must be destroyed."

Santiago reappeared with an unconscious Jordan in his arms. He tried to prop her up in the chair opposite Lucy's, but Jordan slumped to the floor. He left her there, checking the flexicuffs at her wrists, then binding her ankles like Lucy's.

"Thank you," Lucy whispered to him, softly so the others wouldn't overhear.

He didn't so much as glance at her, but she saw him stiffen. He stepped behind her and, in the guise of checking the cuffs at her wrists, slipped his knife into her hands. Lucy's pulse leapt as she furled her fingers around the haft, hiding it from view. *God bless you!*

He stepped casually away from her. "The hostages are secured, sirs."

The *capitán* glanced at his watch. "Three hours to daylight. Let's go!" he commanded, striding out the door.

The lieutenant followed with a parting leer. Santiago risked a glance over his shoulder as he extinguished the lights and shut the office door.

"Jordan," Lucy called, scraping her chair toward Jordan's limp form. "Wake up," she urged, nudging her with her foot even as she worked to cut the tough plastic encircling her wrists. They had about ten minutes to get out of the building before it blew.

Chapter Seventeen

✦

Jordan felt like an ax had been wedged in her skull. "Oh," she moaned. It hurt to talk. She pushed into a sitting position, and her stomach roiled. "Where am I?" she asked, making out a dark room. She remembered with a gasp. "Where's Miguel?"

"We're in the office of the warehouse," said Lucy, quietly, quickly. "Listen to me, Jordan, I need you to stay calm and stay focused."

Goose bumps ridged Jordan's skin. How she wished she'd just dreamed it, but she hadn't. They were still in serious trouble.

"We're going to get out of here," Lucy reassured her, breathing hard, leaning over her, "but we can't be seen."

"Where's Miguel?" Jordan repeated. Panic roared through her bloodstream, driving back the pain in her head. She squirmed to her knees and promptly gagged.

"Calm down," Lucy ordered. Jordan could just make out her silhouette. "I'm almost loose. I'll cut you free in a minute."

"Tell me," Jordan gasped, "where Miguel is."

"He's safe," said Lucy.

"Where?" repeated Jordan, her volume climbing.

"They're taking him with them."

"No!" She'd come so far, given so much of herself to bring him home. She sank to her knees as the will to persevere drained out of her. "I can't do this anymore," she whispered, too heartsick to cry.

"Yes, you can," Lucy countered. *Snap!* She stood up suddenly, bent down to cut the cuffs at her ankles, then groped in the dark to free Jordan. "Let's go." Something warm and wet plopped on Jordan's neck.

"You're bleeding," Jordan realized, suddenly concerned.

"I cut my head," said Lucy shortly.

Outside the office, the volume in the warehouse swelled. Men shouted. Large metal doors rumbled open. A truck with a noisy muffler backed into the cargo bay. "What's going on?" Jordan asked.

"They're loading up and shipping out," Lucy explained.

"We can't let them take Miguel," said Jordan, pushing shakily to her feet.

Lucy seized her arm and propelled her into a chair. "Listen to me, Jordan," she commanded, putting steady hands on either side of Jordan's shoulders. "This isn't about Miguel right now. This is about us getting out of here before this building explodes. I'll help you find Miguel later, but right now we need to get out of here. Understand?"

"Why would they blow up the building?"

"To keep people like me from finding out who's supplying them with weapons. Now, come on, you're going to get out through the window."

"What about you?"

Lucy hesitated. "I have to do something first. I'll be right behind you."

"Are you kidding me?" Jordan squeaked. "You just said they're going to blow up the building."

"I won't be long," Lucy promised. "Now, move." She urged Jordan toward one of the two large windows overlooking the lot of abandoned boxcars. "Get up on the desk," she instructed, tugging on the glass pane. A warm, sulfurous breeze blew in as the window slid open.

Kneeling on the desk, Jordan peered two stories down. The area behind the warehouse looked quiet and deserted, but her heart beat with dread. "I can't," she whispered.

"Do it for Miguel," Lucy insisted. "You want to get him back, don't you?"

Even given Lucy's motivating words, it took all of Jordan's courage to stick her feet out of the window and squirm backward, so that she dangled into nothingness.

"You can do it," Lucy repeated.

Peeking down at the tremendous drop to the ground below, Jordan balked. She clung to the metal window frame until her knuckles ached. And then she plummeted, swallowing her scream.

In the next instant, she slammed into the ground. The breath whooshed from her lungs. Darkness filled the corners of her eyes. She fought to remain conscious, to get up and run, but her mind went blank, her muscles limp.

Crouching in a clump of sea grass at the front right corner of the warehouse, Solomon watched a soldier swagger out of the building to speak with the driver of the loaded truck. Something about the man's demeanor struck him as familiar. Solomon's nape prickled. Well, son of a bitch! If these weren't the Elite Guards whom he and his men had trained a month ago, back before they'd been bought off by the Populists.

He thumbed his mike, reporting his discovery to Gus.

"Are you sure?" Gus asked.

"Positive," Solomon snarled. He listened to Gus inform their commander over the SATCOM radio. The Elite Guard had betrayed them—soaked up the tricks of the trade the Navy SEALs were willing to teach them, then switched sides.

"We should put 'em out of their fucking misery," Harley opined from his sniper position.

Solomon agreed. The traitors deserved sound punishment.

"Yo," Haiku suddenly exclaimed. "Someone just dropped out of the second-story window. They aren't moving, either."

Solomon's heart stopped dead. Not Jordan! He longed to leap up and check, but moving would expose his position.

"Vinny, go in to take a look," said Gus. "Haiku, you cover him."

It took Vinny a full four minutes to report while Solomon suffered through hot and cold sweats, thinking something awful had happened to Jordan, wondering where Miguel was.

Vinny finally reported. "It's Jordan Bliss," he said, freezing Solomon's blood. "She's unconscious, possible broken bones, big bump on the back of her head. But her vitals are good."

Solomon wilted into the sea grass, clutching the stalks as the earth seemed to spin. *Thank you, God*.

"Pull her to safety," Gus instructed, grimly.

Solomon could tell by his tone he was wondering where Lucy was.

Shouts from within the warehouse snared their attention. The Venezuelan Elite Guard was loading up, preparing to pull out with whatever goods they'd recovered from the warehouse. Canvas-covered trucks revved their motors and eased away. A dozen or so soldiers swarmed the armored cars. One of them was carrying a child in his arms. Solomon blinked in disbelief through his NVGs. That couldn't be Miguel...

But who else would it be? Jesus, Jordan would rather die than lose him again.

"Sir!" he hissed into his radio. "They have the boy. We have to stop them."

"Negative," said Gus. "No time for a firefight. The CO wants us to recon the warehouse. Our gunships will take out the convoy."

"No gunships," Solomon refuted on a raw note. "I repeat, they have Jordan's boy with them!"

"Our orders are to search the warehouse, Senior Chief," Gus repeated. "There's nothing we can do for the boy if he's not American."

Fuck the orders. Solomon had followed them to the letter once before and regretted it ever since. He edged out of his hiding place, keeping low.

In the next instant, he was on his feet, sprinting parallel to the slow-moving convoy, moving through the shadows to remain hidden. He heard Harley, who had the only clear view of him, report to Gus that he was following the convoy.

"Mako," Gus hissed. "Turn back *now*!"

Solomon pretended not to hear. He lengthened his stride, his heartbeat doubling and then tripling to meet the demand of speed. But the convoy was getting away from him. He couldn't keep up.

But he had to. How would Jordan ever return his love if he let Miguel die while in the clutches of the enemy?

He gasped for oxygen, felt the muscles in his thighs burn as he continued to pursue the trail of lights now half a mile ahead of him. Every footfall on the uneven terrain jarred his spine and tested his resilience. "No!" he roared, painfully aware of his limitations. He wouldn't be able to keep this pace up much longer, let alone overcome them.

Then, to his immense relief, brake lights flared, and the convoy slowed to a stop, right there on the open road.

Wary of having been sighted, Solomon cut away, circling around. He couldn't afford to die, either. Silas needed him to come back home. As he crept toward the truck that held Miguel, he kept an eye on the action taking place behind the last vehicle. A soldier was hoisting a missile launcher on his shoulder. Another man was helping him to arm it.

Solomon breathed a swearword. "Sir!" he whispered hoarsely into the interteam radio. "Incoming missile, sir! They've stopped to fire on the warehouse!"

"Roger that, Mako. We're inside right now looking for Lucy. Harley went after you. Harley, can you hold them off?"

"Yes, sir," Harley huffed. "I'm almost within range."

"Fire at will," Gus instructed.

* * *

"Lucy!" Gus called. The warehouse was immense and mostly empty now. There was no telling where Lucy might be, only that she had to be unconscious not to hear him and Vinny calling for her.

He'd recovered a backpack that probably belonged to Jordan. He found traces of blood in the office—Lucy's blood?—and an open window. He was stepping out of the office when her voice called out to him.

"I'm right here."

He spun around in astonishment. She stood in the shadows, and he recognized her silhouette, still as slender as she'd been in college, but more athletic. She took a step toward him, and the light from the office illumined her face. Shock strangled his vocal cords at the sight of blood streaming from her forehead, down the side of her nose. One eye was little more than a slit. And she was still the most beautiful woman he'd ever known.

"James Atwater," she exclaimed in a steady, almost serene voice. "What the hell are you doing here?"

But then she swayed ever so slightly, and he leapt forward to catch her if she fell. Of course, she didn't. She put her arms around him, however, and he could feel her heart hammering. She wasn't as unperturbed as she sounded. "We need to get out," she warned him. "The captain of the Elite Guard gave orders to blow up the building."

"Let's go," said Gus. He'd fulfilled his orders to find the missing CIA agent.

Pulling her down the stairs with him, he spoke through his interteam radio. "I found her, Vinny. Exit the building, pronto. She needs medical attention."

"I'm fine," Lucy insisted. In the next second, an explosion rang out, vibrating the hull of the warehouse. "This exit's closer," she said, tugging Gus toward a hidden door.

Sweeping his NVG's behind him, Solomon caught sight of Harley sprinting toward him. The sniper dove into a berm, elbow-crawled to the ledge, and opened fire on the enemy. *Tat-tat!* The soldier bearing the missile launcher staggered and fell. The missile misfired with a roar and slammed into the ground nearby.

Kaboom!

The explosion prompted a flurry of activity. Soldiers poured from the vehicles to defend their goods. Harley promptly mowed them down.

Solomon kept a finger on the trigger of his MP5, but he was more intent on clearing a path for himself than killing the traitors. Running in a zigzag pattern, he ran full speed into the truck that held Miguel. The officer in the truck shouted in astonishment, clutching Miguel as he cringed from the open window.

"Give me the boy," Solomon commanded, recognizing him as one of the young men he'd trained, a promising soldier. "And then I suggest you run, Santiago."

Santiago passed Miguel wordlessly through the window. It was Miguel who protested. He took one look at Solomon's painted face and screamed in terror. It was all Solomon could do to hold on to him with one arm as he pulled him clear, leapt off the sidewall, and retreated, firing to cover himself.

He probably would have been shot—both he and Miguel, if Harley's eagle eye wasn't trained on the shooters firing from inside the vehicles.

"Mako and Harley, pull back now!" said Haiku, who was apparently manning the SATCOM. "I repeat pull back. The Cobras are en route."

Over the clatter of continuous machine-gun fire, Solomon detected the gunships' approach. Following an all-out sprint, he slid, butt first, into the berm next to Harley. Miguel shrieked and struggled in his arms. He hushed him, putting his gun aside to hold him with both arms, gently but firmly. "It's almost over," he reassured him in his ear. "I'll take you to Jordan. Jordan's waiting for you." *For us,* he added mentally, hoping that was really true.

Miguel grew still at the sound of Jordan's name. The eerie, otherworldly throb of the Cobras grew louder.

Gus and Lucy burst out of the warehouse, setting off an alarm. The sound of a nearby firefight made the wail of the alarm seem negligible. By now the entire Populist Army knew where they were. He checked his watch and thumbed his mike. "Haiku, request Trident 1 to pick us up at the LZ in twenty minutes. We have two, maybe three civilians with us," he amended, just in case Solomon was able to retrieve the little boy.

"Yes, sir. Speaking of civilians, sir, this one is waking up. I needed Vinny."

"We'll be there in a sec." But then he looked up at the sky. "No, we won't. Here come the Cobras. Get down."

Solomon peered up, making out the Cobras' silhouettes—no running lights—as they coasted high overhead. Fire flashed suddenly in the muzzles of the missile launchers.

Solomon clapped his hands over Miguel's ears and rolled overtop him to protect his little body.

Just in case.

But the gunships rarely missed. With a *zing* and a *boom, boom, boom, boom,* they took out the four trucks in an instant, turning them into hunks of twisted, burning metal.

It became immediately apparent what was in the trucks. The Cobras vanished, but subsequent explosions continued to shake the earth.

At least twenty minutes passed before a deathly silence descended. Fires flickered over the charred remains of the convoy. The stench of burned flesh made Solomon cringe. He eased apologetically from Miguel and found him catatonic.

Cradling him like a baby, Solomon rose on rubbery legs. He cut Harley a grateful but grim look and struck out toward the warehouse.

When they'd sprawled to the earth, it hadn't been clear whether Gus had shielded Lucy with his body or she'd shielded him. Both lay half-over, half-under the other as the earth shook and multiple explosions lit the sky, battering their eardrums. Throughout the ruckus, he studied his college sweetheart, marveling at just how much she'd changed.

"Why didn't you answer me inside the warehouse when I called for you?" he asked during a temporary lull in the chained explosions.

"I think I blacked out for a minute," she replied.

But he sensed that she was lying. Why would she lie?

Something in Lucy's pocket was gouging his thigh. He could only assume she'd found whatever she'd come for. Good for her.

Finally, silence settled in the dusty, foul-smelling air. Gus pushed to his feet, helping Lucy up. "Echo Platoon, rally up at the Hummer," he commanded. "Let's get out of here while we still can. Do you have your car key, by any chance?" he asked Lucy.

"Not anymore, but I keep a spare under the bumper."

"Excellent," Gus murmured, relieved not to have to carry the wounded all the way back to the LZ.

"I need Dramamine," Jordan pleaded as she peered through watering eyes at the physician standing over her. She'd been whisked, half-conscious, from a helicopter, dreaming she was trapped in a wind tunnel. She could sense the exact moment she'd been wrenched from Solomon's arms and conveyed on a stretcher into this cold, sterile chamber. *Where am I?* she'd asked, as a balding man in uniform examined her.

You're aboard the USS Theodore Roosevelt. *It's an aircraft carrier.*

Immediately, the queasiness she'd fought to keep at bay got the upper hand. She couldn't exactly feel the pitch and roll of the vessel, only hear the throbbing of its engines, but just knowing she was on a ship at sea made her ill.

"I'm sorry," he apologized now. "I can't give you Dramamine."

"Why not?" she cried, battling the urge to vomit.

He hesitated. "Because you're pregnant," he said, gently.

Jordan snatched her head up, then cringed at the pain it caused. *Pregnant!* "What? But that's impossible."

"The test is ninety-nine percent accurate," he patiently replied.

A soft, fuzzy feeling tickled Jordan's insides. How could she be pregnant? Well, duh, but...It had been impossible with Doug.

"Any guess as to how far along you are?" inquired the doctor.

"A couple of weeks at most," she breathed, caught up in amazement. Oh, my God. She was pregnant with *Solomon's* baby!

"And have you ever been pregnant before?"

The question doused her in cold reality, and fear followed on the heels of joy. "Once," she admitted, closing her eyes. Nausea welled up immediately, and she spent the next few minutes emptying her stomach. "I miscarried," she admitted, hoarsely, "at sixteen weeks."

"We're going to put you on an IV drip," decided the doctor, nodding at his female assistant. "We don't want you dehydrated."

They moved out of her line of sight, opening drawers, wheeling an IV holder next to her cot.

As the needle slipped into the vein on the back of Jordan's left hand, tears swarmed her closed eyes. *Why now?* she agonized. *How?*

Memories of her lovemaking with Solomon drifted warmly through her mind. She'd never experienced passion so complete. Solomon was one of a kind. He'd blown into her life, caught her up in his energy, and swept her off to his kingdom, *Camelot,* where everything had intense and overwhelming quality to it.

What would his reaction be if she told him she was pregnant? She winced, wondering if he'd just assume that she had lied to him or that she'd intended to trap him into marriage. God forbid, though he had every right to be suspicious, given his history with Candace.

And yet the odds of carrying a baby to full term were slim, anyway. Chances were she'd lose their baby regardless of Solomon's reaction.

Oh, how could fate do this to her now? And why, when it only meant more heartache, more despair?

"I want to see Miguel," she begged, needing to be reassured that the child she had was in one piece and unharmed from their ordeal.

"In a moment," the doctor promised. "Let's get you comfortable first."

She seized his sleeve as he reached across her. "I. Want. To. See. Miguel. Now," she articulated fiercely. But then she promptly retched, thrusting him aside to lunge for the pan on the counter by her cot.

"Put the boy on the table," ordered the female physician in the adjoining examination room.

Solomon, who cradled Miguel like a baby, didn't move. "You can examine him in my arms," he insisted. He'd sworn he wouldn't relinquish the boy to anyone but Jordan. The gesture was symbolic of his repentance. He should never have separated the two in the first place.

The doctor opened her mouth to reprimand him, caught the dangerous gleam in his eyes, and thought better of it. "Fine," she acceded, stepping close to flash a light into

Miguel's vacant eyes. "Hey, little guy," she crooned, getting no response. "You doing okay?"

"He needs to see Jordan, ma'am," Solomon growled. "The sooner the better."

The officer frowned at him as she ran her fingers over Miguel's skull and beneath the blanket he was wrapped in, checking his spine and legs. "She's being evaluated at the moment, Senior Chief. I'm sure you'll be able to visit her soon."

"How soon? Until Miguel sees her and knows she's okay, he's not going to respond." The same was true for him, only, thanks to his training, he was capable of walking and talking and looking like he wasn't going irrevocably out of his mind.

The physician sighed and moved away. "The boy's in shock," she diagnosed. "You're doing the right thing keeping his feet elevated, keeping him warm. I'm giving him a mild sedative."

"No needles," Solomon growled, pulling the boy protectively closer. "—ma'am," he added at the officer's exasperated glare. "Please, all he needs is Jordan."

"I'll check with Commander Sperry," she snapped, stalking away.

As she disappeared into the adjoining room, Solomon detected the sound of Jordan retching. He leaned against the wall and closed his eyes. *Please let her be okay.*

Miguel stirred, and Solomon's eyes snapped open. They exchanged a startled look. But then Miguel filled his lungs with air and shrieked in terror, nearly flipping out of Solomon's arms.

Tightening his hold on the boy, Solomon thrust his way

into the examination room and nodded. "*Mira,*" he said to Miguel. "Look. Here's Jordan."

Miguel stilled and stared. Solomon did likewise.

Jordan was curled into a fetal position, her cheek on the edge of the mattress, her lip bruised, her face green, her eyes bloodshot. She extended a trembling hand toward them. The other was connected to an IV tube.

"Senior Chief!" scolded the female officer. The balding doctor and his assistant also glared at him.

"What's wrong with her?" Solomon demanded, even as he stepped forward, so that Jordan could put her hand on Miguel's cheek and murmur reassurances. Miguel's tense body immediately relaxed.

"She has a concussion," answered the commander, "a bruised rib, and a twisted ankle. The concussion is making her queasy," he added.

"And I'm seasick," Jordan croaked, struggling to sit up, to take Miguel from him.

"Lie back down," Solomon commanded with concern. "I'll put him next to you."

As he deposited Miguel on the bed, she drew the little boy against her, hushing him as he started to cry, this time with relief. Her own eyes flooded with tears that slid down her cheeks, unchecked.

Leaving Solomon helpless. He hooked a foot around a stool, dragged it closer, and sat down, making it clear to the others that he wasn't leaving. "We'd like to be alone," he said to them.

The commander glanced at Jordan first. "We'll give you five minutes," he agreed, waving the others out before him.

Solomon waited for the door to clang shut before he threw

an arm around both Jordan and Miguel, holding them fiercely. "Jordan?" he queried. "What can I do, sweetheart?"

To his dismay, she simply shook her head, turned her face into her pillow, and silently wept.

What the hell? She was supposed to be happy. He'd done everything in his power to ensure that she was happy. He'd taken on the Elite Guard, for God's sake, to rescue Miguel. What more could he do?

"I saved Miguel's dossier," he blurted, thinking maybe she was still worried about getting Miguel into the country. "It's in your backpack, in Vinny's locker."

She sniffed and pulled her face out of the pillow. "He told me on the chopper what you did to get Miguel. Oh, Solomon. How am I ever going to thank you for that?"

Marry me. He caught back his proposal in the nick of time. For a man who'd lost his faith in love before meeting Jordan, maybe he was moving a little too quickly.

"You don't owe me anything," he refuted, brushing back the hair that was stuck to her damp cheeks. He frowned at the cut on her lower lip and the bruise on her cheekbone. "What did those assholes do to you?" he wanted to know.

That made her face crumple and more tears brim.

"Oh, Jesus, Jordan." The blood drained from his face as the worst possible scenario formed in his head.

"No." She fluttered a hand and vehemently shook her head. "No, Solomon, they didn't rape me."

"You're sure." That would explain her emotion, her tears.

"Positive."

He believed her. Still, recalling the danger she'd put herself in, he scolded her with belated rage, "God damn it, Jordan! You could have died by going back. Miguel could've died. You're goddamn lucky this turned out as well as it did!"

"I'm sorry," she cried, reaching for him, pressing her damp face into his shoulder. "I'm sorry I left you without telling you first. I hated not being honest with you—"

He hushed her, cutting her apology short, loving the feel of her head on his shoulder. "Stop. You don't owe me an apology. I should have let Miguel come home with you last time, or at least found a way to bring him back earlier. It's my fault."

His apology made her cry harder.

She was exhausted and shell-shocked, Solomon decided, wanting desperately to cheer her. "Look, sweetheart," he cajoled, speaking in a gentle voice that would have raised the eyebrows of teammates, "you're scaring Miguel. He needs you to be strong for him. See?"

Miguel leaned against her, his dark eyes reflecting confusion as he looked back and forth between them. Jordan lifted her head with a sniff and a forced smile. "I'm okay, Miguelito. *Estoy bién.* I'm just so happy that you're here with me, and that Solomon is here with us." Her eyes immediately overflowed, belying her words, making Solomon extremely uneasy.

"We'll talk more after you rest, Jordan," he decided, unable to witness her distress any longer.

"Don't leave!" she implored, clinging to his wrist. "I still can't believe I'm alive, and you're alive, and Miguel is safe with us. Please stay."

"You're exhausted," he insisted, hoping rest would put a happier expression on her face. He couldn't stand to see her like this. "And I haven't slept in forty-eight hours," he added, knowing she would put his needs above her own. A knock sounded at the door.

That was Solomon's cue to leave. He stood up, leaned over, and kissed Jordan's clammy cheek. "It's going to be okay, love," he whispered, amazed to hear that four-letter word slip off his tongue so easily. "Soon we'll be back at home. Silas will be so happy to see you. Everything will be exactly the way it was before."

She nodded, but for some reason, she was crying again, crying like her heart was breaking.

Chapter Eighteen

✦

Jillian wiped the back of her hand across her moist fore-head, then heaved the saddle off the horse's back and turned toward the table with it. A rending sensation in her lower abdomen made her gasp and hesitate. Tenderness transformed into a sharp, unaccustomed pain, and she dropped the saddle, clutching her abdomen and doubling over as the pain became intense.

She waited for it to ease, panting with shallow breaths. She'd had two babies before. This pain was not familiar.

She shuffled slowly toward the office, thinking that perhaps she could just sit and rest and she'd be fine. Rafael had been right to caution her. She was working too hard, considering the baby was due in four weeks.

She never made it to the office. Rending agony brought her to her knees. She stared at the dust motes rising out of the straw to sparkle in the late-afternoon sunbeams. The pungent scent of hay and horse manure filled her nostrils as she dragged in a breath and called feebly for help. "Graham!"

Of course, he was probably on his computer, wearing headphones, and he couldn't even hear her. "Agatha!"

Warm moisture crept down her thighs. Her water must have broken. Glancing down, she was horrified to see the crotch of her shorts turning scarlet. It was blood. She was bleeding.

Trained as an ER nurse, she guessed immediately what was wrong. *Abruptio placentae*. The placenta had detached itself from the wall of her uterus. As a result, her baby would be deprived of oxygen. She, herself, could bleed to death.

"Oh, no." She had to get help—now. She tried to get up, but the pain was too intense, and movement brought blood gushing out of her. "Help!" she cried, dragging herself toward the barn's open doors. "Graham! Agatha! Someone help me!"

She was about to pull herself twenty more feet into the office when Graham thumped out of the house. "Mom? Are you calling me?"

"Help me!" she cried, fighting to subdue the panic that coiled around her throat. "Hurry!"

In the next instant, his shadow fell over her. "Mom!" he cried, his voice breaking.

"Call 9-1-1 from the office phone. Hurry. I need an ambulance."

"Oh, shit," he breathed, his voice an octave higher. "There's blood!"

Too much blood, thought Jillian, keeping that fear to herself. The baby was her biggest concern.

Twenty minutes later, Graham stood in the driveway clutching his little sister as they watched the ambulance tear away, red lights flashing. The sudden quiet was almost eerie. He could feel Agatha's wet face through the fabric of his T-shirt. "Is Mama going to die?" she whispered.

The words sent a tremor of denial through him. "No!" God wouldn't be that hateful. Or would He? Graham hadn't exactly been a model son lately. He'd known his mom was working too hard, and he hadn't lifted a finger to help, preferring to nurse his grief and sulk over his mother's burgeoning romance with another man.

None of that seemed to matter now, not with his mother's ashen face so fresh in his memory.

Maybe she would die. The paramedics had rushed her gurney into the ambulance, shouting, "She's hemorrhaging. Call ahead for a blood infusion and an ultrasound!"

"What about my children?" Graham had heard her cry, as they went to close the doors.

"They can't ride in the ambulance, ma'am. It's against regs. Have their father bring them."

"My father's dead!" Graham had snarled up at them.

"I'm sorry, kid. Call a neighbor or something."

"Call Rafael, Graham," Jillian had suggested just before the doors clanged shut, leaving brother and sister by themselves.

They'd been alone before. But never like this.

Graham trembled. He would call Cameron's mom. Maybe she could take them to the hospital.

"Come on inside, Agatha," he murmured, keeping an arm around her as he urged her into their quiet home.

He left her on the couch to call Cameron's, but no one answered the phone there. Aunt Jordan was in Venezuela. Who else could he call?

Hearing Agatha's sniffles, he went to soothe her, to

think. The same thing had happened the night their father had died. He remembered comforting Agatha, feeling dazed and confused, wondering how everything could have changed in an instant.

What if he never saw his mother alive again?

Fear propelled him off the couch and back into the kitchen. He dialed the number off the business card pegged to the cork board.

"Jillian," answered the agent with warmth in his raspy voice.

Graham clasped the phone tighter. "No," he said. "This is Graham. My mother said to call you."

Hesitation. "What's wrong, Graham?"

Graham was embarrassed to hear his voice break. "An ambulance came and took Mom away," he choked out. "They said she was hem—hemorrhaging," he added, recalling the word. "But they wouldn't let us go with her."

The agent whispered something that sounded like a foreign curseword. "I'll be right there," he said, hanging up.

Lucy prowled the aircraft carrier till she found a satellite connection in a small cubicle off the mess hall. She placed a call to Headquarters informing them of her whereabouts and braced herself for a verbal reprimand.

"We know," said Gordon Banks, her immediate supervisor.

"You know?" Lucy repeated, surprised. "What, did you slip a microchip into me at some point?"

"No, no. The SEAL we sent in to retrieve you is one of ours."

A finger of awareness raked Lucy's spine. "Which

one," she asked, though intuition had already supplied an answer.

"Lieutenant Atwater."

So, James Augustus Atwater wasn't just a SEAL—a fact that was astonishing in itself. He'd also been trained by the CIA, just like her.

"We're glad you're okay, Lucy. We want to see you just as soon as you can come in," Gordon instructed.

"Of course." She would be debriefed, chastised for ignoring orders. Hopefully the information she'd downloaded in the warehouse—proof that the Shia Liberation Party had funneled weapons to the Populists—would do more than salvage her career. It might even see her promoted.

Solomon stirred and stretched and rammed his elbow into the steel wall that hemmed in one side of his bunk. He kicked off the standard-issue wool blanket and swung out of his bed, careful not to smack his head on the low overhead.

Jordan! The fact that she was here, on this carrier, safe and sound in the company of Miguel, was so deeply satisfying that he'd shed tears of joy into his pillow when he'd collapsed into his bunk last night. Her emotional state, on the other hand, had prompted disturbing dreams.

He jammed his feet into the boots beside his bed and clomped into the bathroom that adjoined the chief's berthing area, wanting to get to her as quickly as possible.

His bedraggled reflection prompted him to shave, shower, and brush his teeth. With a torn bit of toilet paper fluttering on the end of his chin, he grabbed a fresh jacket and hurried to sick bay.

The balding commander started guiltily as Solomon stepped through the portal. "Senior Chief," he greeted him, with little enthusiasm.

"How's she doing, sir?" Solomon asked, crossing to Jordan's open door. He drew up short to find the room empty and clean, the bed remade. "Where is she?" he demanded, whirling. "Where's Miguel?"

"The, uh, the embassy workers were all transported back to the States via chopper. Miss Bliss and the boy went with them."

Solomon's blood pressure soared. "And no one thought to inform me of this?" he growled, incredulous.

"She asked that you be left alone, to...to rest," the doctor stammered.

"And what about the boy's adoption papers?" he inquired, through his teeth.

"Your corpsman got them out of his locker for her."

Solomon had to glance down at the man's insignia to remind himself that Commander Sperry was a high-ranking officer. It wouldn't behoove his career to rearrange his face. He turned and stalked out of the room, not bothering with a parting salute.

Special Agent Valentino's Lexus had leather seats and an excellent sound system. Too bad the music coming out of it was stuff that only old people listened to. It gave Graham goose bumps. He drove really fast, though, ninety miles an hour, which would have been really cool under different circumstances.

Graham had told him exactly what had happened, what the paramedics had said about a blood infusion. The agent's swarthy skin looked kind of yellow in the late-afternoon sunlight. Tiny beads of sweat shone on his temple by his hairline.

And Graham realized, with mixed guilt and fright, that the agent was just as scared as he and Agatha were.

"We're here to see Jillian Sanders," said Rafe to the hospital receptionist. "She was brought by ambulance half an hour ago."

The woman conferred with her computer and informed them that Jillian was up in Labor and Delivery. She called upstairs. "I'm sending up Jillian Sanders's family," she relayed.

Rafe glanced at Graham, expecting the boy to correct the woman's assumptions, but Graham kept his mouth shut.

No sooner did they step out of the elevator than they were greeted by a stocky, grim-faced nurse who bustled them into L&D. "You can come on back, Mr. Sanders. Your wife's undergoing an emergency C-section, so the children will have to remain out here. We have a television and games for them."

Again, Rafe met Graham's gray eyes. "Is she going to be okay?" asked the teen, still holding his sister's hand.

"Her condition is critical," retorted the nurse, with the barest suggestion of empathy.

Graham grabbed Rafe's sleeve. "Don't let her die," he commanded, his eyes bright with tears he held in check.

"No," said Rafe, stricken by a terribly familiar sense of helplessness. He wanted to hug both children and offer reassurances, but the nurse was hustling him through a secure doorway and down a sterile hall.

"I want you to wash from your hands to your elbows,"

she directed, admitting him into a cubicle with a sink, "and put on these scrubs. Then step through that door, there."

His stomach was twisted into knots by the time he edged through the other door, wearing a blue cap and matching paper outfit, even booties. His gaze flew to the figure draped in cloth and lying under glaring lights. Jillian's long blond hair had been stuffed under a cap like his, with one long tendril escaping.

Rafe approached her, averting his gaze from the great quantity of paper sheet around her lower half. He didn't know what to expect or whether he was even welcome. She appeared to be sleeping. But when the doctor called out a greeting, "Mr. Sanders, come on in. Pull up a stool," Jillian's eyes snapped open and she turned her head, her startled look turning into a smile of wan relief.

"Rafael," she breathed, lifting a hand to him.

He sank onto the stool, relieved that the partition blocked his view of the incision they were carving into her belly. But Jillian's face, so devoid of color, struck fear deep into his heart. He kissed her knuckles, battling the sudden urge to weep.

"Did you bring the children?"

"Yes."

"I'm surprised they let you—"

"Shhh," he whispered, lowering his mouth to her ear. "They'll make me leave. Unless that's what you want."

She shook her head, then closed her eyes, dragging in a deep breath. "It's so hard to breathe."

"Baby's almost out," announced the doctor, glancing up at the monitors. He sent a pointed look at the nurse. "Her BP's low. We need to move faster."

Despite his matter-of-fact tone, Rafe caught the message: Jillian's blood pressure was dropping.

"Here we go. And it's a baby girl," announced the doctor. He pulled a pink, wet ball out of Jillian's midsection and presented it briefly to Rafe and Jillian. The tiny wrinkled face inspired amazement.

"Did you see her?" Rafe exclaimed, as they whisked the baby aside to examine her.

"She's not crying," Jillian observed on a faint but worried note. "Why isn't she crying?"

Not a soul answered. Rafe looked over at the crew working on the baby.

"Oh, God," Jillian moaned. Tears seeped from the corners of her eyes. The machine monitoring her vitals gave a sudden, ominous chirp. "It's my fault."

The doctor glanced over at it, then went back to work. "We need to cauterize this. She's bleeding too much." He tried to be discreet in speaking to his assistant, but Rafe heard the words clearly. Chilled to the marrow, he looked at Jillian to see whether she'd also heard, but she appeared to have fainted.

"Jillian!" he cried, patting her cheek, lightly. Nothing. "She's unconscious, Doctor," he announced.

"That's not unusual, Mr. Sanders. She's lost a lot of blood," the doctor answered. His movements remained confidently urgent, his manner brusque.

The sights, the smells, ignited deeply buried images, sending a tremor through Rafe. Memories of a similar nightmare flashed through his mind. His wife had lain like this, blood draining steadily out of her, only she'd been shot in the gut by mobsters. His baby, Emanuel, was still in her arms, shot in the head. Tito and Serena lay on the couch, with Tito on top, their blood intermingling.

"Please!" he rasped, startling both himself and the doctor. "Don't let her die!"

"Easy, Mr. Sanders," soothed the doctor. "We're gaining the upper hand."

But Rafe hadn't really been talking to him. Folding Jillian's cold hand between his own, he bowed over the fragile bond between them and prayed as he'd never prayed before. He prayed to a God who he believed had stopped hearing his prayers long ago. He prayed until everything and everyone in the room faded away, until reality was just his fervent prayers of whispered desperation over their clasped hands.

It was the baby's loud cry that brought Rafael's head up. The sound of it, so hearty and healthy, gave him something he'd lost long ago—hope.

"How's she doing?" he asked, taking comfort from Jillian's steady breathing.

"The bleeding has slowed, Mr. Sanders," the doctor replied. "Your wife's going to be just fine."

Rafe wilted with relief, tears spiking his lower lashes. *My wife,* he thought, amazed that the title felt so right, so natural. It was as if God had planned for this woman to be in his life all along.

Her lashes fluttered. "Wake up, beautiful," he whispered, tucking the escaped tendril of hair behind her ear.

The jowly nurse who'd originally greeted him now beamed with accomplishment. "There's a little girl who wants to see you," she crooned, depositing the swaddled baby in Rafe's arms. "You hold her, Dad. Mom's still a little shaky."

He took the baby, terrified by how small she was. "*Dio mio,*" he breathed. Gray-blue eyes peered out of an itty-bitty round face. Downy, golden hair topped her head. "She's an angel," he murmured in utter amazement. None of his brood had ever been so tiny.

"An angel," Jillian repeated. "Maybe that's her name." They met each other's eyes and smiled in mutual agreement.

Rafe's eyes watered with tears of joy. "Yes," he whispered. Perhaps God had shown him favor, after all.

"Angel Grace Sanders," Jordan marveled, gazing down at the baby in her left arm, "you are one lucky baby." Having heard her story of survival, it seemed a miracle to find Jillian and her baby both doing so well.

"Well, enough about us, Jordan. Tell me all about your trip and the adoption process. Is everything official?"

"Almost," said Jordan, glancing at Miguel, who sat on her right knee, staring at the baby. "I couldn't get Miguel's dossier signed by Immigration in Venezuela, but my lawyer's working on a waiver."

"Has he spoken yet?" Jillian asked, fixing Miguel with a look of concern.

"No, not yet," Jordan admitted. She watched with amazement as he bent forward and placed a gentle kiss on the baby's cheek. "Good boy! Did you see that, Jillie? That's the first voluntary act he's made since our return!"

"Maybe he likes babies," her sister suggested.

"Agatha has been trying to get him to play with her baby dolls," Jordan admitted.

"I'm so glad you came home," Jillian exclaimed with feeling. "I had nightmares—" She waved a hand, signifying they were too horrific to put into words. "And I can tell just by looking at you that it was every bit as bad as I thought it was."

Emotion clogged Jordan's throat.

"What happened?" Jillian pressed.

With her gaze on Miguel's profile, Jordan recapped her harrowing adventure, finishing it off with Solomon's heroic rescue of Miguel.

Jillian gaped in disbelief. "He's in love with you," she decided. "Either that or he's crazy."

Jordan's stomach clenched. "Not in love," she replied, recalling Solomon's fervent assertion that love was an illusion. True, he was generous with his endearments. He'd called her sweetheart more than once, but she was certain he'd assume the worst if he learned that she was pregnant. "He's just a man with a powerful conscience and a good heart," she added, forcing those words through an aching throat.

"But you love *him*," Jillian guessed, pushing herself higher on her pillows, her gaze astute.

Jordan drew a painful breath and kept her gaze averted.

"Oh, my God, you do. Jordan, I'm so happy for you! Is he back yet?" Jillian persisted. "Have you talked to him?"

"No and no," Jordan answered on a dampening note.

But he'd called her, every day for the past week, from locations he couldn't disclose, demanding to know why she'd jumped ship. Was she okay? Why wasn't she answering her cell phone? The worry in his voice was giving her a guilt complex.

Jillian's pleasure dimmed as she contemplated her. "Honey, what's wrong? Please tell me you're not running from this guy because you think you'll get hurt again. I've told you, not all men are like Doug."

Jordan sighed. "Look, I didn't come here to talk about my love life. I came to visit you and the baby and see how you're doing."

"I'm doing great, considering. It's you I'm worried about," Jillian insisted.

"Don't," said Jordan, managing a smile. "I'll be fine." Once she figured out what to tell Solomon, how to keep him from thinking she'd intended to trap him all along. Then there was preparing her heart for the inevitable heartbreak of losing the tiny life in her womb.

"Well," Jillian conceded, "I'm glad you're home, little sister. And thank you for watching Graham and Agatha while I'm stuck in the hospital. It didn't feel right to put that off on Rafe."

"My pleasure," Jordan reassured her. The fact was she had nowhere else to go with her condo rented out. Nor could she return to Solomon's houseboat the way things stood between them. "I'm going to take Miguel to see Silas while Graham and Agatha are still at grief camp," she announced, glancing at the clock on the wall. "I'd better get going," she added, putting Miguel on his feet to hand back the baby. "She's just precious," she added, placing the tiny bundle in Jillian's arms. What were the odds that the fetus in her womb would also defy the odds?

Jillian regarded her closely. "Jordan, you know you can talk to me anytime," she offered perceptively.

"I know." It was all Jordan could do not to spill her secret, but she'd put Jillian through enough worry as it was. "Come on, Miguelito," she called, holding her hand out. "Let's go play with Silas."

Play was perhaps too strong a word. Miguel's virtual unresponsiveness had Jordan scrambling to find him the best children's psychologist, one who specialized in trauma. Seeing him kiss the baby was the most promising sign yet.

As they crossed the baking-hot parking lot, Jordan turned her cell phone back on, hoping that the psychologist—the one she really wanted for Miguel—had called back to say there was a cancellation. The phone chimed to indicate that she had voice mail. With it tucked under one ear, she unlocked the door and let the hot air out.

"Jordan," said Solomon on a peremptory note. "I'm pulling into port today. Stop avoiding my calls and call me back. I want to talk to you." Impatience had clearly gotten the better of him.

With a firming of her mouth, Jordan deleted the message and dropped the phone in her purse. "You're forgetting your manners, Solomon," she muttered.

If she called him back, he would demand to know why she was avoiding him. He would hound her until she blurted the truth. And then what? She'd either have to listen to him accuse her of lying to him, or he would do the noble thing and ask her to marry him. Either outcome would bring its share of heartache. She wanted him to marry her because he loved her, not out of some obligation to their unborn child, a child that—most likely—would never survive.

Leaning into the car, she buckled Miguel into his booster seat. "At least I've got you," she whispered, kissing his cheek. She just wished she could have *everything* her heart desired and needed to be truly happy.

Chapter Nineteen

✦

Solomon hurled his duffel bag into Sean Harlan's truck bed, got in the passenger side, and slammed the door.

"What the hell put a burr up your ass?" Sean demanded from behind the wheel.

Solomon cranked the window down, but it was almost as hot outside as it was in the cab. He was also steaming mad. "The woman won't return my calls," he growled. He'd left dozens of call back numbers, and she hadn't bothered dialing a single one of them. "Something's going on with her, and I don't know what the hell it is."

"Have you told her you love her yet?" Sean drawled, flicking him a wry look as he turned the key. The engine gave a throaty roar.

Solomon glowered at him. "She knows I love her," he retorted. "I took on a battalion of the Elite Guard to get the kid back, didn't I?"

With a shake of his bald head, Sean drove them away from the terminal at NAS Oceana. They were finally home, after a week at sea, training with regular Navy personnel aboard the carrier *Teddy Roosevelt*. "You don't know much about women, do you?" he lamented.

Solomon opened his mouth to deliver a caustic retort. But his assertion that women were all grasping, ambitious creatures like Candace didn't apply at all to Jordan, who was loyal, passionate, and generous to a fault. She was also ridiculously stubborn for holding out on him. "Oh, and you do?" was the only comeback he could summon.

Sean's response was a low, satisfied chuckle. "Yes, I do."

"So, that's the answer, is it, Romeo?" Solomon mocked sarcastically. "I just tell her that I love her."

"It's that simple," Sean said with a nod. "You do that, and the dominos will all fall into place."

Solomon sent him a suddenly suspicious frown. "You'd better not play that game with Ellie Stuart," he warned.

"Her?" Sean looked incredulous. "Hell no. You know I don't date women with kids."

"She's been through hell as it is," Solomon added, recalling Ellie's spare trailer home with a shudder.

"Enough said," Sean retorted with a stern look that made Solomon close his mouth abruptly.

He turned his head to glower out the window. How would Jordan respond to a declaration of love? he wondered. And was that really all she needed to hear? His heart tripped over itself in its haste to find out. "Can't you drive this piece of shit any faster?" he snapped at Harley. "I haven't seen Silas in over a week," he added, disguising his real reason for wanting to get home.

Sean gunned the accelerator, flinging his passenger against the seat. "Be honest with yourself, Mako," he shouted over the wind rushing through the window, "you haven't been laid in over a week."

Graham's job was to muck the barn in advance of his mother's homecoming. He finished well before noon, left his boots in the mudroom and went to gauge the progress in the nursery. Aunt Jordan was painting the trim white, to offset the peach-colored walls. Rafe was putting together the crib for the baby. He looked up as Graham sidled into the doorway.

"I'm done," Graham announced.

Rafe glanced at his watch. "Would you like to come to the hospital with me to pick them up?"

"Is there something else I can do?" Graham asked, unwilling to afflict his ears with opera music.

Aunt Jordan looked up from the baseboard. "You can babysit Agatha and Miguel," she suggested with an innocent smile. He could hear Agatha in her bedroom, dressing Miguel up in her play clothes.

Graham grimaced. "I'll go with you," he said to Rafe, braced for aural torture.

"Pick a station," Rafe offered, as they cruised down the driveway en route to the hospital several minutes later.

"You mean, like, my kind of music?"

"Show me what you like," confirmed the agent with a nod.

Graham tuned into a light rock station, avoiding the heavy metal that he sometimes listened to. He settled back into his seat, aware of a certain tension in the car as the Lexus flew along the country road.

"Do you think she'll notice the front porch?" Rafe inquired. He struck Graham as nervous.

"Maybe not right away," Graham decided. They'd fixed the listing porch together yesterday, jacking it up with cinder blocks and trimming the foundation with latticework. "But she will eventually."

The tension was barely alleviated by the thrum of a guitar and the hum of tires.

Rafe spoke up again. "I wanted to show you something," he said, drawing his wallet from his back pocket. He flipped it open, revealing photographs inside, and handed the wallet to Graham.

"That's my oldest son, Tito," he said, in a voice that roughened perceptibly. "He was your age when he died."

Graham looked into the dark, intelligent eyes in the photograph and felt pressure on his chest. His mother had mentioned that Rafe's children were all killed by the goons of the notorious mob boss, Tarantello. Graham hadn't quite believed her.

"The next picture is Serena, my daughter. She was eight."

Serena's mischievous smile reminded Graham of Agatha.

"And that's Emanuel."

The curly-haired tot looked like one of those babies that made you smile. "Mom said that they were all shot," he ventured, with a quick glance.

"They were," Rafe confirmed, gravely. "By men who worked for the mafia."

Graham didn't know what to say to that. It was too awful to conceive.

"I thought that God had turned his back on me," Rafe finally added, his voice more gravelly than ever.

Graham stared down at the pictures and drew a hidden breath. That was how he felt sometimes.

"I know what it's like to lose the ones you love, like someone punched a hole in your heart. I wished, so many times, that I had died with them."

Tears stung Graham's eyes, blurring the photographs.

"I could never take your father's place, Graham," the agent added, gently. "I wouldn't even want to try. But you and I have something in common. We both love your mother very much."

Graham looked up, blinking furiously. Suddenly he knew where this was going, and he wasn't ready for it.

"You've been part of your mother's life for fourteen years," Rafe added. "That's much longer than I have known her. That's why I want this to be your decision. If you don't think you can share her right now, then I will wait until you're eighteen. But if there's room for the two of us, I'd like to marry her now, to help her with the ranch, to help her with Agatha and the baby. And to be a friend to you, if you would allow me to."

Graham closed the wallet and handed it back. Turning his head, he gazed out the window at the dark green trees filtering the August sun. As a fellow cop, his father would have thought that Rafe was a hero for what he'd done. He wasn't such a bad guy, really. They'd shared a couple laughs jacking up the front porch yesterday.

But all he had to do was picture his mother's face lighting up when Rafe stepped into her hospital room, and he knew, with dwindling resentment, that they—her children—weren't enough. She deserved the love and support of a husband, a partner in life. Agatha and Angel needed a father. And Graham supposed he could always use a friend.

He sent Rafe a sidelong, considering look.

"It's up to you," Rafe repeated.

"Would you teach me some Italian cursewords?" Graham asked, looking for personal profit.

Rafe pursed his lips, considering. "Fair enough," he conceded. "Just don't say them around your mother."

"Okay, then," said Graham. "You can marry her."

A smile of relief transformed the agent's face, making him look ten years younger. "Thank you." He stuck out a hand for Graham to shake.

"It's like this," Graham said, showing him how the cool kids shook hands.

"Ah," said Rafe, practicing. "Do you want to see the ring?" he asked, confirming Graham's guess that he was nervous. He opened a compartment on his dashboard and handed him a velvet box.

"Whoa," breathed Graham, cracking it open. "What are the green stones on the sides?"

"Peridots, the baby's birthstone."

"That's cool." It struck him that Rafe would be the only father baby Angel ever knew. And yet, his father had planted the seed. So he was still part of the whole. How weird was that?

He supposed he'd get used to it. Like they'd assured him at grief camp, it took time for changes to feel familiar. At least he didn't feel like God had abandoned them completely. There was hope for healing.

*   *   *

Silas sat on his knees on Ellie's couch, gazing out the window as Caleb played beside him with a Matchbox car. He drove it up Silas's elbow, over his shoulders, and down his other arm, stepping over Silas in the process. "You're in the way," he pointed out.

Silas wasn't moving till his daddy got home. Aunt Ellie said she thought he'd be back today.

Sure was taking him a long time to get here. This morning they'd been to the beach. They'd had ravioli for lunch, and Silas had eaten so much that his stomach bulged, but he still felt empty inside from waiting so long. It was fun playing with his cousins, but he was ready to go home now.

Home, he thought, musing over the word. *I live on a houseboat with my daddy. He can hold his breath under the water forever. I'm gonna do that, too, when I'm bigger.*

He couldn't wait to go home. He hoped Jordan would be there. Aunt Ellie said she didn't know if Jordan would be. Who would watch him if she wasn't? He liked Jordan. Her hair smelled like strawberries. He even liked it when she hugged him close and said, *Great job!* though he pretended not to.

A car swung into the driveway, and Silas jerked his chin off of the windowsill. But it wasn't Daddy.

The glare on the windshield kept the driver hidden till the car door opened and Jordan got out. Silas's heart jumped up, and he sprang off the couch and ran for the door. "Aun' Ellie!" he shouted. "Jordan's here."

He struggled with the lock on the door till Ellie got there and helped him. "Easy, Silas," she warned.

He dove out the door and ran into Jordan, throwing

his arms around her waist. A shoe bumped him in the head, and he looked up, realizing she had a little boy in her arms.

"You found Miguel," Ellie exclaimed, sounding surprised and pleased.

"Sure did. Hi, Silas." Jordan smiled down at him, her pretty eyes crinkling at the corners. She pulled him against her and squeezed him hard. "I've missed you, big guy! How's it going?"

"Okay." Silas was assessing Miguel. He didn't look at all like he'd pictured. "He's sure small," he volunteered.

"Come on in," urged Ellie. "It's hot as blazes out there."

Jordan steered Silas back inside. In the living room, she went down on her knees, putting Miguel on his feet. The boy hung on tightly to her neck and wouldn't let go.

"Everyone, this is Miguel," Jordan announced, letting him cling.

Christopher wandered up, and Caleb stopped driving his car long enough to stare hard at the stranger. Colton started belly-crawling toward them.

Silas looked into Miguel's dark eyes and wondered why he looked so afraid. He dropped to the floor to see his face better. "You're sure small," he said again.

"He's only four," said Jordan.

Silas looked him over. Small and skinny. "Can he talk?" he asked.

"He'll talk when he's ready," Jordan reassured him, reaching out to stroke the top of his head like she sometimes did, her eyes growing wet.

"Don't cry," Silas said in alarm.

"I'm just happy," she replied, with a smile that warmed his insides.

Colton had dragged himself across the room on his elbows, drawing Miguel's interest as he groped for the little boy's shoelaces and tugged them toward his mouth.

"Silly baby," Jordan said.

Miguel reached over and softly touched Colton's yellow hair.

"He likes babies, huh?" Silas deduced.

"And big kids, too," Jordan reassured him.

"How 'bout cars," said Silas, pulling a shiny red hot rod out of his shorts pocket. Miguel regarded it with interest but didn't try to take it.

"I hope he likes books," said Silas, remembering that he had news to share. "Hey, I can read now!"

Jordan gasped her amazement. "You can?"

"Yep. Wanna see?"

"Of course, I do. Let's sit down, Miguel. Silas is going to read to us."

Happy as he'd ever been, Silas bounded to the attached playroom and pulled his favorite book from the bookshelf.

With Silas seated snugly against her, stammering his way through *Where the Wild Things Are,* and Miguel in her lap watching him covertly, Jordan experienced contentment and relief, at last.

Silas was happy, and Miguel was going to be okay, she told herself. Recovery was a process, made possible with the help of the best child's psychologist in the area.

As for her pregnancy and her relationship with Solomon, she'd just take life one day at a time and see what happened. But she wasn't holding out for a miracle.

The rumble of an engine caused Caleb to leap onto the couch to look out the window. "Mr. Sean's here!" he announced, excitedly.

"Oh, Lord," Jordan heard Ellie exclaim from the bathroom she was painting. She appeared at the door pulling a paint-speckled bandana off her head. "I swear, that man has got the worst timing." She opened the door and flicked Jordan a look of concern. "Silas, your papa's here, too," she announced.

"Daddy!" Silas exclaimed, dropping the book to race for the door.

Jordan's mouth went dry. Her heart started to gallop, her palms turned moist. *Here goes,* she thought, braced for anything.

She came to her feet, drawing Miguel up with her. Something told her that Solomon wasn't going to wait to settle this quietly, later. The sound of his voice as he greeted his son, giving Silas all the love that he deserved, made her insides jitter.

Sean Harlan was the first to step inside. "Caught you workin' again," he observed, giving Ellie a quick once-over as he wiped his feet on the doormat.

"Just paintin' the bathroom," she muttered, edging behind the door.

"Ma'am, how are you?" Sean added, sending Jordan what was clearly a sympathetic grimace as he headed toward the boys. "Hey, fellas," he exclaimed, as they jumped up and down and shouted his name. With a bear-like growl, he tackled both Christopher and Caleb and bore them to the rug.

A shadow appeared at the doorway, and there was Solomon, holding Silas on one arm, still wearing his battle dress uniform. He directed what was meant to be a pleasant smile at Miguel, who gripped Jordan harder. "We need to talk," he said, skewering her with his silvery eyes. He put Silas on his feet and whispered something in his ear. With a grin, the boy shot across the room to join the ongoing melee.

Jordan drank in every feature of Solomon's suntanned face. How she'd missed him! "I'm watching the boys," she demurred. She wasn't ready for this.

Sean Harlan lay flat on the floor, dangling the baby and making him squeal. "Don't drool on me," he pleaded.

"Harley will watch them," Solomon insisted. "Why don't you step outside with me?"

Jordan swallowed hard. "Miguel won't let me go." But, to her surprise, Miguel squirmed out of her arms to lie down next to Silas, who wanted to see the baby from Sean's perspective. The SEAL roared with mock horror as a string of drool started its descent.

Solomon stalked into the house, grabbed Jordan's hand, and pulled her inexorably outside. He led her across the grass, into the shade of a big oak tree, where it wasn't so hot.

She tried to jerk free. "Solomon, you can't order me around like some—" He swung her around, put her back against the wide trunk, caught her chin, and kissed her hard, cutting her off midsentence.

Jordan braced herself. The magic, the animal instinct to mate, whatever horrible phrase he'd once called it, was as potent as ever. Desire spiraled through her, drugging and confusing her, till she was clutching him rather than pushing him away.

"Jordan," Solomon rasped, against her lips. "I have something to tell you."

"What?" she asked, realizing that for better or for worse, this man owned her heart. There was no pretending otherwise.

"I was wrong," he said, startling her by admitting something so unexpected. "What I feel for you isn't biology, although there's no denying that component," he added, with a brief, lascivious grin that gave way to earnestness. "I love you," he declared. "Not blindly. Not the way I thought I loved Candace. But as a man who can see just how beautiful and special you are, how much knowing you has enriched my life and Silas's." His voice grew husky and a sheen of tears made his eyes seem translucent.

Jordan reeled. She opened her mouth to speak, couldn't figure out where to start, and closed it again.

Solomon's ruddy countenance slowly paled. "You're not saying anything," he noted hoarsely.

"Solomon," she murmured thickly, "God knows I love you, too. But it's not that simple."

He scowled at her response. "What's not simple about it?"

Could she tell him? She dreaded the effect it would have, terrified that it would somehow cause him to rescind his unexpected declaration.

"I'm pregnant," she whispered, dropping her news like a bomb. There just wasn't any other way to do it.

It was his turn to be speechless. "But you said—"

"I know what I said," she cut him off. "And I thought

it was true. I wasn't out to trap you or anything like that, though I'm sure that's the first thought to cross your mind—"

He seized her shoulders. "Don't even say that," he retorted, giving her a gentle shake. "Don't even put yourself in the same category as Candace. Jordan," he added in amazement, lifting his hands to gently cup her face. "When did you find out?"

"On board the aircraft carrier when they took my blood."

His expression shifted from astonished to comprehending. "No wonder you were so emotional," he realized out loud. "I thought it was something else, something awful."

To her immense relief, he pulled her into his arms and held her, rocking her gently back and forth. He wasn't hurling accusations. Wasn't taking back his words of love.

"What do we have to do to keep this baby?" he asked in her ear.

She gave a watery laugh. How typically Solomon—as if pure determination would keep their baby alive. "I'll know more after I see a doctor," she told him. "It's still early. But I can't stay in bed the whole time. I have a child to care for—"

"Two children," he corrected her. "Silas needs you, too."

She leaned into him, her heart pounding with anticipation.

"Right?" he prompted.

"Right," she agreed.

"So you'll marry me," he growled with confidence.

Jordan snatched her head off his chest and glared at him. "Solomon," she warned.

"Okay, okay." Heaving a sigh, he sank down on one knee and gently clasped her hand. "Jordan," he said, stopping and clearing his throat. He pressed her knuckles to his lips to give himself more time. "Would you please take mercy on my pathetic, lonely soul and make me the happiest man alive?"

Touched by his earnest vulnerability and enjoying his groveling, Jordan took her time answering. "Well," she equivocated, "I suppose." Bending over, she kissed him with all the tenderness and relief overflowing her heart. How she loved everything about him, from the tickle of his moustache to the tremor in his touch as he cradled her head and kissed and kissed and kissed her! "But only on one condition," she added, belatedly.

He looked suddenly concerned. "What?"

"We get a real house, so I don't have to worry about our children drowning."

He shot to his feet, confident again. "I'll build you a great big house," he swore. "At this rate, we're going to need it," he added optimistically.

Giddy with happiness, Jordan threw herself into his arms and wrapped her legs around him. "I love you!" she declared.

"Careful," he warned.

"That won't hurt the baby."

"Oh, I'm not thinking about the baby," he countered, backing her against the tree. "I'm thinking about making love to you, right here, right now."

"Mmmm," she agreed, losing herself in the desire that warmed his eyes to quicksilver. "Let's go home, then."

He dropped her like a hot potato, pulling her behind him as he strode to the door. "Silas, Miguel, we're going home."

They had to wait, though, because the children were taking turns riding Sean Harlan's back. The chief looked up and grinned, displaying dazzling, white teeth. "Took my advice, did you?" he said to Solomon.

"Remind me later to buy you a beer," Solomon growled.

"Oh, hell no. I want to be the best man," said the bald chief, making Jordan wonder how he'd known there was a wedding in the making.

Epilogue

✦

"God damn it, Jordan, take something for the pain!" Solomon implored. Watching her endure increasingly ferocious contractions was hurting him nearly as much as it was hurting her.

"No," she gasped, clutching the upper edge of the mattress as if to pull herself up and out of the pangs that gripped her.

"It's almost over, Mr. McGuire," soothed the nurse, gauging Jordan's progress. "She'll be able to push in just a minute now."

"Jesus," Solomon swore, swimming in a clammy sweat. He couldn't wait for it to be over. Watching Jordan suffer for fourteen hours of labor was worse than any SEAL op he'd ever been on. He'd done everything he could think of to make it easier for her—massaged her lower back, held her in a warm shower. But the pain only got worse, and there was nothing he could do, this time, to protect her.

"I need to push!" Jordan suddenly cried, sounding panicked.

"That's fine," said the nurse. "Push with the next contraction, as I count to ten."

"Where the hell is the doctor?" Solomon raged, alarmed at the thought of proceeding without him.

"He's with another patient," said the nurse. "He'll be in shortly."

"Now!" Jordan gasped.

"Take a deep breath and push. One, two, three, four…"

Solomon gripped Jordan's hand as she bore down for ten seconds.

"Draw another breath and push again," said the nurse.

Jordan made a sound like a moose in mating season. *Oh, dear God, when would this nightmare end?*

"I see a head," said the nurse, sounding surprised. She stepped over to a speaker on the wall. "We need a doctor in room 114, right now!" she called.

In the same instant, Jordan let loose with a scream that turned Solomon's blood to ice. The baby's head appeared abruptly between her legs. Solomon raced to the foot of the bed. Being a SEAL hadn't prepared him for *this*.

Jordan screamed again, and the entire baby slipped out of her with a gush of clear liquid. With an exclamation, Solomon caught the warm, squirming bundle, and gaped, incredulously. "It's a girl!" he croaked. "With red hair. Look!"

As he showed his catch to Jordan, the doctor burst into the room, donning gloves as he hustled over.

"You're late!" Solomon growled, relinquishing the slippery baby with reservation.

On knees that felt squishy, he went to embrace his wife, shedding a tear of private relief now that her agony had abated, though he could still feel her trembling. The echo of her screams reverberated in his head, making him shudder. "It's over, sweetheart," he rasped, embracing her, reassuring himself at the same time. "You did it. You did it all by yourself."

She accepted his fervent praise, still quaking. "That was...oh, my God."

From the corner of his eye, Solomon watched the doctor suction the baby's airways. An impossibly sweet cry rent the now-quiet room.

With an expression of rapt astonishment, Jordan reached instinctively for her baby. The doctor obliged her, placing the newborn on her belly. "Hush, sweetheart. Mommy's here," she soothed.

"Mommy and Daddy," Solomon emphasized, wanting acknowledgement for his part in the drama.

"You want to cut the cord, Dad?" asked the nurse, handing him a pair of scissors.

He did the honors with hands that shook. The baby was then whisked away to be measured and weighed. Solomon listened to her cries and stroked Jordan's hair as she avidly watched the nurses tend her baby, her gaze hungry and filled with love.

"My brave wife," he murmured, marveling at her heroism. "Have I told you how much I love you today?"

"A couple of times," she answered, sparing him a wry smile.

"Here she is," announced the nurse, handing back the baby, now securely swaddled. "All six pounds, four ounces of her."

Holding a collective breath, they took leisurely stock

of their daughter. Violet-gray eyes, set in a heart-shaped face, regarded them, uncritically.

"You're so pretty," Jordan exclaimed with boundless wonder.

Solomon couldn't speak. Love had a stranglehold on his vocal cords. Amazing that such a tiny creature could summon such devotion in him. Like Jordan, she was his riptide.

He placed the tip of his finger in her tiny grasp, not at all surprised by the strength of her grip.

Jordan's eyes brimmed with happy tears. "I've waited so long for you," she whispered.

All my life, thought Solomon, his gaze sliding from daughter to mother.

His continued quiet drew Jordan's questioning gaze. "What are you thinking?" she asked him.

"I'm thinking of a poem I'm going to write for you," he admitted sheepishly. "An epic poem praising your heroic feats."

"Careful," Jordan warned, glancing meaningfully at the doctor. Solomon's passion for poetry was a deep, dark secret. "Your daddy is a romantic," she whispered to the baby. "What are we going to name you?" she asked.

The baby blinked at her, clearly receptive to suggestions.

"Isolde," suggested Solomon, his mind on epic poems.

"I don't think so."

"Helen of Troy."

"Helen's the name of your XO's wife," Jordan pointed out.

"Penelope, the wife of Odysseus," he suggested.

"That's the name of your commander's wife."

"Jesus!"

"That's a boy's name."

Solomon clicked his tongue in mock exasperation. "What was the name that you finally settled on, smart ass?"

"Rachel," said Jordan, gazing deep into the baby's eyes. "Rachel Marie McGuire, after my mother."

"Ah," said Solomon, recognizing a perfect fit. Silas had been named for Solomon's father and Miguel, christened just last month, was now Solomon Miguel McGuire. He put an arm around his women and sighed. Their family was complete. "Let's call the boys in," he suggested.

"Let the games begin," Jordan agreed, with a chuckle.

About the Author

Marliss Melton enjoyed an exotic childhood growing up overseas where entertainment meant riding on elephants in Laos, Sunday visits to museums in Paris, and tracking tigers in northern Thailand. With the world her home, Marliss excelled in language, music, and storytelling. She has taught various aspects of language in high schools and colleges, including the College of William and Mary, her alma mater. She has written eight books since becoming published in 2002, branching into two subgenres of romance, medieval historical and romantic suspense featuring Navy SEALs. Marliss lives in Virginia with her navy veteran husband and their five children.

THE DISH

Where authors give you the inside scoop!

♥ ♥ ♥ ♥ ♥ ♥ ♥ ♥ ♥ ♥ ♥ ♥ ♥ ♥

From the desk of Michelle Rowen

Michael Quinn used to be a vampire hunter. Now, he's a very reluctant vampire in search of a magical cure for what ails him in LADY & THE VAMP (available now). He's nursing a bit of a broken heart after being on the losing end of a love triangle in my first two Immortality Bites titles, *Bitten & Smitten* and *Fanged & Fabulous*. He doesn't know that true love is just around the next corner, and she's got a wooden stake with his name on it. To help this tall, dark, and "fangsome" vampire bachelor on his quest for love, liberty, and the pursuit of a hot, blond mercenary named Janie, here is something that Quinn might encounter in your average, everyday vampire bar.

Top Ten Vampiric Pick-up Lines

1. "I don't drink . . . *wine*. But, how about a piña colada?"
2. "Hey, you! You, in the black!"
3. "Didn't I go to your funeral?"
4. "Baby, you don't look a day over 350!"
5. "You have a beautiful neck, mind if I bite it?"
6. "You look just like David Boreanaz!"

7. "Are you one of the children of the night? Would you like to be?"
8. "Where have you been all of my long, tortured existence?"
9. "You, me, a bag of blood. Whaddya say?"
10. "Is that a wooden stake in your pocket or is it . . . ? Okay, never mind."

Then again, perhaps Quinn should just steer clear of vampire bars for the time being. It's just a suggestion.

Happy reading!

Michelle Rowen

www.michellerowen.com

♥ ♥ ♥ ♥ ♥ ♥ ♥ ♥ ♥ ♥ ♥ ♥ ♥ ♥ ♥

From the desk of Marliss Melton

Dear Reader,

It has been said that every novelist draws on what she knows and that her stories are, in some ways, autobiographical. So, reading any author's work is a bit like glimpsing the skeletons in her closet or her underwear hanging out to dry! This often-embarrassing phenomenon couldn't be truer for me than it is in DON'T LET GO (available now), the fifth book in my Navy SEAL series.

I've never been to Venezuela to do mission work like Jordan (the heroine of DON'T LET GO), but I did study abroad in Ecuador during college. I never adopted a child like the little boy Jordan wants to adopt, but I cherished my little Thai foster sister, who went on to be adopted in the United States. I've stood in her sister Jillian Sander's shoes, a widow with young children, hoping to carry her boys through their grief in the most positive way possible. I've watched a relationship develop between a fatherless boy and a man willing to fill a giant's shoes. But, most obviously, I've loved a man like Solomon McGuire, a man who is passionate in all things, secretly romantic, and sometimes hard to live with.

My second chance at love, my husband, most profoundly influenced the development of Solomon's character, from his black moustache to his New England dialect. Of course, I had to pair Solomon with a woman who resembles me, at least in regards to her hair color and the speed at which her baby was born. Not every reader is going to fall head over heels with this commanding character, but there'll be plenty who do. All I can say, ladies, is, "Sorry, Solomon is all mine."

To see a real–life photo of my inspiration, just check out the photos page on my Web site www.

marlissmelton.com. And while you're there, check out a preview of my next SEAL Team Twelve book, featuring the blue-eyed, baldheaded Chief Sean Harlan.

Did I mention that my husband is also bald?

Yours truly,

Marli Melton

♥ ♥ ♥ ♥ ♥ ♥ ♥ ♥ ♥ ♥ ♥ ♥ ♥ ♥ ♥

From the desk of Elizabeth Jennings

Dear Reader,

Charlotte Court, the heroine in PURSUIT (available now), is a truly gifted artist, who perfected her craft in Florence, Italy. Art is her entire life until a murderer comes after her and she has to go on the run to Baja California. That's where she meets Matt, a former Navy SEAL, a rough, tough guy, who falls head over heels for her and is blown away by her talent.

Like Charlotte, I spent a number of years in Florence, Italy, immersed in an artistic environment. My mom worked at a US graduate school of fine arts—now, alas, defunct—in a beautiful villa nestled in the green hills just below Fiesole, Villa

Schifanoia. Legend has it that this was the villa where the young Florentine noblemen and women fled to avoid the plague in Boccaccio's *Decameron*.

We lived around the corner from a fabulous international art school that was in itself a small masterpiece. It was in a 16th century deconsecrated church in the Borgo San Frediano, simply a stunning place to study art. Just a glimpse inside felt like being magically transported back to a Greek or a Roman temple.

I'm arty, but not visually gifted like the students I grew up around. I love words. At the time, I was learning characterization, hooks, and motivation, studying the masters, going over the writing again and again and again, revising and rewriting until I got it right.

I founded a writer's group in Florence that met in the basement of the American church—quite an eclectic group of people. I was the only one writing romance and it did me good to pit myself against those who had no sympathy for or knowledge of the genre. It stiffened my spine. And, boy, did I learn how to tighten up my writing.

Since I was putting myself through this intense apprenticeship, exactly as a young Renaissance artisan working in a *bottega* or the young artists in that beautiful school, I had an enormous amount of sympathy for the work involved in becoming proficient at an art.

Charlotte Court was born then in my mind, all

those years ago. A beautiful woman, exceedingly gifted and hardworking, who lives for her art. I had her study at this wonderful art school. She was alive to me—her drive to paint and draw almost obsessive, yet totally understandable.

I have held Charlotte in my head and heart all these years, and in this, my eighth book, I have finally given her life.

She is put to the test in PURSUIT. Wounded and hunted, she shows immense courage and fortitude. I like to think that her art gives her strength and grace.

Happy reading!

Elizabeth Jennings

Dear Reader,

I hope you enjoyed reading DON'T LET GO as much as I enjoyed writing it. Between the gut-wrenching drama and the heart-thudding action, this book reminded me of a roller coaster.

So, on to the next wild ride . . .

Did you happen to notice Sean "Harley" Harlan again in this book? His gorgeous baldness first appeared in NEXT TO DIE when he gave Joe a dressing–down for taking his place on that fated mission. In uniform, Sean is all business flashing blue eyes, and he can out-perform any officer on the teams. In DON'T LET GO, we see Sean in his civilian-mode: a laughing, teasing hunk of fun, as laid-back as a guy can get. And he loves kids, taking immediately to Ellie Stuart's fatherless boys. But Ellie herself is off limits. Sean has learned the hard way not to date women with children, regardless of their appeal. He hates breaking little hearts when his relationships end. But there's something about Ellie that keeps Sean coming back. And when Ellie's three boys are mysteriously kidnapped and Ellie herself is being framed, Sean spearheads a wild and ultimately deadly search to reunite mother and children. But with Ellie constantly at his side, his self-restraint is wearing thin. Will he violate his rule and sleep with her? Will he break the hearts of the boys he's determined to save? Read the next rollercoaster ride in my SEAL series, coming in Spring 2009.

Enjoy!

Marliss Melton

http://www.marlissmelton.com/

Want to know more about romances at Grand Central Publishing and Forever? Get the scoop online!

GRAND CENTRAL PUBLISHING'S ROMANCE HOMEPAGE

Visit us at www.hachettebookgroupusa.com/romance for all the latest news, reviews, and chapter excerpts!

NEW AND UPCOMING TITLES

Each month we feature our new titles and reader favorites.

CONTESTS AND GIVEAWAYS

We give away galleys, autographed copies, and all kinds of fun stuff.

AUTHOR INFO

You'll find bios, articles, and links to personal websites for all your favorite authors—and so much more!

THE BUZZ

Sign up for our monthly romance newsletter, and be the first to read all about it!